Unshakeable

M. MARINAN

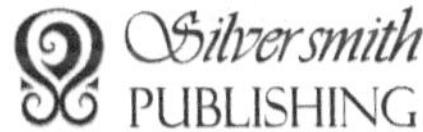
Silversmith PUBLISHING

First published in New Zealand in 2019 by Silversmith Publishing
Mass market paperback edition.

A catalogue record for this book is available from the National Library of New Zealand

ISBN 978-0-9951196-9-7

Unshakeable

Seventeen-year-old Iscendra's world is shaken
when she's illegally conscripted into
a spoiled Martian ruler's private army.

With her entire future under threat, it takes
all her strength not to fall apart.

But when the opportunity arises for real
change, will she have the courage to risk not
just her own life, but her family's too?

Across Time & Space series
The Eternity Stone
Mountain of Glass
Desert of Fire
Desert of Ice
The Hidden Door

Fairytale Memoirs series
The Mostly Forgotten Memoirs of Rose Red
Viola Sends Her Regrets
Gifted

Standalone books
Breaking the Glass Slipper
Unshakeable
Tyger

For information on new and upcoming books,
go to **mmarinanbooks.com**

Unshakeable *is dedicated to Deborah,*
who is as tough, determined and
soft-hearted as this book's heroine.

And as always, many thanks
to Kate and Anne-Marie for their
invaluable time and feedback.

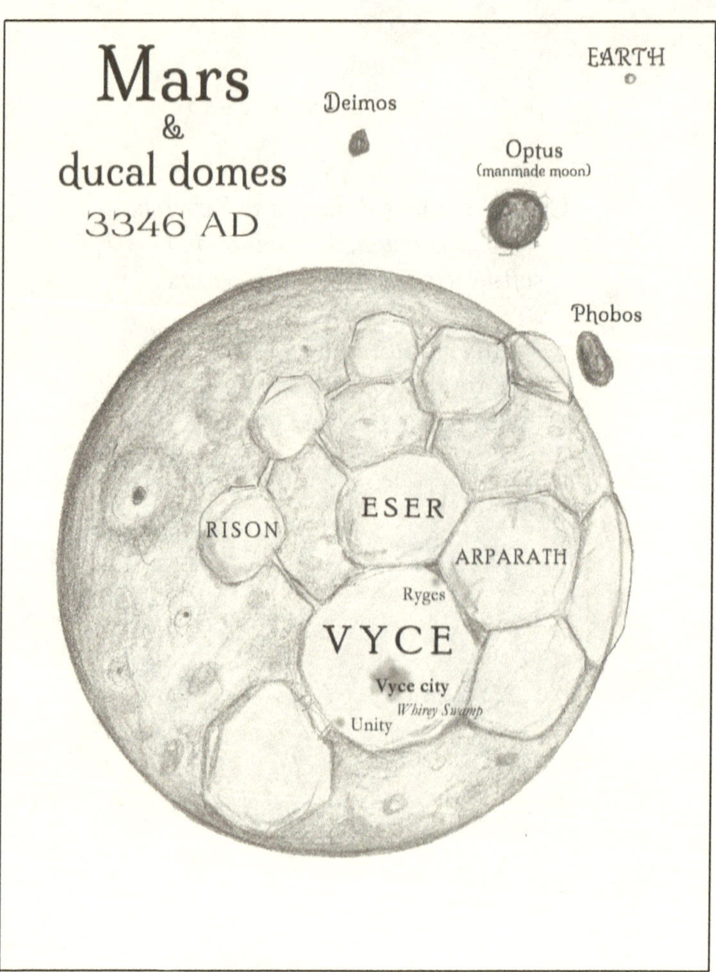

Mars
&
ducal domes
3346 AD
EARTH
Deimos
Optus
(manmade moon)
Phobos
RISON
ESER
ARPARATH
Ryges
VYCE
Vyce city
Whirey Swamp
Unity

# Contents

Glossary

To help you navigate the weird and wonderful world of the distant future.

Breaker – a soldier in the High Duke of Vyce's army

Farlac – a six-winged horselike creature native to Mars

Grawlix – an unpleasant person

Older – someone from Earth

Old World – slang for Earth

Optus – a man-made moon orbiting Mars, a popular holiday destination

Pog – a pig/dog hybrid, a popular pet

Ruges – an Earth-run town within Vyce Dome

Shriekn', shrieking – yet another vague swearword, work it out yourself

Suds – damn (or worse, depending on your mood)

Swamp-mare – a huge aquatic predator native to Mars

Unity – an Earth-run town within Vyce Dome

Vyce Dome – a territory on Mars, ruled by High Duke Shandlin

Wolcrox – a horned, ox-like creature known for stubbornness

PART ONE
Iscendra

ONE
The Crate

* * *

The town of Unity, Vyce Ducal Dome
Mars, 3346 AD

Ten minutes until the gondola left. Ten minutes until I was on my way across dangerous country, leaving the safety of this Earth-owned town and crossing miles and miles of Martian wilderness, all for one goal.

Making money. It was a good goal, right? But I couldn't be late, or all my work would be for nothing. The gondolas across the atmospheric domes didn't come often in this part of the world, and the tickets weren't transferrable.

I checked once again that my precious red crate was still strapped to its hover-carrier, then ran for the kitchen. Even from a distance I could smell the delicious scent of just-heated fruit bread, AKA my breakfast. But when I moved through the doorway, my younger brother Nik stepped into my path. At fifteen he was two years my junior, but annoyingly also quite a bit taller…and I wasn't short.

"Where are you going in such a hurry?"

"You know where I'm going! I'm taking a crate of sketches to Ruges, to sell them at the big opening festival. Now get out of my way, or I'll miss my ride." My words were harsh, but my tone was light. Nik made a hobby out of irritating me, and I did the same back. It was our job as siblings.

Naturally he didn't move, so I shoved him aside then headed for the food-heater. But when I opened it, it was empty.

"Sowwy, were you wooking for vis?" Nik said around a mouthful of fruited bread. He swallowed, then grinned at me.

"Thanks for breakfast, Sis'."

"Argh – you!" I grabbed a frozen chunk of bread off the nearby counter, then threw it at his head.

He ducked, and it bounced off the wall behind him. "Too slow, as always. Are you going to throw food when *Felix* comes to visit, fizzy Iscee?" The ridiculous rhyming nickname was leftover from my childhood, but it wasn't what caught my attention.

I paused halfway through throwing the third roll. "Who?"

Nik grinned annoyingly, revealing that he hadn't swallowed all of his see-food. "You know. Felix, the amazing and handsome grandson of our neighbours Brant and Trudi. He's coming to visit tonight, and Trudi thinks *you* would be a perfect match! When's the wedding?"

This time the bread hit him right in the forehead, but unfortunately that was when my mother walked in. She was half a head shorter than me, and fair-haired where I was dark, but her unimpressed expression was still enough to make me take a step back. "Are you throwing food, Iscendra Cole?"

"Sorry Mum, but he started it," I said humbly. "Um… gotta go! I'll miss my gondola."

"Are you *sure* you need to go?" she persisted, setting her hand on my arm. "Can't you just post the crate? It'll get there before the festival, and then you won't be in danger…"

"I have to go," I repeated patiently, just as I had the last three times she'd asked. "The chances of the crate making it all the way across the dome to Ruges without me is pretty low. At the very least, some of the sketches will be missing. They're still worth a bit, even if they're not real paper. Besides, I'll be safe. I'll stick to the main route, and won't get off at all except for the gondola changeover in Vyce City."

Mum's lips tightened into a straight line, then she sighed. "And you'll avoid Breakers, and you'll keep your valuables hidden separately from your ID, right? I know you're an Earth citizen and they have no legal right to bother you, but it doesn't mean they'll always respect that."

"Right," I agreed, even though I knew I couldn't exactly

avoid Breakers, if they didn't want me to. The local police force AKA disaster squad went where they wanted, and bothered who they wanted; whether Earth-born or Martian. In fact, as an immigrant from Earth – or an 'Older' in Common slang – I felt like more of a target than any local girl just travelling across the vast domes that made this world liveable. I would try to keep my head down and hope they ignored me.

"And if you do run into any," Mum continued, "don't lose your temper!"

"Yeah," Nik piped up from his safe spot behind her shoulder. "Otherwise you might end up breaking someone's arm, just like you did to me."

"I was eight, and it was an accident!" I rolled my eyes, then quickly leaned in and gave my mother a kiss on the cheek. "Gotta go. See you at dinner."

"And don't forget *Felix*," Nik sang.

"Oh yes," Mum called after me as I left the room. "You remember him from when you were ten, right?"

I muttered something purposely incomprehensible, then ran for it, grabbing the handle of my hovering crate as I did so. Sure, I remembered some dark-haired kid, but that was as far as it went. And while my family loved me, I'd rather not be set up with a stranger just 'because we'd make a cute couple'.

I passed my youngest brother Alek where he sat quietly at his desk, his fair head bent over a game of bright orange toy soldiers. "Bye, Alek."

He didn't respond, but I hadn't expected him to. Alek might look twelve, but sometimes he acted like he was much, much younger, or like he was in another world. Most of the time, he just acted like Alek.

I ran out the front door, hearing its distinctive *swish-click* as it closed behind me, then jumped onto the descending platform that would take me down the cliff towards the nearby town centre of Unity. I passed rows and rows of climbing garva vines, the dozens of round fruit currently a sickly pale green. In a month it would start to turn pink, indicating ripeness, but now it was good for nothing but a sore stomach. The occasional white, spidery shape moved amongst the vines – not actual spiders, but tiny robots designed to keep bugs off the plants. And in the distance I could see a small figure, looking shadowy within the massive greenhouses lining the edge of our plantation. It was Dad, but I knew he wouldn't be able to see me from here.

The moving platform finally reached the bottom of the cliff, and I didn't wait for it to stop before leaping off and running towards the Unity gondola station, dragging the hover-carrier behind me. The large, white gondola cabin marked with its destination 'RUGES' still had its door open, but the flashing light indicated it was a matter of seconds before it would leave. Uh oh.

Luckily I had long legs, and determination gave me energy. Picking up my pace, I made it onto a seat right before the doors closed. *Phew*. I was the only person on board, so there was no one to notice me squeak in alarm as the gondola cabin suddenly lurched up into the air. I dug my fingernails into the seat cushion, closing my eyes as it rocked back and forth in the air, hanging from that single strong cable.

"Suds," I murmured to myself, trying to settle my pounding heart. "That was too close." And to make it worse, I'd missed breakfast. Thanks a lot, Nik.

"You are now leaving Unity," a polite automated voice informed me as the gondola rose higher into the air, now moving with a smooth hum. "In three minutes you will leave Earth territory and enter the Ducal Dome of Vyce. Please scan your ID."

I obediently raised my wrist to the scanning block set into the wall, waiting until its distinctive 'beep' showed it had read the chip embedded under my skin.

"Earth citizen Iscendra Cole. One return ticket to Ruges," the automated voice informed me. "Changeover at Central Station, Vyce City. Be aware that there have been hijackings on this journey. We recommend that you do not carry any valuables on you while using public transport."

Gee, thanks! Now that was a new and very unwelcome

addition to the auto-spiel. But then we were well up in the air, flying at high speed across the Martian landscape. Since I didn't come this way often, I leaned back in my seat and watched the scenery skim by beneath me.

Seeing the green and blue forest interspersed with the occasional outpost, it was hard to believe humans had once called this 'the Red Planet'. But that was back before we'd built the hundreds of colossal domes that made the air breathable; that made this world warm and damp and so very liveable. Now it was all so lush and green, the jungles between our little town and the main cities growing absolutely wild and uncontrolled.

That was why the gondolas were always at such great heights, skimming along cables strung between enormously tall pillars, sticking out well above even the tallest trees, but still well below the sheer domes. Those were high enough for swirling clouds to form at most times of the year, and too high to be reached by anything except air shuttles or ships.

"Good thing I'm not afraid of heights," I said to no one in particular. Perhaps I was only trying to convince myself. But from up here I could see *everything*. The Vyce Dome was one of the largest in Southern Mars, yet I could see the nearest edge of the dome shimmering faintly in the distance, just beyond where my town would be. Past the dome was desert, but all I could make out was a faint orangish haze.

In the other direction was Vyce City, home to almost ten million people, and looking rather like a wasp's nest. Even from here I could see the faint shapes of what must be thousands of air vehicles, so tiny they looked like dust motes in sunlight. Most of them wouldn't have the clearance to leave city limits. With the domes keeping everyone alive, we couldn't risk anyone getting drunk then ramming a hole in their protective layers – or even worse, doing it on purpose as had happened up north five years ago.

They'd fixed the breach before any real damage was done, but I remembered how it had been all over the news vids, and how my parents had spoken about it in low, frightened tones when they'd thought we weren't listening. The solution in Vyce had been to automatically shut off power to any air vehicles lacking the correct clearance. They'd get too close, and then suddenly they'd be falling.

You could see why I preferred the gondolas, even though it meant I had to go through the city. I reached up a hand to my aching jaw, then realised I'd been scowling at the thought. So I intentionally turned away from that view, leaning against the clear windows of the gondola and studying the vegetation below instead. These gondolas were purposely strung high above the landscape, not just because of the afore-mentioned air vehicles, but also because humans weren't the only ones to thrive on this colonised planet.

Centuries ago, back when the domes were first built and the first forests thick enough to hold animal life, some idio- I mean, *colonists* brought along multiple species from Earth. My old school teacher said that at the time, people had been terrified of the apocalypse – of the Earth overheating or overcrowding, and every species being lost. So naturally they'd released them into the newly created Martian wilds.

While clearly Earth survived – just ended up overly busy and expensive, in my opinion, hence my family moving here – a few of those imported species had also survived the slightly lower gravity and cooler temperatures. Then a few scientists had really got inventive. They'd created weird and wonderful creatures specially to survive in the worst the Martian domes had to offer. Why? I didn't know, but I squinted at the scenery below, trying to spot something more interesting than trees.

Just then a fluttering white shape came into view, holding pace alongside the gondola. It was a four-winged wild farlac; its horselike head wearing an expression of blind panic. But then farlacs always looked worried. Perhaps they were scared that they'd be captured and ridden by a crazy Breaker, because no other normal human would consider doing that.

I watched it curiously for a while, admiring how it matched the gondola's incredible speed, occasionally ducking lower and vanishing into the jungle canopy before rising up again to meet the gondola.

But then up ahead I saw an expanse of black water with white cliffs marking one edge. The water was still, but even from here I could see something pale moving under the surface…

I closed my eyes just as something colossal burst from the water. I felt the impact of its movement rock the cabin, and I sucked in a breath and dug my fingers into the padded seats. But then when I opened my eyes again the wild farlac was gone, and the black water was frothing white and bubbling from whatever had just grabbed its breakfast.

Suds. And that was why the gondolas really needed to be higher here, I thought again with a shudder. If a predatory swamp-mare could make the jump to catch a farlac, then who was to say it couldn't catch a gondola cabin? And to think someone had made those things on purpose and let them loose on Mars centuries before. Nice one, unknown scientist.

Just then a soft purple light flashed on my wrist; my plain communicator bangle quietly signalling an inbound call. I smiled to myself. I knew who was calling, because I'd programmed a different coloured light for each of my favourite people.

I tapped the screen twice, and a holographic image of a girl shot up to fill the air in front of me. She looked an awful lot like me, except that she was a bit curvier, and instead of messy dark hair in a ponytail, hers was…

"Purple, Aria?" I scrunched up my nose, half-smiling. My choice of a purple alert had been more appropriate than I'd anticipated. "What happened to the green?"

"My parents didn't like it," my cousin said casually, running her fingers through the violet strands. While the hologram's mouth was moving, the sound of her voice went straight into my ears via two tiny implants. "I figured this was better."

"And everyone thinks you're the nice cousin," I muttered. "Ha! *You're* the scary one. Do you see me giving myself rainbow hair?"

"You should," Aria retorted, her holographic form setting its hands on its hips. "You're looking a bit dull. Come to Optus! I'll give you a makeover, and your own mother won't recognise you."

Considering that our own mothers were twins, and that Aria and I had been mistaken for the same... "You know that sounds like a threat, right?"

Aria smiled cheekily, then blew lightly on her nails. Even with the transparent image I could see they glowed yellow. "So are you coming?"

"The whole family's coming in July after the garvafruit harvest, and then you can do what you want." I paused, considering my statement. "No, wait. I take that back-"

"Too late! You can't take it back! Iscee, I see you with... orange hair. Orange and pink spikes, oh yes..."

"Again, who is the scary cousin?" I rolled my eyes. "Not going to happen, Aria."

"You're the scary one," she pointed out. "Because I don't go punching holes in walls when I get angry."

"That happened once, and I was twelve!"

She shrugged. "Still counts."

We chatted for a while as the gondola made its way into the city fringes. Aria was my age, but unlike me, she was an only child. We'd grown up together on Earth in a busy, smelly, expensive Pacifican city. Tiny homes, dangerous streets, not so much fresh air. Then the new treaties were made with some of the Martian domes. Earth would stop taxing so many Martian imports, and Mars would allow Earth to keep small territories within the domes – completely under Earth rule, subject to Earth laws, safe from the Martian version of chaos.

To my parents it had sounded like an incredible opportunity. They'd packed up Nik and I, since Alek hadn't yet been born, and had begun a new life in what had seemed like a simply colossal home, set in a simply colossal plantation, in the luxurious town of Unity – one of the Earth-run territories. It was tiny compared to the surrounding Martian-ruled Vyce Dome, but safe and clean and all those good things. And it *was* good, I told myself. I wouldn't want to live anywhere else.

"What's got you looking so serious?" Aria teased.

"I was just thinking about how we moved here. Do you ever regret that your parents moved to Optus instead?" When we'd left for Mars, Aria's parents had taken a different opportunity to buy a resort on the tiny, glamourous satellite of Optus. It orbited Mars along with its two natural moons, and wow, was it beautiful. But perhaps a little lonely too…

She shrugged. "It's quiet here, and people only come for a holiday, then leave again. But it's safe, Iscee. How long do you think Earth will keep its territories down in those domes?"

My eyebrows shot up. "Negative, much?"

"I'm just being realistic. You're the one who tells me about the issues between the locals and the immigrants, never mind that you've lived there longer than you ever lived on Earth. The problem is your Earth ID. Maybe you need to just take the plunge and get a local citizenship instead."

I just stared at her, waiting for the punchline to the joke, because I'd always been proud of my Earth heritage, and the feeling of safety it brought. But after several seconds went by when she didn't so much as smile, I shook my head. "You know that Unity is fenced off. Nothing gets in there that's not chipped for entry, not even animals."

"And are you in Unity now, Iscee?"

My eyes narrowed. "You think I would be better to be at the mercy of the local rulers? Have you *heard* about the Vyce High Duke, Aria? He doesn't exactly treat his people well."

Her lips tightened, but then she laughed. I knew her well enough to know it was forced. "Or maybe move to Optus with us, or else one of the other colonies. There are always options."

I rolled my eyes. "How about when there's a real problem, then I'll consider it. But for now, life is good. We've finished school, and our futures are free and open. So why don't you wish me luck instead ?"

Aria sighed. "Sorry, I don't mean to be so anxious. It's just that I see the Mars news vids, and they never have anything good to show."

"The news vids produced by Earth, you mean?" Everyone knew that Earth was resentful over losing control of their former colony like they had. The ancestors of the current High Dukes and Duchesses had actually been put in power by the same people who'd built the atmospheric domes, and Earth never missed an opportunity to insult their former countrymen. Barbaric, undisciplined, criminal…

"Um…yes."

"Then it's a good thing I don't watch those news vids," I said cheerfully, "because everything seems just like always. But we're coming into the city now, so I'll talk to you later, OK?"

We said our goodbyes and I shut the communicator off, then carefully stowed it under my clothing. I hadn't forgotten that early warning about hijackings on these gondolas, and I knew that some people considered such communicators signs of wealth. I didn't want to attract the wrong sort of attention.

Down below me the forest had long turned to scattered houses, then apartments, and the gondola began to slow as we were surrounded by tall buildings. The city grew denser and busier, full of bright colours and air vehicles moving in their lanes. Gondola lines ran in every direction, marked with flashing holographic lights for better visibility.

On a distant hill loomed the massive shape of the Ducal Residence with its high fortified walls. It was squat, unmissable and ugly, probably a lot like its owner. High Duke Shandlin was young and reckless, but also notoriously secretive. I didn't think I'd seen a recent picture of him, but I figured he must resemble a leprous toad, if his looks matched his behaviour.

"Two minutes to Vyce Central Station," the automated voice informed me pleasantly. "Prepare to disembark and transfer to any connecting gondolas, and don't forget to guard your valuables."

"Thank you," I retorted a little sarcastically, but I pulled my precious crate closer to me anyway.

"You're welcome."

Outside the open air was exchanged for high buildings, dozens of other gondolas, and then finally a massive enclosed space. Vyce Central Station. By the time the gondola came to a halt I was already on my feet, with my plain tunic jacket latched around my waist, my sheer hood up over my hair, and my hover-carrier's handle tight in my fist. I paused, then tapped my wristband a couple of times until the jacket's colour faded from deep red to a muted, easily-missed rust-brown, all the better to blend in around here. Just another ordinary girl on her way to nowhere in particular…

This part of the city was always a shock compared to quiet, green Unity. Just like the city itself, the gondola station was large, chaotic and dirty. Rubbish flew around in the light breeze, holographic advertisements flashed on the walls or popped up in front of unsuspecting pedestrians, and the buildings and paved areas were mismatched and ugly.

The other people down here looked like me. Hoods up, heads down as they quickly moved around, probably hoping not to be noticed. Criminals, ordinary people, who knew? I took the chance to use the bathroom and to buy food from a nearby dispenser. But as it whirred away, assembling my nutrition bar, I spotted an unexpected blur of green near my foot. Leaning in, it was revealed to be a tiny fern; smaller than my palm and perfectly formed in spite of its location. It appeared to have lodged in a mix of dust and condensation from the dispenser.

Something about that struck a chord with me: that miniature, fragile thing surviving exactly where it wasn't ever meant to be, and I watched it right up until the dispenser ejected my nutritious (but not so delicious) replacement breakfast.

It was going to die, wasn't it? Nothing could survive for long in a place like this. Or more likely, someone would spot it and scrape it off the ground, then throw it away. It would die, just because it had grown outside the designated areas, and that felt like a tragedy.

Don't be silly, I scolded myself. *It's just a stupid fern.*

I took the bar, its degradable packaging crunching in my hand, and an idea occurred to me. Checking that no one was watching, I quickly knelt down and scooped up the plant, roots and dirt and all, then tucked it inside the firm packaging. Then I slipped the whole thing into my pocket, feeling a devious little smile curve my lips. *Iscendra, fern-hero. Another job well done.*

Silly, yes. But still, rescuing that tiny fern made the day seem just a little brighter, and I made my way onto the next gondola with a skip in my step.

Two hours later, the skip had vanished entirely. This second part of the trip from Vyce city to Ruges seemed to take forever, and it didn't help that I was squashed into the smallest, most uncomfortable bench on the gondola.

The first gondola from Unity had been empty, so I'd happily taken the closest, widest seats, the sort usually reserved for the elderly or injured. But this one was packed full with a dozen people, my little detour to the bathroom and food dispenser having lost me valuable seat-choosing time. But rather than stand, I chose to wedge my crate up on one of the highest benches, like a shelf up one wall of the gondola. Then I climbed up the short ladder to squeeze in next to it. The top bench was always uncomfortable, with the added risk of falling out if the gondola lurched and the support barrier wasn't working properly. So no one else wanted to sit with me, which was fine.

We skimmed our way out of the city, through the outskirts then through more jungle. Beyond that were miles and miles of planted fields, complete with green-towers just like in my parents' plantation. Not *all* of Mars was wild and untended.

But even though the view was pretty, I was more than ready to escape once we finally came to a gentle halt at the Ruges station. I waited for everyone else to disembark, then unfolded myself from the awkward bench, trying to find the ladder down without falling on my head. As the blood came rushing back into my limbs, I let out a pained groan.

"Need a hand, Izz?"

I paused mid-movement then smiled down at the guy standing in the gondola's open doorway. My old friend Lanny was short and stocky, with a face that smiled easily and a crop of very curly hair, perpetually in need of a trim. But not today… "You've had a haircut!"

"Yes, I've been known to do that," he said dryly, raising a hand to help me down.

"Not often," I countered as I carefully manoeuvred down the ladder. "What's this one for, trying to impress a girl?" I waggled my eyebrows, and he rolled his eyes in response. We'd been fast friends since I'd moved to Unity twelve years before, and if he was trying to impress anyone, it certainly wouldn't be me.

"The girls love my hair, long or short," he retorted. "But Dad said I had to look tidy for the opening festival. He didn't want people put off entering our store because it was run by a hulligan."

"A what?!"

"Hulligan? Um…maybe it was hewlligun. You know, a messy young person who screws things up."

I had to laugh. "That could describe half our old class, including myself – and don't forget the Breakers. But sure, cut your hair if he thinks that will help."

Lanny took my hover-carrier, studying the crate with interest. "So this is what brought you all the way here, huh? How was your trip?"

When he moved as if to open it, I smacked his hand. "Open it inside. As for my trip, it was long and mostly boring, but we didn't get hijacked by anyone or eaten, so I suppose it went well." Just then we stepped out of the gondola, and I finally took in my new surroundings. "Ooh, this place is beautiful! Show me around."

"Bossy as always." But I saw the pride in his posture, and he proceeded to do just that.

Like Unity, Ruges was a tiny patch of Earth territory within the much larger Vyce Ducal Dome. Until recently it had been made up of farms and plantations with a small town centre. Maybe a little depressed, maybe not quite as wealthy as Unity. But then someone had the idea to create a themed town centre – the sort with ancient-style, vehicle-free cobblestoned streets, houses with thatched roofs (!) and boutique stores selling unusual and interesting goods.

The local shop owners had taken to it with gusto, especially once they'd seen how much it increased their trade. In the last six months, Ruges had finished its upgrade – now pretty much everything you saw within the town centre and initial rings of houses had the same style.

"And here's our art gallery," Lanny said, gesturing towards a nearby building. "Dad bought it last year, and now it's finally ready. It'll sell old-fashioned art only; the sort made by hand, that you can actually touch. No holo-art at all."

He'd told me some of this by communicator, when he'd offered the chance to display my own pieces, but we hadn't really spoken at length. I studied the small building appreciatively. It was beautifully built, complete with a colourful, abstract mural spiralling across its front façade. "Did you paint that, Lanny? It's gorgeous."

We'd been neighbours until his father had moved him here at school-end, but our common interest in art had given us a deeper connection, and I recognised his style at once. I also knew that he needed encouragement. Heaven knew, I did too.

"Thanks!" he said, beaming. "Now come inside, and let's open that crate of yours. If they're as good as the samples looked, I bet they're going to sell brilliantly at the festival next weekend."

The well-advertised festival that promised to bring thousands of visitors…and exposure for me as an artist. If my work caught the eye of the right person, it could mean a whole new life for me – and that I wouldn't have to find menial work once my school-end holidays were over; something I'd been dreading.

My stomach did a little flip, and I glanced down at the solid red crate, still quietly sitting in its hover-carrier. "I hope so."

But ten minutes later when we were in the back of his cute little shop, and we opened the crate, what was inside was all…wrong.

Lanny frowned down at the colourful paintings and drawings, his brows drawing together tightly in confusion. "Oh. These aren't…the same style as what you showed me before. Is that a…finger painting?"

"That's because they're not my work," I said flatly. My stomach was churning, and I could feel heat rising through my chest and face. Anger. Disappointment. "I mean, they are my work…but it's the wrong crate."

I closed my eyes briefly, turning away from the horrible sight. I'd brought the wrong crate. All my work. All that careful design, all those pictures. All wasted…all back at home in Unity.

The wrong…crate!

"Um, Iscee…are you OK? 'Cos your face has gone all funny, like that time when you threw our history teacher's pot plant through the window, and got suspended from school. You're not about to do something stupid, are you?"

"Why is everyone reminding me of things I did when I was a kid!?" I shouted suddenly, throwing my hands in the air. "Suds and shrieking grawlix, Lanny! I brought the wrong frarking crate! All this time, all this money to get here, and I brought a collection of stupid finger paintings I did when I was six! I don't even know why we still have these!"

"*Oh.*" His eyebrows shot up, but he didn't comment on my language. And I could hear the world of disappointment in that one syllable.

I could see him out the corner of my eye looking in the crate again, but I stomped away across the shop, my arms wrapped tightly around myself and my jaw tight from gritting my teeth. I was so *angry*! How could this have happened?

How could I have been so *careless*? I knew exactly what was riding on this, and still I'd messed up. I'd failed.

I pulled my communicator out of my jacket and slapped it on my wrist again, then tapped the code for the direct home number. Ten seconds later my mother's face popped into view. Pleasant, familiar. "I'm sorry," her holograph said politely, "but I'm unavailable right now. If you call-"

It was her recorded message. I tapped to end the call, then pulled the wristpiece off again and pulled back my arm to throw it. I felt overwhelmed with fury, like I was boiling inside. I was literally an inch away from hurling it at the wall when I felt a tap on my shoulder.

"Hey, Iscee," Lanny said apologetically. "Try not to destroy anything in a rage, OK? So you brought some childhood rubbish instead of your cute, sellable art. It's a shame, but not the end of the world. Come back tomorrow or the next day. The festival's not on yet, so we've got time to get things sorted."

My boiling anger simmered down to merely 'hot'. "I can't come back, Lanny," I said flatly. It was embarrassing to admit it, but I had to tell the truth. "At this time of year the plantation's broke. We're waiting on the garvafruit harvest. I can't pay for another ticket."

"Oh." There was a brief pause, then he shrugged. "Then I'll pay it, and take it out of your future sales. No biggie, Izz. I reckon it'll take about ten sales to clear the cost of a return ticket from Unity, and how many sketches did you have for me?"

I felt my mood lift a little more, turning as quickly as the fury had come on. Yes, I had a temper. I was working on it. "Eighty-five."

"Then I'd say we can afford it," Lanny said sardonically. "Now will you come and have lunch with me, or do you need to punch something first?"

"The way you people talk, you'd think I had anger issues," I retorted lightly, now feeling almost normal again. I glanced longingly at the stupid, false red crate that had somehow got itself mixed up with my precious, precious sketches. "I'll have you know I almost never punch things anymore. I would burn those stupid finger paintings, but I think my mum would be upset. She's probably the one who kept them. So sure, I'll settle for lunch."

But then something else occurred to me. Something important, although not art-level important. I pulled the now badly crumpled package out of my pocket, holding it sheepishly up to the light. "Do you have a place I can plant this first?"

"I can't believe you carried that weed all the way here," Lanny said again. He was shaking his head, a grin splitting his face. "Wall-punching Iscendra almost misses her gondola, just so she can save a fern from destruction."

"It's not a weed," I countered, feeling my cheeks heat. "And I almost never punch walls anymore. I told you that."

"Anything's a weed if it grows where you don't want it. But wall-punching or not, you're such a contradiction. You seem so tough sometimes, and next thing you're sobbing over some dead leaf. Do you cry during children's story-vids too?"

I scowled and looked down at my lunch on the table in front of me, because Lanny knew better than anyone that, yes, I might shed a tear or two during the sad bits. But who didn't?

I hadn't answered, but he let out a hoot of laughter. "Of course you do! Staunch, unshakeable Iscee rescues weeds and cries during children's story-vids. Shall I put that on your artist's bio?"

He referred to the personal description that would accompany any of my art pieces. "Don't you dare, Lanny. And since when am I unshakeable?" I shook my head ruefully, remembering my earlier temper tantrum. "I'm emotionally unstable. You said it yourself."

His smile widened, and he leaned back in his chair. "Sure, you have strong feelings about a lot of things. I know that. But nothing seems to scare you, and you don't hold grudges. It's probably why we're still friends."

I didn't list off all the things that *did* scare me, because he'd just argue more. Besides, he had a point. I wasn't scared by things that seemed to frighten others, probably because I tended to think things would work out OK…unless you were eaten by a swamp-mare like that wild farlac. That probably wasn't fixable.

"I just wish my emotions were unshakeable too," I said instead. "That I could stop and think before I'd let myself get upset. Life would be so much easier."

"Then you'd be boring, and I wouldn't want to hang out with you. But Iscee, you *do* stop and think. You didn't throw your communicator against the wall earlier, did you?"

"It's too expensive to break," I replied automatically, then brightened. "Ooh, then I did stop and think first! I guess I am improving." I narrowed my eyes at him, leaning back comfortably in my own chair. My tummy was full of good food, which was halfway to happiness, in my opinion. "Thanks for the feedback, Doctor Lanny. Now it's your turn. You seem to have settled in here well. You don't mind the distance?"

He shrugged. "I've made new friends. Besides, I'd rather be further away from the capital if I can help it. Things are messy there. I've heard rumours of unrest."

"Yeah, but…that's Vyce land. Not Old World."

He shrugged again. "You think the Martians are going to respect our passports and imaginary borders? If they decide Earth doesn't have the power to protect us, then we'll lose everything. That's a fact."

My eyebrows shot up. Lanny had always been a laid-back kid, friendly and hard to faze. Kind of my opposite, really, never mind what he'd said earlier. It was strange hearing him talk like this, and I wasn't sure if I believed what he was saying.

"You know, Aria was saying something similar just this morning. You both could be right, but what can we do about it? Things seem the same as always, so for now, let's just enjoy life." I grinned at him. "And I'll be back tomorrow. Plenty more time to worry."

He smiled back, but this time it didn't reach his eyes. "Not right now there isn't. Your gondola is just about to leave."

"Suds!" I leapt out of my chair, grabbing my belongings in dismay. How did I always end up running late? "I better go."

"See you tomorrow, and be safe!"

"See you!" As for the 'be safe'? I'd been OK on the way here. Fingers crossed.

The gondola ran back over the same route it had taken earlier, stopping for long enough to offload most of its passengers in Vyce city, all except for me and a little old man sitting quietly in the corner. He'd been fixated on his handheld device for most of the trip. I'd dozed lightly most of the way, my hover-carrier stuck between my feet. As long as it stayed there, and as long as my valuables remained in my pockets, I didn't care who sat next to me or how much conversation we had. *Just get home…be safe.*

The door beeped, indicating that it was about to close, but suddenly a long metal blade stuck in the gap. A moment later the door was forced open, and the little old man and I had company.

Breakers.

Be safe? Maybe not.

TWO
Felix

◎　◎　◎

The doors were wrenched open to reveal a couple of teenagers wearing the brown, studded armour of the High Duke's private police force, and with arrogant smirks that said, 'I can do whatever I like, and you can't stop me'.

Suds, suds, suds. As if the day hadn't been bad enough already.

"ID," the first Breaker snapped at us. She looked about sixteen, with reddish hair under her distinctive crested helmet, and a series of scars up her neck and the side of her face. She also held a long stave, the sort with a blade at one end and a hook at the other, so I decided not to comment on her lack of humour.

I held out my wrist silently, trying not to make eye contact as she ran her scanner over my chip, reading out the stats as she went. "Iscendra Cole. Age seventeen, height one-eighty-two, weight ninety-six units, place of birth: Sidnee, Pacifica, Earth. You've come a long way from home, Older."

Only Martians ever used the world 'Older' like she had – with disdain. But I knew the Breaker was just looking for an excuse to cause trouble, and while anger still roiled inside me, my voice was even as I answered. "Settled here with my parents when I was a kid. I think of Mars as home now."

The Breaker sneered. "Once you hold a Martian ID and answer to Martian law, then you'll be home." She glanced down at my crate of finger-paintings in its hover-carrier. "And what's this, Older?" "Nothing of importance."

"Then you won't mind if I look inside."

I minded. But I didn't move to stop her as she flipped the lid open, then began prodding through the sheaves of images with the hook end of her stave. "What's this rubbish?"

"Children's drawings," I said flatly, even though I could feel my neck turning hot. "As I said, nothing of importance."

The other Breaker, a boy about Nik's build, with a face spotted with acne, peered over her shoulder. "Look under the drawings," he suggested. "She could be hiding something."

"I'm not hiding anything!" Except my communicator, my money, and my temper.

But the girl Breaker narrowed her eyes, hooking her stave on the side of my crate. Then she turned the entire thing upside down. Cheap, time-bleached synthetic papers fluttered everywhere, some catching the breeze and being pulled out of the gondola carriage. An oddly-shaped item was at the bottom of the crate, and she bent down to pick it up. "Smuggling goods, Older? That's a capital offense."

"That's a clay pog," I said very politely, trying to hold back a disbelieving laugh as I recognised the object. "I made it when I was seven. While I'm sure it had value to my seven-year-old self, I hardly think it counts as smuggling goods."

The boy Breaker snickered, and the girl's face turned red under her metal helmet. Then she turned and very deliberately threw the little figurine out of the door and across the concrete of the station. It shattered against a nearby wall. Then she dragged her hook stave through the remaining papers, throwing half of them out of the gondola and into the street. "Better clean up, Older. Littering is a punishable offence."

Just then the door beeped again, at a higher pitch this time. The gondola was well behind time, and if I stepped outside to get those papers, I'd have to wait for the next one. I slowly bent down, starting to pick up the nearest cursed pictures and return them to their crate, and feeling the Breaker's eyes on me the whole time.

"Come on, Tresh," the other Breaker said, sounding bored. "I'm hungry."

Tresh the Breaker gave me one last evil glare, then finally… *finally* stepped out of the gondola. The doors slid shut with a happy little beep, and then we were lifting quickly into the air, as if it was trying to make up for lost time.

Then it was just me, a massive pile of damaged children's art, and an old man who was still focused on his hand-held game. They hadn't bothered *him,* at least. They could just have easily have stolen that game and called it taxation.

As for me, I sat there breathing slowly in and out of my nose, feeling my neck and cheeks and ears hot with fury, feeling it boiling in my stomach. To be so helpless…it was the worst feeling.

"From Pacifica, are you?" the old man said into the heavy silence. "You *are* a long way from the starting line, aren't you?"

"You might say the same for yourself," I retorted, my mood foul enough to keep me from politeness.

He chortled, seeming unoffended at the reference to his age. "Don't worry about it, dear. Those Breakers are *such* grawlixes, aren't they? It'll all be alright."

I scoffed, surprised at the use of language from such an old person. But he was right about one thing – the Breakers *were* grawlixes…and hewliguns, too.

My mood didn't improve much as the gondola travelled along, pausing to let the old man off on the next stop half an hour later. I didn't even have the chance to pull out my communicator and sob my woes to Aria, or Lanny, or even Mum or Nik, because someone new got on and took the old man's seat.

This guy was about sixty years younger than the last one, so maybe my age, and kept from being truly good-looking by his height (short, but then most guys were to me) and his baby face. Still, with that black hair and dark eyes surrounded by long, black lashes, maybe he'd be worth looking at in a few years. Except now he was staring quite rudely at me and my messy pile of 'art', which hadn't all made its way back into the crate.

"What are you looking at?" I snapped. "Never seen the

outcome of a Breaker visit before?"

"Is that what that is? I thought it was…finger paintings."

I shrugged, then bent down and began stuffing them back into the crate. "Something like that."

"Besides," the boy continued. "Breaker is an insulting term. You should say 'the Ducal Guard'."

I snapped my gaze back to him, certain he must be joking, but his expression was serious. "Then maybe they should stop breaking everything in their path," I retorted. "Then we can give them some more respect." Weirdo.

I could feel his eyes on me, then he said, "So…going to Unity, are you?"

"That's the plan."

"Ah. And you're…" He paused. "Iscendra Cole?"

I paused mid-paper-stuff, glancing up at him. He was watching me with an intent expression and a slight smile, and I felt a jolt of familiarity. "Do I know you?"

The boy shrugged, smiling. "You don't recognise me?"

I put two and two together. *Dark-haired boy travelling to Unity today, knows who I am.* "Oh, suds. You're not Felix, are you? Trudi and Brant's grandson."

"Something like that," he retorted, mimicking my earlier tone. "And you've got a brother, right? Nik, age sixteen?"

Suds again. Felix might be a total weirdo – because *no one* defended Breakers – but I had to be nice to him, because he was coming over for tea. Suds, suds, suds. "Mm. He's fifteen, actually."

"Oh." Felix's face fell into a slight sulk, then he brightened. "And you're…"

"Not interested in this conversation anymore." I finished pushing all the rubbish art back into its crate, then snapped the lid into place.

"You missed one."

I took the paper he'd held out, pausing to study it in surprise. The paper didn't feel familiar, but I definitely recognised the image as one I'd put up for sale online last year. "Oh. This is one of the good ones." It was a simple sketch of a pog riding a three-wheeler bike, a grin of glee on its fluffy face. "I wonder how this got in with the rest of them?"

"I like it," Felix announced. "Do you have any others?"

He went very slightly up in my estimation. "Not here. But I have more at home." I paused, then added, "I could show you later, if you like."

"Yes."

No 'please'. Just 'yes'.

Just then there was a flash of red from my communicator. The home number. Luckily I'd moved it to my wrist after we'd left Vyce, so I didn't need to go digging around in my clothing. I answered it with voice only, then turned away, speaking as quietly as possible. "Mum?"

"No, it's Nik. She told me to call and see if you're OK."

I felt a wash of emotion rush over me at that, and I actually closed my eyes. Why was it that when life was hard, sympathy made me want to cry? But I didn't. Instead I gave him a very quick, very quiet rundown of what had happened in Ruges, although didn't mention the Breaker attack from earlier. "So I'll go back tomorrow," I finished. "Same time."

"Oh. Well, you'd better come straight home today. *Felix* is going to be here any time. You don't want to disappoint your *one true love*."

"Shut it, Nik!" I glanced over to see that Felix seemed to be engrossed in the scenery, then turned back to the communicator. "He's not my one true love, that's for sure. And guess what? He's actually here on the gondola with me."

Now that shut my brother up, and I ended the call with a smile of satisfaction.

Now Felix was definitely watching me, and he seemed to be wearing a smirk. Had he heard what I'd said? "Family," I said briefly. "So how long will you be staying with your grandparents?"

"Not too long," he replied vaguely. "I'm not going straight there, actually. I have to stop somewhere else first."

Then the gondola slowed to a halt, coming down to rest on the last station before we moved out of Vyce territory, into the outskirts of Unity. Felix got up to leave, and now I could see he was definitely smirking. "I'll see you around."

I would have said 'not if I see you first', but unfortunately he was coming for dinner, and I did have *some* manners. So instead I nodded goodbye.

The doors closed after him, and as the gondola swiftly rose into the air, I saw a couple of figures in brown armour approach him. "And there's your punishment, Weirdo," I said aloud. "A Breaker visit of your own, on the last stop they can."

Ha.

The sun was setting by the time I got home, dimming the sky enough for the twin moons to show low on the horizon. Misshapen Phobos was in the foreground, looking rather like a glowing space-potato, with tiny Deimos almost hidden behind it. I knew that soon I'd be able to see Optus, shining like an oversized star as it orbited Mars, and of course that made me think of Aria. Suddenly I felt a wave of homesickness wash over me.

"Silly girl," I muttered. "You *are* home, and it's time for dinner."

Dinner with Felix the Weirdo, which probably explained my crankiness. It occurred to me then that I hadn't eaten since leaving Ruges, and that would be adding to my bad mood. So I grabbed a large, ripe nectapeach from the nearest tree as I went by, shoving it into my mouth so that I could use both hands to access the lock. Then I stepped onto the small platform that whisked me up the cliff to our front door, then went straight inside to see my brother Nik in the kitchen, serving up portions what looked like pie.

"Felix is here," he grunted.

I rolled my eyes, swallowing the bite of nectapeach and punching him in the side…then quickly regretted that punch. *Ouch.* Nik was bony. "Impossible. He just got off at the previous stop."

"Well, he's here." Nik waggled his eyebrows. "And he

brought his girlfriend."

A girlfriend. I laughed aloud, and he laughed right back. For all that he teased me, my brother was always on my side, and he knew well that I didn't want to be set up with anyone. So when I finally went through to the next room to greet our visitor, I had a big, genuine smile on my face.

But the silver-haired boy in the other room wasn't the same one I'd just met. He had dark roots under that coloured hair, a vaguely familiar face, and an arm around a blue-haired girl about my own age. "Hi," he greeted me, extending one hand. "You must be Iscee."

I stopped in my tracks. "Who the shriek are you?"

Mum made a sound of dismay at my bad manners, and the silver-haired boy's dark eyebrows shot up. "Uh…Trudi and Brant's grandson, Felix. This is my girlfriend Aminda."

"*You're* Felix!?"

"Uh…yeah." The boy exchanged an awkward, amused glance with the blue-haired girl. "Why, do you need to see some ID?"

"Brant just dropped him off half an hour ago," Mum explained, shooting me an evil glare. But then she didn't know about what had happened on the gondola, because I'd spoken to Nik instead. "What's going on, Iscee?"

My heart sank, and I finally realised what had happened. *You must be Felix*, I'd said to the weird boy on the gondola, and he'd agreed. He'd never volunteered that information.

"That's a really good question," I answered finally.

"You're definitely not going on that gondola tomorrow morning," my dad said later that night, after our real visitors had gone. We all sat around our small dining room table, the remnants of dessert left abandoned on our plates. "You said the boy might have overheard what time you were planning to go. He could be waiting for you with friends. You could be robbed."

Unfortunately I couldn't argue. All I could think about was the fake-Felix's stupid smirking face, and trying to remember exactly what I'd said. "I'll call Lanny and tell him I'm not coming," I said instead, feeling my shoulders slump. "And I'll miss the opening of the festival." Suds, suds, suds.

"I'm so sorry, Iscee," Mum said with genuine sympathy, which of course made me want to cry. "If only I'd seen Alek rearranging the crates, then you would have delivered everything today."

We'd finally figured out that he was the one who'd unpacked my precious art, had put it all back up on the walls of my tiny home studio, and then had filled the crate again with the junk that had been in there previously. Why? Because Alek did not like change, and that included the contents of *my* crate, apparently. Lesson learned.

"Yeah, but we were all home too," I countered. "Nik and me and Dad. We didn't see it." I shrugged, too depressed to force a smile. "So it's not your fault. And Alek is who he is. I should have kept the crate in my room until the last minute."

"Why don't you go on Friday instead of tomorrow?" Nik suddenly suggested. "Take a late gondola. You can do the turnaround fast, and still be back in time. 'Cos if this weirdo *did* listen to what you told me, then he thinks you're taking the first trip tomorrow. Even if he's up to something, surely he's not going to check every gondola for the next three days. That'd be really expensive."

My eyebrows shot up. That was…a good idea, actually. I glanced hopefully at my parents. "Can I…?"

"I don't see why not," Dad said thoughtfully. "But we'll take a few precautions."

And that was why I found myself on yet another gondola two days later, swinging high above the Martian landscape in a repeat of my first trip. Except unlike that time, this time I had a siren baton strapped to my wrist, a spare, cheap communicator in my underwear, a shocking device strapped to my *other* palm, and the now-black crate of sketches was double-sealed and painted to look like a fruit delivery. Yes, fruit. But then we had a lot of fruit boxes around the plantation.

I felt rather more cheerful too, munching on a nectapeach as the gondola sailed across those same forests and swamps as before. Lanny was expecting me, I was armed to the gills, what could go wrong?

But then about halfway between Unity and Vyce city, the gondola slowed to a halt mid-air. I looked around warily through the clear walls, my hand moving to turn on the shocking device. The audio had mentioned hijackings, and what was that I could see in the distance, above the forest canopy? I was alone in here…

The gondola cabin beeped a couple of times, signalling that it wanted to keep moving, and I huffed under my breath. "I'm with you on that one, gondola."

Then finally the cabin lurched back into motion, and I heaved out a sigh of relief. That lasted only two minutes, until we reached the point where two gondola lines intersected. I was meant to keep moving straight, towards the capital then beyond it, but instead the gondola slowed and abruptly began moving right, down one of the side lines.

Suds. I checked the flashing destination light again, but it still read, 'Ruges', just the same as when I'd first got on. But this was *definitely* not the way to Ruges.

Suds, suds, suds…and a few words worse than that too. I quickly lifted my communicator to my mouth, tapping in home, Aria, Lanny, and the emergency contact for gondola services. The more the merrier. Chances were no one would respond to the last one, out here in the middle of nowhere, but I didn't have any other choice.

"My cabin's been pulled down a side path," I said urgently into the group contact. "On the intersection near the Whirey Swamp. This doesn't look good. Send help ASAP."

Now the gondola seemed to be slowing again. Up ahead I could see a tall platform rising from the trees. The large, flat space was almost bare except for a small building and some kind of vehicle. I squinted at it, but the angle wasn't good, and I was coming in at high speed.

I sucked in a breath, my heart pounding, and squeezed the shocker in one fist. A *zing* of electricity showed it was live. *Surprise, grawlixes.* If only I could startle them for long enough for the gondola doors to shut, for it to keep moving…

There was silence from my communicator, and I realised that I'd only opened it one way. Probably that was good, because the screams of horror from my mother and cousin would make this harder to deal with.

And then the cabin lurched to an abrupt halt, sending me flying sideways onto the floor as the platform's magnetic grip stopped the gondola dead, and the doors slammed open. Suddenly there was a long metal spear tip right in my face. I looked up its length to see…brown armour? "Use that shocker and it'll be the last thing you do," the blonde soldier informed me flatly.

I didn't move from my awkward position. Really, lying on the floor with one leg on the seat, and my fake fruit crate stabbing into my back wasn't the way I'd choose to deal with this situation. But still…

"You're kidding me," I blurted out. "I'm being robbed by *Breakers*? Don't you have anything better to do?"

The soldier just stared at me flatly, much in the same way that other, redheaded one had days before. But this girl was much shorter, with a round face that might have been cute if it hadn't been so emotionless. "Put your hands in the air and get up."

I tried to obey, really I did, because I couldn't see anything from where I was. Besides, I didn't want to get skewered by the pointy end of the stave they all seemed to carry around. But getting up from a lying position, without using your hands? Not easy.

"Get up!" the girl shouted again.

Fine, fine! I did so, moving back into my seat. But even from here, I couldn't see past her. Couldn't see what was behind. I could just see more brown armour; could hear voices or perhaps laughter? "I haven't broken any laws," I said in a low voice. "Why have you brought me here?"

The girl gave me a flat look. "Unclip that shocker, and whatever you've got strapped to your other wrist. Hand it over along with your communicator."

Suds, suds, and shrieking grawlixes. This was bad. "Am I being robbed? You know I'm an Earth citizen, right?" I said as I unclipped the shocker and the two wrist pieces, then dropped them on the cabin floor. "You'd better believe people will find out about this. You got a name, Breaker girl? Or shall we just call you 'the one who caused an interplanetary incident'?"

She didn't respond, instead using her foot to scrape the items off the floor and kick them outside.

"Oh no," a new voice said from somewhere outside. It sounded amused. "You can call *me* the one who caused an interplanetary incident."

The blonde Breaker moved back from the doorway, and then I could see who was standing behind on the high platform, along with a large open-air vehicle parked behind. There was a tall, male Breaker with cropped fair hair and a bored expression.

And next to him, barely reaching his shoulder, was The Weirdo. The fake Felix from days before, and he was grinning. "Welcome, Iscendra Cole. We've been waiting for you."

I blinked at him in shock. One second, two passed as my temperature rose to boiling point. "You!"

"You were supposed to catch the first gondola two days ago," The Weirdo said as if I wasn't going red with fury. "And we had to keep tabs on the records since then. Well, not me. But Bloom here has been, and she hasn't liked the task."

Bloom, AKA little blonde Breaker, didn't respond.

My voice was low and hoarse as I finally managed to speak. "Are you seriously saying that you've waited all this time for *me*? What exactly did I do to annoy you so badly, whoever you are?"

The boy frowned, his dark eyebrows coming down low over those thick-lashed eyes. "I'm not Felix."

"Yeah, I figured that!"

He still looked perplexed. "Don't you know who I am?"

I blinked at him. Perhaps that face *was* a bit familiar, but there was still no recognition when I looked at him. Only dislike. "The guy who's tried to ruin my day not once, but twice? The guy who's going to get his face plastered all over the news vids for what he's doing right now?"

I was serious, but he just laughed. Next to him Bloom glared down at my communicator where it sat on the platform. "This thing's on." And then she flipped her weapon and smashed the communicator's surface with one sharp blow.

"Ruined your day?" And now the boy laughed. Like a full-on, wide, hilarious-joke kind of laugh. "Oh, but it's about to get better. Congratulations, Iscendra. You've just become the newest member of the Ducal Guard."

But that didn't make sense… "What?"

"The Breakers," the tall male guard said, sounding bored. "You've been conscripted."

THREE
Conscripted

I just sat there on the gondola seat for a few seconds, staring out at the three of them.

The tall, male Breaker still looked bored. The short, blonde Breaker was emotionless. And the middle-sized, dark-haired fake Felix? He was grinning. Still grinning, as if he'd made a wonderful joke.

Finally I found my tongue. "You can't conscript me," I said in disbelief. "I'm an Earth citizen. You can't compel me to do anything."

"Yes. Well. That's where the interplanetary incident comes in, right?" The Weirdo spread out his palms in front of him as if performing a magic trick. "And we'll see how much power the Old World still has here in Vyce, when one of their own precious daughters is snatched up by the local government. Will they or won't they? I'm betting they won't do a thing to save you."

Just then the gondola began to beep, signalling the doors were about to close. I looked up at it in hope, but then the male Breaker lifted his weapon. Three short bursts of light and sound, and the beeping stopped. Those staves weren't just hooks and blades – they were also guns.

"Get out of the gondola," the girl ordered me.

But I didn't move. "You can't do this," I said again. "It's illegal."

"And yet here we are, Iscendra." The boy pouted. "Come on, then. We've waited long enough."

The male Breaker stepped in and grabbed my crate of sketches, and suddenly I was spurred into action. "Hey!"

But he ignored me and yanked the whole thing out onto the platform, and I followed after it. "Hey, that's mine!"

"What's in here?" The Weirdo mused. He kicked at the crate. "More finger paintings?"

No, sketches that might be worth six months' wages for me, if they sold. "None of your shrieking business!"

The boy's dark eyes narrowed. "Really." He turned to the taller Breaker. "Toss it off the platform."

"*NO!*"

But I was too slow, and the Breaker had already moved faster than I'd thought he could in that bulky armour. The precious crate of sketches was hefted off the platform and tumbled down into the thick forest below. It vanished into the canopy within a second.

My eyes were so wide that they hurt; overwhelmed with anger, or maybe a little fear. My sketches. My work. Gone.

"You should have just told me," The Weirdo informed me casually. "Now get on the transport, and-"

I punched him in the nose. *Crunch* went the cartilage, and there was a wonderful spray of blood as he howled, doubling over and slapping both hands to his face.

"*Those were important!*" I shouted at him. The two Breakers were both between us now; the girl blocking The Weirdo, and the boy pointing his weapon at me. But I ignored them. I was so angry I felt like I could literally explode, like I could tear something apart, and I tried to push the weapon aside so I could have another shot at him. "You stupid, stupid, *stupid-*"

ZZzzzt. Suddenly blue lights flickered in my eyes, and my whole body convulsed. They'd shot me with someth-

My eyes were heavy, and my head hurt. There was something hard underneath me, and I heard the sound of laughter, of clanging metal. I blinked, squinting against the shafts of bright light that jabbed at my eyeballs, then groaned. Oh, my stomach...

"Throw up in the bucket," someone ordered.

I wasn't going to throw up...I didn't think. "What

happened?" I managed to ask.

"You sucker-punched the High Duke, Older." The female voice sounded gleeful. "Wow, are you in for it."

"Whuh...?" But now I'd properly woken, so I pushed myself to my elbows and looked around, blinking in pain and confusion. I was on the floor in a dark room. Just in front of me was an open door, which was where the bright light was coming in from. Through the door were colours, shapes; people playing a game? Fighting? Hard to tell. And right next to me was a smiling face. Female. Reddish scars down her neck, reddish hair. Had we met?

"The stunners always pack a punch," a different, male voice said. "You can go, Tresh."

"But don't you need my help?" Tresh persisted. "I could slap her around a little. Fair's fair."

"Fair would be letting the High Duke punch her right back, and he passed on that," the male voice said wryly.

I'd punched a High Duke?

Suddenly I remembered what had happened, and I groaned again, this time in dismay. I'd punched The Weirdo...who was apparently also the ruler of Vyce. The selfish, secretive, disaster-breeding teenage ruler of Vyce, and the one who ran the Breakers. And he'd deserved it, because he'd had the stupid idea to conscript me. *Me!* And he'd ruined my day...

Then I remembered something worse, and I sat bolt upright. A wash of nausea came over me, and I almost fell sideways again. "My sketches!"

He'd had them thrown off the gondola platform into the wild greenery below, never to be seen again. They'd probably been eaten by something.

I slapped a hand over my mouth. Now I *did* want to be sick.

I wasn't, though. Instead the guy who was in the room with me waited a few moments, then tapped me on the shoulder. "Try this. It'll make you feel better."

'This' was a shot-glass full of an orangey-red liquid. I

eyed it suspiciously.

"We call it Magic Juice," the guy continued calmly. "So drink it, and feel better. Or don't, but you're going to have to get off that floor anyway. You've been there for three hours."

That would explain why I needed the bathroom.

I drank the glass, and it tasted like tomato…plus something that set my mouth on fire. "Argh!"

"Yeah." The guy was now grinning. "That's the usual response. And I'm Zavier, by the way. You can thank me now, or later. Either is fine."

But I did feel better, and I finally managed to focus on his face. Not unhandsome, with short-cropped light brown hair and no helmet, and the remnants of acne scarring on his cheeks. He was young, like these Breakers all were. But then I finally placed where I'd last seen him.

"You threw my sketches off the platform!" I accused, stabbing a finger towards that face. "You absolute grawlix!"

The grawlix swiped my finger away with a casual brush of his hand, then stood and moved back. "I was directly ordered to do so by the High Duke Shandlin. I wasn't going to say no, Older. And if you were smart, you wouldn't have tried so hard to make him angry."

"I didn't know who he was," I muttered. And truthfully, I didn't blame this guard for the sketches. I blamed Fake-Felix. I stood cautiously, then when the room didn't spin, stretched. Ouch. Even my fingernails ached – whatever had been in that stunner, I didn't want to get hit with it again.

"Well, now you do. And if you want to last the full two years as a Breaker, you'll need to do the smart thing. Stay alert. *Listen.*" The last part was said with emphasis because I'd already moved over to the open door, squinting outside into the sunlight.

I could now see that we were inside some kind of compound. There was a large, paved space with high walls all around it, and buildings rising higher still. They were functional rather than lovely, and those high walls were sprayed with multi-coloured slogans. 'Breakers rule!', 'never stop' and for some reason, 'study hard' featured quite a few times. But in the empty space, brown-armoured teens were fighting with those double-ended staves, while others gathered around them and cheered or booed depending on who they supported.

I felt a hand grab my arm and pull me back inside. "What did I say about listening?"

"I shouldn't be here," I said automatically. "Seriously. You know that, right? Earth citizens can't be compelled to do *anything* by Martian authorities, except keep their laws while within their territory, which I've done. There's nowhere, *nowhere* that says you can grab some random girl off a gondola and try to make her a soldier."

"Might means right."

"What?!"

Zavier smiled at me, kind of. It was the first truly friendly expression I'd seen since that horrible moment on the isolated platform. "It's a Breaker saying. Basically, the High Duke's decided that he's going to test your government's strength and interest by keeping you here. He doesn't think they're going to charge on in to save you. So if he wants you here, then you're here, until someone strong enough comes to get you back. You know that, right?"

He'd mimicked my earlier statement, and I felt my lips tighten. Because that was the crux of the issue. *Was* Earth strong enough to get me back, or did it just rely on ancient peace treaties that no longer had any power? Would it even *try?*

"I hate this," I clipped out.

"Yeah. When I was conscripted at sixteen I felt the same way. But then I got used to it." He grinned at me, and I upgraded him from 'not unhandsome' to 'definitely cute'… if he hadn't been a crazed Ducal guard. "So when I finished my two years three months ago, I decided to stay. I'm with the High Duke's personal guard, I get paid well, and it's interesting. Give it a month or two, Older. You might feel the same way."

"Iscee."

"What?"

"Iscee, not Older. You may as well get my name right, if you're wrong about everything else. Because I will *never* feel the same way. And if your High Duke thinks I'm going to fight *for* him, then he's got another-"

Zavier's hand slapped across my mouth, and he was once again sombre. "Seriously, Iscee. I get that you've got a temper, but show some sense. Keep your mouth shut, will you?"

I looked around, and realised that even though we were inside, we definitely had attracted some attention from those outside. And he was right. I did have a temper, but I did have some sense too.

I nodded. "So you're with Shandlin's personal guard. Why are you out here with me?"

"I'm here to teach you a few things, and make sure you don't get killed the first day. Olders aren't popular around here."

"Yeah, I'd noticed," I muttered. 'Killed the first day'? That didn't sound so good.

"So I'll be with you for the afternoon, then you'll be on your own. And if you want to last, like I said, you need to be smart. It doesn't matter how you feel! You need to *act* right. The rules are, once you're in the Breakers you stay in the Breakers. No friends, no family visits, no dating, no deserting. Two years in and you get promoted out. Understood?"

'No dating' was about the only thing I could accept. As for the rest of it, no, I didn't understand, and I didn't like it. "You mean if I don't get killed before then, I get to not-die some more. Fantastic. Or even better, I get some wonderful facial scarring like everyone else around here."

Zavier shrugged. "If you don't like the scarring, then wear the full-face helmet." He pointed to a pile of something on the floor behind me. A moment later I realised what it was – a uniform. "I'd put that on if I were you."

I looked at the brown metal armour that symbolised everything I currently despised, then back at my own simple clothing. "I don't think so."

He sighed. "Then don't. It's your funeral. Come on, I have somewhere to be."

"Wait!"

"What is it now?"

I felt heat rise in my cheeks, and I lifted my chin. "I need the bathroom."

Zavier pointed silently at a nearby door.

Once inside the tiny room, I locked the door then took a moment to switch on the taps. They were the sort that'd turn off the moment you moved your hands away, just like at my old school back in Unity. In front of me was a large, age-faded mirror showing my reflection. Red hooded jacket, wild brown ponytail, spots of pink in each cheek. Angry. But I knew from the expression in my brown eyes that I was scared, too.

Better to be angry, I decided. It meant I'd make things happen – although hopefully not punching a hole in a wall, breaking anyone's arm, or bloodying another duke's nose.

To the right of the mirror was a very small window, partially open to allow air flow. Old fashioned. Crude. It also looked rather like the windows from that same school. And I hadn't liked school all that much…

I crept over to the window and gave it a tap. It swung right open, revealing a wall about three feet away. Cramped, but possible. I'd done it before…

Ouch. Ouch. But with minimal damage, twenty seconds later I'd swung myself out of the window. I now stood on the sill, in the narrow alley created by the two walls. Just below was the hard ground. The building stretched far to either side, like army barracks. I wouldn't fit down there, not really. But above me was the sill of another window, from what must be an upper level. I narrowed my eyes and weighed the distance.

Inside the small bathroom I heard a heavy tap on the door. "Are you done in there?"

Suds. "Nearly," I called back. "Give me some privacy!"

It was now or never. I pressed one booted foot against the other wall, then stretched up to grab the higher sill. With a burst of strength I pushed off against the wall, and just managed to hoist myself up onto that second ledge. But it was only just, and I felt myself falling backwards. My back hit the second wall, and then I was stretched awkwardly across the gap between buildings. *Don't fall, Iscee, or you'll be wishing you wore that helmet.*

My first day as a Breaker and I was already acting suicidal. See, I fit right in.

I muttered a quick prayer then tried again. Even though my position was awkward, I managed to grab onto the ledge and finally lift myself onto it. Whew! And it was easier from up here. This ledge was thicker, and ran right along the length of the building. I shuffled along, careful not to lose my footing, and with an eagle eye out for any possible escape routes. I spotted a wall in the distance that appeared to mark the edge of this compound. If I could make it over, make it out into the city, then perhaps I could get away. Get back to Unity, or to the Earth embassy. Home.

All I needed to do was get to this building's roof, then jump across, I decided. But when I reached the other end of the ledge just outside another blacked-out window, I realised I had a problem. It stopped dead, and I doubted I could climb any higher without falling on my head.

I was practically in front of this other window. It was larger than the bathroom one I'd escaped from, and it appeared to be covered with a thin perforated barrier, or whatever these barracks used. It was also open just a crack. I crouched down, trying to hear if there was any noise inside, but could only hear a faint rushing noise.

"Oi!"

I looked down to see Zavier's head sticking out of the tiny window down below me. A moment later he vanished, and I knew my time was limited. Without worrying about what was inside, I yanked the window in front of me open, then punched my fist straight through that thin barrier. It split like old paper, and I tumbled through to land on the floor of what appeared to be another bathroom, albeit a nicer one.

But I wasn't alone. Just in front of me, standing before the shiny mirror, was the High Duke. He wore an ugly white cone-shape over his nose, and if it hadn't been for those distinctive eyes and eyebrows I wouldn't have recognised him. It looked like I'd interrupted him examining his face in the mirror. His face, which *I* had punched.

Suds and double-suds. I had the *worst* luck!

We just gaped at each other for a moment, me wondering how quickly I could throw myself back out of that window, and him – who knew. Then I found my stupid mouth saying, "Nice nose-piece. What happened there?"

His eyes narrowed. "Come to finish the job, have you?"

Just then there was the sound of running feet from behind him, and two Breakers appeared in the doorway, weapons out. One was Bloom, the small blonde with the emotionless face. The other was a dark-haired guy I hadn't seen before.

"You want me to stun her again, Your Grace?" Bloom offered.

"That depends." The High Duke scowled at me. "Are you here to apologise?"

I carefully got to my feet, my palms outspread in front of me to show I meant no harm. But an apology? That was asking too much, and I couldn't tamp down the simmering anger that had been in me ever since the gondola had been hijacked. "Sure. Right after you apologise for kidnapping me, for destroying my valuables, *and* you pay me compensation for damages done. How does that work for you, *Your Grace*?"

There was a silence, broken by what sounded like an aborted laugh from the other Breaker, and the Duke's eyes narrowed further. Hard to think of him as the ruler of Vyce, when he looked more like a bratty kid who went to school with my little brother – one currently wearing a fake nose. "Get her out of here," he said shortly. "And do something about that bathroom window!"

I didn't fight the rough hands that dragged me out of the bathroom, because there was nowhere I could have gone. But even so, as I was pulled through a much, *much* nicer suite than the empty room downstairs, I found myself looking over my shoulder at him.

He half-raised a hand as if to cover his nose, then lowered it again. "And if the stunner's not enough incentive to behave, Iscendra, how about this? I wanted to take your brother, until you told me he was only fifteen. Breakers have to be sixteen, you see. But I think I don't care anymore. If you don't do what you're told, then I'll make sure he's brought here. I'll make sure he gets the most dangerous jobs, and that he's set to riding an untamed farlac that's sure to throw him mid-flight."

He paused, tapping his chin. "Oh. And shall we say that your parents won't be able to sell their produce anywhere in Vyce, because we'll cut off their exports. Will that do it?"

Fear twisted in my stomach along with anger, and if I hadn't hated him before, then I did then. Either of those things would have ensured my good behaviour, because my family was more precious to me than my own life, or even my sketches. So I just looked at him, and he finally rolled his eyes. "Oh, go away, and don't come back."

I went.

I would have happily gone away and not come back, if only I'd been able to find a way out of this place. But after the High Duke's threat against Nik and against my parents' business, I lost the heart to even try. Instead I let Bloom and the other, new Breaker take me downstairs.

We met Zavier on the way, and his expression was a mix of displeasure and something else. "Sorry, Bloom," he said apologetically. "She sneaked out of the bathroom window. Did she try anything stupid?"

"She insulted the Duke's new look," the third Breaker said. He sounded almost amused. "He didn't like that."

"Watch your mouth, Colby," Bloom ordered. "Or you'll be cleaning the toilets with your tongue."

"Sorry, Sarge."

So Bloom was somehow in charge, in spite of her gender

and small stature. I filed that information away for later use, along with her creative, disgusting threats.

"You've been here a while?" I asked her.

"Five years," she replied flatly.

Wow. I guessed she'd started when she was twelve, then, because she did *not* look twenty-one. The timeframe might explain her hardness; that lack of emotion that seemed at odds with her round cheeks and wide eyes. That made her either as trapped as I was, or incredibly hard-edged to have lasted so long.

We marched out of the building and along the open space. Several of the Breakers in the courtyard turned to watch us pass, and I watched them right back. I recognised the redhead, Tresh, but otherwise they were just blurred faces under those ugly brown uniforms.

"I'll show you to your new quarters," Bloom told me. "Zavier. Colby. Go back to His Grace."

They left, and I followed Bloom along past identical, dark grey buildings. These ones were all single level, and rather ramshackle, especially with the bright slogans painted on them. "So did you get forced to come here too?"

"Nope."

My eyebrows shot up, and I actually stopped walking. "Seriously? You weren't conscripted?"

"People *can* volunteer, Older. I did so when the High Duke's father was in power." Her lips tightened almost imperceptibly. "Things were different then. But I *am* loyal! As for you, girl. I'd recommend you do what you're told. Keep your head down and your mouth shut, and just maybe you'll make it to that two-year mark."

She pressed her palm against a door marked '663' and after a moment it clicked open. "This one has a sticky latch, but lucky you, a space has just opened up. Someone got a little too close to a power line while flying."

Inside the room were four bunk beds, the whole space smaller than my room at home, and empty. "Doesn't look like anyone lives here," I commented.

"You do, now. And you've got fifteen minutes to settle in before evening training begins."

She left me there in that plain, ugly room. I shut the door then sat down on the nearest bunk bed and pondered what she'd said. Her comment about keeping my mouth shut was almost exactly what Zavier had said, but I was thinking about how she'd volunteered to join the Ducal Guard, back when things had been different.

The previous High Duke of Vyce, Shandlin's father, had been in power until about four years ago when he'd suddenly died. I remembered how the news had talked about Vyce, worried about what might happen since Shandlin had been well underage at the time. At thirteen I'd been a bit too young to care, but I remembered my parents talking about it too.

In the end his uncle had stepped in as regent, technically in charge until Shandlin turned eighteen. In reality, the uncle spent most of his time on leisure resorts, doing whatever he wanted. And Shandlin, the current High Duke? He spent his time *here*, doing whatever he wanted. And ruining lives and peace treaties, apparently.

I took a moment to smirk over his new, white nose-piece, then slumped back into despair over my situation. That only lasted until I remembered my other communicator – the spare one hidden in my underwear.

I fumbled to pull it out, then immediately switched the thing on and called my parents. But the signal just flashed once, then went straight to their voicemail. I left a quick message. "It's me. I'm OK, but I've been conscripted by the High Duke. Um, into the Breakers."

It still sounded ridiculous to my own ears. "I haven't been able to escape yet. He's also made threats against you guys. Against Nik, if I don't play along. So I will, just until Earth sends someone to get me." I sucked in a breath, trying not to think the worst, that I'd be here for the full two years. "Contact me back when you can, but I might not be able to answer. Bye."

I ended the call not a moment too soon, scrambling to hide the communicator again even as someone pushed my door open. "Ever heard of knocking?!"

Bloom didn't react, and didn't show any indication she'd overheard my conversation. Instead she threw a pile of something brown onto the floor. The armour. Then she held up another brown item, but this one was shiny and crested. "I hear you don't like facial scars, Older. If that's the case, then wear this. You'll be out in the training ring regardless." She dropped it on top of the pile, and it rolled down to land at my feet. "See you in ten minutes."

I picked up the helmet. It was lighter than it looked, and it had padding on the inside where it would curve up around my cheeks, but would leave my eyes, nose and mouth exposed. A distinctive whiff of sweat came off it – the self-cleaning fabric clearly wasn't doing its job.

My hands curled around the hard surface, then tightened as sudden fury rose up in me. *Smash the stupid thing. Show them how you feel.* Never mind that Bloom had already left, and I was the only one in the room to see any destruction I'd cause.

But another thought quickly chased that; a thought that dampened my anger like water on a smouldering fire. *If you don't play along, he'll go after Nik. He'll stop your parents exporting anything outside Unity, and their business will be done for.*

I sucked in a deep breath through my nostrils, closing my eyes then letting the breath out again. I *would* play along, I vowed to myself. It seemed crazy that only three days earlier I'd been telling Aria and Lanny about how good life was, about how I'd choose not to worry until there was something to worry about.

Well, I'd been conscripted, and let's not forget those threats against my family. Now I had something to worry about, so how was I going to deal with it? Not unshakeably, no matter what Lanny had said, but I'd do my best.

Training ring in ten minutes... Maybe I'd get to legitimately punch a Breaker! Or maybe they'd punch me back...and really, I could do without the facial scarring.

So I sighed heavily, then put the smelly helmet on. "This can't be any worse than wrangling with Nik over fruit bread."

Right?

FOUR
Might Means Right

* * *

"**W**eapon UP, Older!" Bloom roared at me. "You want that pretty face smashed to bits?"

I bit back a squeak of dismay as the guy I'd been paired with lifted his plasti-metal training staff and went for my face *again*. I raised my own staff just in time to block the impact, but I felt it judder all the way down my arms. He hadn't been holding back.

Perhaps not much like fighting Nik after all.

I swore under my breath, taking a step back in the small ring and surreptitiously trying to shake feeling back into my fingers. "What's the point of this again?" I muttered under my breath.

"Self-defence," Bloom said, showing there was nothing wrong with her hearing. "You need to be the strongest one in the room at any given time. Do you want to be at just anyone's mercy, Older?"

I felt my hackles rise at that reminder. I already was at the mercy of these people – and it made me *furious*. I didn't want to defend. I wanted to *attack*. So when my partner's staff came down on me again, I swung my own hard to knock it back, stepping sideways so the impact glanced off me painlessly. Then I swung my staff around low and struck him hard in the ankles. He fell, his staff flying out of his hand, and then I came down hard, slamming the point of my staff towards his neck – and stopped an inch short of crushing his throat.

There was a frozen moment where I waited to be stunned, or for someone to shout at me. But instead the guy on the ground looked at me with…respect?…under that crested helmet.

As for Bloom, her face actually showed some expression: she raised her eyebrows. "Now why didn't you do that in the first place?"

I'd take it as a compliment.

Two hours later I'd been judged to have 'trained' enough. That had meant hitting people with sticks, avoiding being hit back, running around and around the training area, climbing on things, falling off things, and not punching people in the nose when they called me 'Older'.

Finally we were released to go for supper, and I pulled off my helmet, headed towards the nearest water fountain, then stuck my head under the trickle. *"Cold…"*

"You know that's meant to go in your mouth, right?"

I paused, turning towards the speaker, but a spurt of water went straight in my eye instead. "Argh!" I stood, wiping my eyes and pushing my wet hair back off my face, then turned to see who'd spoken.

He was dark-haired and dark-eyed, and for a single furious moment I thought it was Shandlin, the High Duke. Then I realised that this guy was older – probably twenty or so – and taller, without the roundness that youth gave the Duke's cheeks. He was also dressed in casual clothes, with a silvery hooded top and black trousers. "Do I know you?"

The new guy shrugged. "Maybe you've seen me on the news. I'm Derry, Shandlin's cousin."

Cousin. The pieces suddenly clicked together in my mind, and I realised exactly who he was. *"Ohh.* You're the one who wants democracy. The, er, second in line for the Dukedom?"

Derry looked a little pained, but smiled down at me. "That's the one, although don't shout about it. Shandlin's not my biggest fan. As for you – I guess you're one of the newest conscripts. Or did you volunteer?"

The Duke didn't like him? I guessed we'd be friends. "I did *not* volunteer," I said grimly. "I'm Iscendra, but you can call me Iscee. I'm an Old World citizen, FYI, but His Grace thought it'd be funny to see if Earth would step in to get me back."

Derry's eyebrows shot up, and he studied me with evident curiosity. "Oh? And how's that going so far?"

"Well…" I gestured down at the brown armour that I still wore over my street clothes. "It's been half a day, and I'm still here."

"Hmm." His gaze moved from my dust-covered shoes, up my body to my drenched face, and his mouth curved into a slight smile. "No obvious wounds. You seem to be doing OK."

"Thanks." Yes, that was sarcastic, but he was also right. It seemed that Shandlin had picked the right girl to conscript, because so far I could hold my own in just about everything. Thank you, Nik, and thank you, dangerous fruit-picking job. "So what brings you here, if Shan- I mean, *His Grace* isn't exactly a friend?"

Derry laughed. "Please, call him Shan. He'll *love* that. My nickname for him is Shanny."

I couldn't hold back a snicker at that idea. "I guess he loves that nickname too, right?"

"About as much as he loves me coming around here to chat with his Breakers. I'm family, and this palace is Ducal land, so it really belongs to all of us. Besides, he can't ban me even if he wants to. My father is the regent."

"This is the *palace?*" I blurted out in shock, and he laughed.

"You didn't know? This is the ugly, functional part, but good old Shanny seems to like it." He looked around with exaggerated slowness. "Speaking of which, where is he? He usually comes storming out the moment he sees I'm here. Worse still, if he sees I'm speaking to one of the pretty girls."

The girl Breakers, I figured he meant. But with the grin he added to that comment? I knew in that moment that Derry the regent's son was a real flirt. Ah, well. From experience I knew such people could be good fun, as long as you didn't take them seriously.

I shrugged, but then remembered a good reason why Shandlin might be hiding his face. "I hear he had an accident,"

I said lightly, trying to hide my smile. "A broken nose, and he's wearing the loveliest white nose-piece at the moment until it heals."

Now Derry did laugh out loud, slapping a hand against his thigh. "Really? I'd give a lot to see that."

And to get a holo-vid online as soon as possible, because that's what I would do. "I'd show you a picture, but they smashed my communicator," I said apologetically. And it was true, too. My communicator was smashed – the one hidden in my clothing was a backup.

His smile disappeared. "Breakers breaking things again, huh? That's the old 'might is right' philosophy. Shanny's father went by the same belief, except that he at least didn't let his Ducal Guard get in the way of the city running, like these Breakers do."

I felt my eyelids shutter, suddenly taking in his serious tone. He knew. He was second in line, and he knew what his cousin was up to, probably better than I did. I'd only been here a day, but I still knew that the Vyce police force was hampered by the Breakers, and probably just as corrupt.

"Tell me, Iscee," he said in a low voice, moving a little closer to me. "If I asked you to help me, would you-"

But I never found out what Derry was about to ask, because just then Zavier sauntered up. He held a communicator in one hand, and wore a slightly sheepish expression.

"What are you doing here, Derry?" The voice had come from the communicator, and it was definitely Shandlin's.

Zavier shrugged, looking apologetic, but then *he* wasn't in range of the camera, which seemed to be turned off. Otherwise there'd be a pop-up holographic High Duke, which there most certainly was not.

"Hello, cousin!" Derry said cheerfully. He had his hands in his pockets, and once again looked the picture of a carefree, if annoying, young man. "I've come to visit my old home, of course. But you haven't come out to see me today?" He voiced that as a question, as if I hadn't just told him exactly what the Duke was probably hiding.

There was a silence from the communicator. "I'm busy," Shandlin replied testily. "And I don't need you here, interfering with my guards. They've got things to do."

Derry turned to me with eyes exaggeratedly wide. "Oh sorry, Iscee. Am I keeping you from something important?"

I shrugged, trying not to smile. After all, I was the one who'd have to deal with an aggravated High Duke at the end of it. "I have no idea. I was only kidnapped at lunchtime."

"*Conscripted!*" Shandlin shouted from the communicator. "Suds it, Older, there's a difference! Now go to your quarters, or I'll have Bloom find you something to do!"

Probably cleaning something with my tongue, if her repeated threats during the evening were true. I shrugged again, tamping down my anger. "Better go. Nice to meet you, Derry."

"And you too, lovely Iscee."

I could still hear the High Duke shouting at his cousin through the communicator even once they were out of sight. He sounded like any other teenager, especially in that moment, but unlike just any teenager, he had the power of life and death over most of those here. Me too, suds it.

I quickly made my way back to my quiet little room and shut the door. Then I pulled out my hidden communicator, checking for messages. My heart sank when I saw there were none, but there was just a hint of purple showing that I had some satellite reception. Nothing local, but I could try to contact Aria again. Unlike Derry and the High Duke, I actually liked my cousin.

I quickly tapped in her code, but just like with my parents, it went straight to the messaging system. Suds. But I left a message anyway, repeating what had happened and to contact my parents and the Old World embassy.

I paused, then added, "And I punched the High Duke in the nose, before I realised who he was. I'm pretty sure I broke it." I couldn't hold back an evil snicker. "Oops. If anyone overheard this then I'm in big trouble. Better go."

I ended the message with mixed feelings, then carefully

hid the communicator away again. Thank goodness for no bunkmates. And I found that strangely, so strangely in spite of the circumstances, I actually felt alright.

Maybe it was finding out that some of the Breakers were actually human, or that I was fit and strong enough to hold my own, or even meeting Derry. But I wasn't boiling with anger, and neither was I depressed in this moment.

I was going to get through this, I decided, even if I had to break a few more noses on the way. Just as long as it wasn't mine.

Two weeks later

I stood near a cluster of restless farlacs on the outskirts of another little Vyce township, watching as the two other Breakers conversed with a store owner. And by conversed I meant shouted at. I couldn't hear what they were saying from here, except that the middle-aged male owner looked both angry and cowed, judging by his scowl and slumped shoulders. But then no one was ever happy to see Breakers.

Smash. Someone broke the transparent plasti-metal window on the store front with the solid butt of their weapon. The store owner howled in dismay, but the Breaker just leaned in and grabbed something off the display shelf. He said something to the owner, who tugged at his hair in apparent frustration, but then finally stepped away with hands raised. Thirty seconds after that, both Breakers had come back to join Bloom and I.

"I grew up in this town, and I always hated that guy," the Breaker who'd broken the window said cheerfully. He held up a vase-shaped item. "And look! Free stuff."

I stared at him in shock, then turned to Bloom to see if she'd scold him. After all, when I'd first started, she'd made a comment about things being different under the old leadership. But she was focussed on her communicator, and had barely taken it in.

"You can't just rob people," I told the Breaker in disgust. "What are you, a criminal? Now he'll have to pay to fix the window, and for that thing you stole too. What is it anyway?"

The Breaker shrugged, seeming unbothered. "Dunno. A bottle, maybe? My mum might like it."

"Not if she knew you stole it!"

"Stop being so shriekn' uptight," the other Breaker snapped at me. She was a girl, and like the guy, was about a year or two younger than me. Both were new conscripts, although these two seemed to have taken straight to their role. "We don't get paid, do we? We've got to have *some* fun."

I imagined my own hardworking parents being treated in such a manner, and it made me furious. It didn't matter what the shop owner was like; he had a right to be treated fairly. "And this is why people hate Breakers."

"*You're* a Breaker," the boy shot back. "You're wearing the uniform, same as us. Stop acting like you're so shriekn' special."

I opened my mouth to probably say something stupid, but then Bloom finally cut in. She was the shortest of the four of us, but still held that authority as sergeant. "Enough! Now get on your farlacs, and get back to the palace. Last one there does *all* the dishes tonight."

The other two cheered, then both ran for their mounts where they were tethered behind me. I was a bit slower. It had been hard enough to get onto that thing this morning. It didn't have a name, just a number on its saddle, but it shied away and stumbled on its six short legs as I moved towards it.

"Keen to do the dishes, Iscee?"

I glanced over my shoulder at Bloom. "Keen not to fall off the thing and break my neck. They're hard to steer." There was no point arguing that sane people didn't ride farlacs. We'd already had that conversation, and I'd lost. They'd been created in a lab 800 years ago. I didn't know what those long-dead scientists had been intending, but they'd made something wild, panicky and weird-looking. Farlacs had white horse-shaped heads and were fine-boned and tailless, with six short legs that were only good to stop them falling over when they settled on the ground. But Breakers rode them, and that was that.

We both watched as the other two trainees managed to mount their farlacs and lift off the ground, only hitting each other a couple of times as they did so. One veered into the roof of the trading post, barely missing it as they gained altitude.

"The trick is not to try," Bloom said finally. "Let the farlac lead you. They know the way back, and they follow the gondola lines."

I watched as the other two figures disappeared into the distance, at a right angle from the lines. My brow creased in confusion. "Are they going the wrong way?"

Bloom didn't answer, but she almost looked like she was smirking, so I'd take that as a yes.

Five minutes later I'd finally got my farlac up high into the air and pointing in the right direction. I crouched low on its back, feeling the breeze from the two sets of frantically beating wings and trying to minimise air resistance. It was cold up here even though the day was otherwise pleasant, and I finally realised the reason for that odd crest on the Breaker helmets. It cut the air like a knife, and the farlacs could move far faster than you'd imagine from such an odd-looking creature. Good thing I was strapped on.

Up ahead of us stretched three thick, perfectly smooth cables, spanning across the Vyce landscape of mountains, forests, and swampland. And without the slightest nudging from me, my farlac was following those cables at high speed, dodging the occasional swinging white gondola going in both directions.

I realised Bloom was right. I couldn't direct it, and it was better not to try. Besides, I was in front, so no dishes for me. I just hunkered down in the saddle and tried to enjoy the view. Beneath me I could see glimpses of sunlit glades, dark ravines, the occasional movement of an animal…and something red, white and blue with the curved horns of a wolcrox.

I blinked – had I actually seen a multicoloured animal

down amongst those trees? But then I realised what it must have been, and let out a short laugh of surprised delight.

Centuries ago, when troubles had begun with the then-Martian colony, Earth had sent in hundreds of surveillance robots in disguise (and a few animal-shaped weapons, too). I'd heard that a few of them survived; still 'living' within the Martian wildlands even though their artificial hides had long worn away. All that remained now were decrepit old cyborgs with ancient Earth flags printed on their sides, the remnants of a colonial age now long gone.

"Amazing," I murmured aloud. I'd have to tell Aria and Lanny about that…if I ever got the chance to.

I glanced over my shoulder and spotted three tiny figures in the air behind me: Bloom and the other two Breakers, now apparently heading in the right direction. I thought again of how those last two had treated that shop owner, and felt a wash of disgust come over me. I'd been thinking about animals, but really, the other Breakers were just as dangerous as any swamp-mare or ancient cyborg. But you could avoid those – and you couldn't avoid the Breakers.

In my short experience, it seemed they were mostly a bunch of lawless, careless teens. Unbelievably, a good number of them had actually volunteered to join rather than been conscripted. From the roughest areas of the dome, it seemed they preferred to become legal bullies and thieves rather than live under others' rules.

I'd read once that some teens might look like adults, but their brains were still maturing. So they'd make poor decisions on the fly; they'd be far more vicious than an adult might be in the same situation, because they couldn't judge what was appropriate.

In that moment, I thought how most of the Breakers were a perfect example of half-brained stupidity and aggression. They'd egg each other on long past what compassion or even sense would dictate. Last night a simple fight over a towel had left someone without vision in one eye; each fighter being encouraged by the onlookers to 'fight the grawlix! Have another go!'

Idiots. I'd just moved to the back of the room and kept my head down, as I'd been advised. So far I was still in one piece, so that method seemed to be working. But here, so high in the air and at the mercy of an equally half-brained animal, all I could do was hang on tight…

Just then my farlac veered wildly to the right to dodge a swinging gondola and I dug my feet into the stirrups, sweating a little as I'd slid almost to the edge of the saddle. I should be used to this by now; this wasn't my first ride, and I was going at breakneck speed – not by choice. I could now hear the beating sound of wings behind me as the others gained on me. It seemed my farlac was determined to keep its first-place position.

We flew over an area filled with massive, dark patches of water, and I immediately recognised the Whirey Swamps from my trip to Ruges a few weeks earlier. Since then I'd found out it was also a suicide spot for people who didn't want to leave behind a body. Rumour had it that if you flew too low here, or jumped in that water, then the local swamp-mares wouldn't give you the chance to reconsider. The gondola lines were definitely too low, I decided again. Just high enough to avoid a swamp-mare lunge, but only by metres. And you'd never know until the moment they chose to-

Suddenly a massive white form lunged out of the black water below. Its vast mouth was open wide enough to swallow both me and my steed, and it snapped shut a second later, missing by mere feet and then falling back to vanish below the swamp's surface. I shrieked in fright, clinging to the saddle as we spun sideways, seemingly out of control. The farlac flapped madly, then finally straightened just long enough to run into a nearby gondola.

This time I couldn't even scream. The breath left my lungs as it lurched upwards at the last moment, and I could swear I saw the fascinated expressions on the faces of the gondola's occupants as we passed by close enough that I could have touched the cabin's clear sides. No one liked Breakers, and to

those passengers, that's what I was – a Breaker about to fall into the dangerous Whirey Swamp.

A Breaker trying desperately to remember that I was *strapped on* as my farlac spun in circles, more like. Then finally, finally it righted itself. We were well away from the lines by now, somewhere over the white cliffs edging the swamp. Safe enough, especially since swamp-mares were basically just mouth and gut, and they didn't bounce.

That one that had almost caught us wouldn't have the strength to lunge for us again, I told myself. Probably. But that didn't take away the cold sweat running across my brow under the stinky helmet, nor the chills down my back, nor my trembling hands where I gripped the reins.

Unshakeable Iscendra.

Yeah, right.

"Come on, farlac," I told my steed. "Get moving, or I'm on dishes tonight." A specially devised punishment no doubt, since even the Ducal Guard barracks had dishwashers.

The farlac obediently headed back towards the gondola lines, and was beginning to pick up speed when the two caught up. They passed us with a rush of wings and a jeering roar, and I knew that I couldn't catch them up this time. Not unless they ran into a gondola or two themselves, and really, I shouldn't wish that on the gondola passengers.

Just then Bloom's farlac caught up to me, slowing a little so she didn't pass. "Looking forward to those dishes, Older?"

Not particularly. I pressed myself flat against the saddle, eyes fixed on our destination…and hoped that the other two would crash into each other, and save me instead.

FIVE
Treason

◎   ◎   ◎

We finally arrived back at the palace well after Breaker Thugs One and Two, and my farlac settled in the stable courtyard as peacefully as if we'd not almost been swallowed whole. I unstrapped myself then stumbled off the saddle onto the mercifully solid ground, pulling my helmet off and sucking in deep breaths of air. My hair was wet, but this time it was sweat rather than water. Sticky, clammy, panic-induced sweat.

Nice.

Bloom's farlac came to rest next to mine thirty seconds later. She'd been right behind me the whole time, probably making sure I didn't try to escape. (If I'd thought I had a chance, and that my family wouldn't suffer for me escaping, then sure, I would have.)

"What happened there, Older?" she asked me snappishly. "You were winning."

"I was overcome with the desire to clean dishes," I retorted just as sharply. "So I arranged for a swamp-mare to startle my farlac. Good move, right?"

She didn't laugh. "Then you've got what you wanted. Twenty-five trays of baked-on grease, waiting for you to make them sparkle. And if they don't sparkle, Older, you'll be-"

"Cleaning them with my tongue?"

The snap of the sergeant's proctor rod sizzled by my ear, and I barely held myself back from blinking. Yeah, so I shouldn't have been talking like that, but I was still angry, and being angry kept me from falling into a useless, sobbing pile over this whole shrieking situation. "Got it. Moving."

I stomped my way into the kitchen and picked up the dishwand, prodding it roughly at the pile of trays stacked in the large sinks since last night's dinner. Oh, I hated it here, I thought furiously. I hated the people, I hated the place, I hated, *hated* stupid arrogant High Duke Shan…

Beep.

It took me a moment to realise what the sound was since I hadn't heard it in almost two weeks, and when I recognised it I scrambled for my communicator. They'd not searched me well enough or perhaps they didn't care if I did keep it, but even so I never used it when the others were around.

I'd been making loads of outbound contacts, but I'd never been able to get through to anyone. Something about the isolation of this place, or perhaps the signal disruptors around the walls. Or perhaps it was the tracking device they'd implanted in my upper arm two days after I'd arrived. 'For safety', they'd said, but I knew what it really meant. If I left, they'd find me again.

I finally retrieved my communicator and tapped twice at its flashing surface. At once a holographic image of my parents sprang up.

"Mum? Dad?" I whispered, tears pricking at my eyes. I was ecstatic to see them, and it had only been two weeks. "What's happened?"

But they weren't responding the way I thought. Instead Dad said, "Iscee, darling, we can only hope that you'll get this message at some point, although it would be a miracle if they let you keep your communicator. We've-"

"We've been in touch with the reps back on Earth," Mum rushed in. Her eyes looked red and swollen as if from crying. "They said that there's- there's probably nothing they can do, but that they'll follow it up."

"So- just keep safe," Dad said, his expression tight. "Do what you have to, but don't compromise what you know is right. And don't worry about us! We'll get by just as we always do. Come visit us as soon as you can."

Mum might have said something more, but the image

flickered and blinked out, replaced by another. It was a symbol of a black star on a white background, the long spines curving out almost like a spider's legs – the Earth government's logo. It looked like I had just a few minutes of reception, and I was getting all the messages at once.

This second message was from the aforementioned Earth reps, and it was automated. "Thank you for your enquiry," the pleasant man's voice said, "but at this time we are unable to take any action. If the situation changes, you will be notified. Have a good evening, and we wish you the best with any further ventures."

Then the Earth symbol vanished and I was treated to a few fuzzy seconds of my mother crying and Alek saying something in the background before the holograph switched off entirely.

Message end.

I was crying now too: angry, despairing tears. What had Dad said, 'to do what I knew was right'? It wasn't right that I should have to be here, but all I could think was that to protect my family, I had to stay. I had to do more than just play along for a little while, but possibly for the whole two years.

Two. Shrieking. Years. I turned and picked up the nearest dinner tray, hurling it at the kitchen floor with all my might. But instead of shattering, it bounced and hit me hard in the shin, and then I was crying from the pain as well as at the hopelessness of the situation. Two years minus two weeks, and if I was still in one piece I'd be able to leave…maybe. But would I even be the same person after all that time?

As for Earth – those useless shrieking bureaucrats. It seemed they didn't even care enough to send a personal message. Instead they'd sent one so vague it could have meant anything, and so meant nothing.

Just then I heard quiet footsteps behind me, and I quickly dashed a hand across my face before hunching back over the sink. Whoever it was bent down and next thing the tray was being held out in front of me. "You dropped this."

It sounded like Zavier, but I couldn't even look at him. I

wouldn't. Then the tray was set down with a clunk, and he said quietly, "You've got to make the best of this. Who knows what good could come out of it?"

He walked away and I still didn't look up, only picking up the tray once I heard him go. I shoved it angrily into the water, noting that the patterns in the grease looked awfully like letters-

Suds. I pulled it out again, just able to read the faint text. It read; *254 – 7pm.*

Two-five-four, seven PM. What...?

A moment later it sunk in. *Meet at cabin 254 at 7 pm...* That was only ten minutes away, and I suddenly wished that I'd taken the chance to at least glance over my shoulder, to see who'd been speaking to me. If it had been Zavier, then why would he want to meet? Even if he was *interested*, he knew well that Breakers weren't allowed to date. Bloom had told me three or four times, as if without the warning I'd be overcome by the urge to make out with the nearest male Breaker. (Mmm, sweaty brown armour, my favourite!)

Of course I'd rather punch most of them than kiss them, and based on how vicious training could get, it seemed that the feeling was mutual. My helmet had taken quite a few knocks, but it had done a miracle – kept my face unscarred.

But now my curiosity managed to overcome my despair, and I attacked the dishes with vigour, pretending that a certain High Duke's stupid face was in place of the hard metal trays.

Twelve minutes later I made it to cabin 253. But past it was an empty space, with no 254 to speak of. I studied the darkened space curiously, noting the ramshackle shed in one corner, and that the graffiti covering these barracks had made it here too. *Breakers rule! Good luck for exams!*

The last one made me do a double-take until I remembered something I'd overheard at breakfast a few days earlier. This part of the palace didn't just look like an old school – it had been one, founded by a previous High Duke a hundred years before, then transferred out into the city proper. When the Ducal Guard had been moved here, it seemed no one had bothered to update the décor.

I wandered over to the graffitied shed, feeling amused in spite of the situation. "Good luck for exams," I mimicked aloud. "As if Breakers know how to re-"

Read, I'd been going to say, but as I'd passed nearby the shed, suddenly the world had changed. I was no longer alone. Now I stood with two tall figures and one short one, all in Breaker uniform. One held a round device that shone light all around us; a holographic reflection of the 'empty' space.

Even as I took that in, suddenly I was grabbed by both arms, pulled in and a hand was shoved over my mouth. I opened my mouth to bite, but then Bloom's distinctive voice hissed in my ear. "Don't say a word! Just go along with what we're saying. If we're caught, then we're punishing you for having an unlicensed communicator, understood?"

I nodded warily, and the hand was removed from my mouth. "You didn't need to grab me like that," I told her quietly, my tone hiding my irritation…and curiosity. "I came here voluntarily."

"Ugh, what part of 'don't say a word' didn't you understand?"

I narrowed my eyes. I'd understood, but it had seemed unreasonable since *she* was talking. "Was that a rhetorical question?"

"Enough!" one of the others cut in. I recognised Zavier, the partial shadows barely hiding his face. Next to him stood Derry, also in Breaker uniform, and I blinked at him in shock. He winked at me.

"We don't have time for this," Zavier said, his words quick and quiet. "We have two minutes tops before we can risk being found, and you're late, but nothing more about that. Iscee, how do you feel about the High Duke?"

"What?" This surely had to be a trick question, but why bring me here to ask it? I raised my eyebrows. "You have to know I don't like him." That was an understatement.

The others exchanged glances, and Bloom said in a low voice, "I don't like this, bringing her in. She can't control her temper or her words, and she'll be useless to us."

"I don't know about that," Derry countered casually. "We've never had an Older conscripted before. The other Dukes always thought they'd end up being spies." He looked at me, and his dark gaze was warm and almost amused. "Would you end up being a spy, lovely Iscee?"

I felt my cheeks heat, but not with anger this time. I covered my embarrassment with a scowl. "Are you offering me a position?"

"A perfect position to help bring democracy into the New World for the first time," he replied. "And who better but someone so close to the symbol of Vyce Dome's weakness?"

"I'm not close to the High Duke. I haven't seen him since I got here." Since I'd left him with that lovely white nose-piece. And since he'd shouted at Derry via communicator, I hadn't even heard his voice. It was no loss.

"You will if we arrange it," Zavier told me sombrely. "I'm the head of his personal guard, and he trusts Bloom like no one else. Will you work with us, Iscee?"

I laughed with scorn. "I say yes, and next thing I'm being flogged for treason, never mind that I don't owe Vyce any loyalty. Forget it. I just want to serve my two years and go home, if Shandlin doesn't get sick of me sooner. Although I bet he's already forgotten about me, that little grawlix."

The others exchanged another glance, and Derry sighed. "She called him a grawlix: it's a shoo-in. I have to go, but you two tell her whatever needs to be told. I'll see you this time next year." He nodded at me warmly. "Good luck, lovely Iscee."

"Er…thanks," I said automatically, but I was watching him go in confusion. I turned back to the others. "Why's he dressed like that, and what is going on? And don't mess with me on this one, *please.*"

"Too late not to tell her," Bloom said crankily. "Go on then, Zavier." He looked uncertain, and she snapped, "Two minutes until Shandlin notices you're gone. Hurry up."

Zavier sighed, then he looked right at me, his expression

a little rueful. "You know if you tell any of this, even to save yourself, we're probably dead."

"I won't tell, I swear." I met his gaze, trying to show my sincerity through my expression. "I'll do whatever you need. Except for stealing, or killing people."

"But you'll punch whoever you need to punch, right?" Zavier quipped. "And you're good with those training staffs. We've been watching you."

My eyebrows shot up. "We, as in you and the High Duke?" That idea was…very disturbing. Did he mean watching me in training along with the others, or just *watching* me? Because the second option was not OK.

"Zavier, stop messing around!" Bloom sighed, then shoved the taller Breaker aside. "It's like this, Older. I said to you before that I signed up under the old High Duke. Things were different then. The Breakers tended to be older, and they were his specialist guard, not just a bunch of hooligans that smashed things wherever they went. But things still weren't perfect. That High Duke took advantage of his position. He didn't have integrity. He didn't *care* about people, and he ignored the needs of the common folk for safety, food, and free movement."

She lifted her chin, looking up at me intently, and in that moment she had my full attention. "Shandlin's worse, of course," she continued. "But that's because he's just a kid who's been given too much power. He's not evil, he's just selfish and clueless. If he'd been raised differently…but that's not the issue. It's hereditary leadership that's the issue. Leaders should be chosen by the people, not born."

"I agree," I said. "But if this is leading up to an assassination, I'm not helping."

"No killing," Zavier agreed quickly. "But it's like this, Iscee…"

And then he told me about the Freedom Movement. A group of people at every level of society – including the second-in-line Derry – who wanted a new way of governing every dome on Mars, not just Vyce. They wanted more safety, less feudalism: a world where everyone had the same chance to flourish, and they weren't ruled by whoever the genetic lottery picked as the next heir.

"And as Bloom said, Shandlin's not even the worst of the High Dukes," Zavier added in a low voice. "He has something of a conscience, but it'll ruin even the best person to have so much power at such a young age."

"A conscience?" I hissed. "He practically kidnapped me!"

"He didn't kill you and burn down your plantation," Bloom retorted. "That would've got Earth's attention, don't you think?"

I stopped, waiting one, then two beats as I remembered the automated message from the Earth reps. "About that." I sucked in a deep breath, feeling the burn of impending tears at the back of my throat. I pushed it back ruthlessly, because I would *not* cry in front of these people. "Shandlin was right. Earth isn't going to challenge Vyce over one girl, even if the law has been broken. They don't care what happens to me. I just-" and I almost choked for a moment, "...I just got the message proving that."

The other two exchanged glances, and for a moment I thought perhaps they held a little sympathy for my plight.

"Oh yeah, the communicator," Zavier said finally, sticking out his hand, palm up. "Bloom figured you had another one somewhere, but we didn't bother searching you. They never work in the palace unless you've got access. There are signal blockers everywhere."

"Oh." No sympathy, then. I stared at his hand for a few seconds, and he sighed.

"Give it to me, Older. It's not like you can use it."

I pulled it from my pocket and reluctantly handed it over. It disappeared somewhere inside his armour. "So this is serious?" I asked. "Some sort of rebellion – and you want me to be a part of it? I don't even know what I could do."

"Just be a good Breaker, and *listen,*" Bloom told me flatly. "Like me. When you need to do something, you'll be told. And if the Old World won't help you, won't you help yourself?"

It didn't take more than a moment to decide. "This better not backfire on my family."

"It won't," Zavier promised. "But if you tell what we've said to even one person…"

"Of course I won't," I said grumpily, but on the inside I was excited. A snippet of hope was enough to make me feel determined rather than despairing. "Should I go back to the kitchen now?"

"Mm. Just a moment," Bloom replied, and then her fist shot up and struck me hard in the eye.

"*Ahh!*"

I doubled over in shock, and as the pain began to set in she said loudly, "That's what you get for smuggling in a communicator. Any more rule-breaking and it'll be something permanent."

Then with a brief nod in my direction, she and Zavier stalked out of the shed, and I finally understood what had happened. I was being 'punished' – a good excuse for why they'd be talking to me out here, but a painful one.

Hey, at least it wasn't my nose.

The following morning I stood in the communal bathroom, studying my reflection in the brightly-lit mirrors. Bloom might be short, but she sure could pack a punch. Not only did my face hurt like crazy, but the skin around my left eye had swollen and turned blackish red, complete with flecks of blood leading away from the bridge of my nose.

I could still see from that eye, but only just. As a kid I'd fallen and hit my face on a stepladder at the plantation. That black eye had taken weeks to fade, and I'd bet this one would be the same.

I sighed, and my lopsided reflection sighed with me. The bruise had been gained for a good cause, probably, so I'd deal with it.

I left the bathroom and headed towards the dining room. Just like with my old school, this too was a big, open room full of long tables. It was always half-full of noisy, hungry

Breakers either heading to or coming back from training, and the food was mediocre except on those rare occasions the High Duke would deign to eat with us.

That had happened twice so far, and each time the meals had gone from sub-par to pretty decent, although they still didn't know how to make a good fruit smoothie. Both those times Shandlin had sat at one end of the room, surrounded by his three or four personal guards, and had eaten along with us. It didn't make much difference to me, since I'd sat as quietly as possible in the far corner, but I'd noticed that there was less fighting than usual amongst the other Breakers.

I'd also noticed that his white nose-piece was missing, and his nose now looked regrettably normal. Perhaps I hadn't hit him hard enough, or perhaps his medical care had been really good. Either way there was no lasting mark of my displeasure. Considering how he showed *his* displeasure, that was probably a good thing.

This time the room was mostly empty, and so were the trays of breakfast food. I grabbed a tray and studied the remaining selection with distaste. My options were something sloppy and baked with cheese on top; something sloppy and unbaked, possibly with fruit; and something that might once have been bread, but now resembled dry brown circles. I sighed, then went to grab a piece of the breadish-stuff, but just then something hit me hard from the left, shoving me aside.

"Watch yourself, Older," a female voice snapped. "You almost knocked my plate out of my hand."

"Sorry," I began, because I actually hadn't seen whoever-it-was. Swollen eye, and so forth. But then I turned to face her, and recognised that red hair, red scarred neck and ever-present scowl. This was one of the few Breakers whose name had actually stuck in my memory, and not for a good reason. She'd been the one to scan me that day on the gondola, and had first brought me to the High Duke's attention. "Oh. Tresh."

Her eyebrows shot up as she took in my new, improved

look. Then she began to laugh. "Who did you annoy this time, Older? Or did you trip over your own feet?"

Now I was the one scowling. Tresh seemed to take every opportunity to cause me trouble, although she'd never done so in front of any leadership. But she *had* tripped me several times in training, and had claimed I was just clumsy. I hadn't forgotten, but I also didn't have a pithy comeback right now. "Get lost, Tresh," I said instead.

Her mood changed like lightning. "I don't think I will," she snapped in a low, ugly voice. "I think you should get lost, Older. No one wants you here, and I don't think your skinny bones need any breakfast this morning. So get to training, or I'll give you a matching set of eyes."

Oooohh. With every word she'd spoken, I'd felt my muscles stiffen and the anger rise inside. But I held my temper…sort of. "Big words, Red. But if anyone should skip breakfast, it'd be you. Then maybe your farlac could finally get off the ground."

Tresh's cheeks turned so pink that her scars almost disappeared. She was stocky, although not really overweight, but yesterday there were supposed to be more of us on that flying trip. Her mount had flatly refused to go anywhere, and Bloom had told her to stay behind rather than saddling another one. I'd kept my mouth shut then, but I hadn't forgotten *that* either. Ha.

Her eyes narrowed, and I saw the flash of movement from the corner of my eye just in time to bring up my breakfast tray. Her fist hit it hard, sending it flying out of my hands and onto the floor. The sound of it hitting the hard surface was like a crack of thunder in the almost-empty room.

But not empty enough. "Fight!" someone shouted, and then I heard other voices join in. "Fight, fight, fight!"

Uh oh. But now Tresh was coming for me again, a roundhouse punch from my blind side, and I blocked it with my elbow, the impact shuddering up into my shoulder. But she'd let out a cry of pain, and encouraged, I stepped forward. Sometime over the last two weeks I'd learned to attack rather than fight defensively, because Breakers just didn't give up, and sooner or later you'd need to end it. And me? I'd rather not be the one ended.

So this time I shot the heel of my hand up into her face as hard as I could, aiming for her nose. I didn't wait to hear the crack of cartilage. Instead I pulled my knee up and stepped into her, turning my face away as I did so I didn't break *my* nose on her chin.

My knee hit her in the gut and I heard another groan, but it hadn't been hard enough. It *mustn't* have been hard enough, because her hands were grabbing at the shoulders of my training armour. She was strong, and she was pulling me away-

"Break it up, Iscee!" someone snapped in my ear, and I finally got out of my anger-panic haze enough to see Tresh in a bloody, snarling mess five feet away with two Breakers behind her, holding her by the arms. They'd dragged us apart.

I threw up my hands, even though I still couldn't see who was holding me. "I've stopped!" I'd been winning, anyway. I thought.

But the arms holding me finally loosened, and I turned to see Zavier smiling down at me. OK, it was just a hint of a smile, but it was definitely there in his blue eyes. "Battling over the last slice of fruit bread, Iscee?"

I smirked back. "Is that what those brown things are?"

"So they tell us. But your timing could have been better."

"Why's that?" As the Breakers would say, there was no bad time for a fight.

"What happened here?!"

Uh oh. Now that voice wasn't so friendly, and I felt my spine stiffen in protest. But still I turned and politely nodded at the newcomer. And now I saw why it was a bad time for a fight – we had a Ducal visitor joining us for breakfast, and he didn't look happy to see us.

Tresh didn't volunteer an answer, and neither did I. But I could see the moment when High Duke Shandlin saw my black eye, because his own shot wide open…and surprisingly he didn't look pleased.

"Older, you look a complete mess," he said to me in disgust. "Fighting over breakfast. Who started it?"

Now there was a way to become entirely hated. Breakers might fight, but they didn't snitch on each other. Not over this kind of thing. In my peripheral vision I could see Tresh's lips tightening under that mask of blood (hooray, it'd been a perfect shot!) but she still didn't speak. It was up to me.

"Nobody started the fight," I answered finally, with just a hint of sarcasm. "We jostled each other in line for this delicious food, then I accidently slipped and hit Tresh in the face. And kneed her in the gut. Isn't that right, Tresh?"

She scowled at me but didn't comment, and I smiled blandly at the High Duke. Either we'd be punished or we wouldn't, because the whole thing would be recorded somewhere. My answer didn't really matter.

His eyes, so much like Derry's, narrowed. Then he focused on the least important part of what I'd said. "What's wrong with the food?"

Really? I mean, *really*? I pointed at the congealed trays of something. "See for yourself."

The fight seemingly forgotten, Shandlin stepped forward and studied it with raised eyebrows. "What the suds is this stuff?"

There was a silence, then some brave soul ventured, "Breakfast?"

But the High Duke was shaking his head. "You don't usually eat like this. *I* eat with you sometimes, and the food's not...ugh. Three days old?"

"The food's better when you're here," I piped in, because at least this distracted him from my little fistfight. "Or it has been since I arrived."

"It's not usually bad," Zavier said hastily. "Or not terrible, anyway."

"I see," Shandlin said. One second ticked by, then two, then suddenly he shouted, *"We're all supposed to eat the same food! That's the whole point of this thing! Somebody fix this!"*

I jolted in surprise, but no one else seemed bothered by the outburst. Perhaps this was normal. But then the universe showed that 'somebody' was listening, as the trays of unappealing food began to slide out of sight into the wall. Ten seconds later they were replaced with the much nicer food we'd enjoyed when Shandlin ate with us.

We're all the supposed to eat the same food, he'd said, but that didn't make sense. Since when did High Dukes eat like conscripts?

"Good," he said shortly. He nodded towards one of his personal guards who I'd briefly met on that first day. "Colby, serve me up. You know what I like." He turned as if to go to his usual seat at the far end of the room, then paused. He glanced over his shoulder again, catching my eye. "Iscendra. You come see me after the meal."

I'd really rather not. But I nodded, then waited for him to take his seat. Then I got in the line with everyone else, because I was hungry, and the new food actually looked good.

Three minutes later I'd taken my seat in the nearest corner, the one farthest away from the Duke's table, then hoed into my full tray. Usually I sat alone, with a sizeable gap to the nearest Breaker, but today someone plunked their tray next to mine, then sat down. It was a guy who I'd met a couple of times while training, but we'd hardly spoken. A moment after that another few Breakers sat too, then suddenly I was sitting in a group.

Hmmm. I paused mid-bite. Was this a good thing, or a bad one?

But then the first guy said, "Nice eye, Older."

There was no nastiness in his tone, so I just shrugged. "Thanks. But you can call me Iscee. It's not like I can call you 'Newer'." No one ever used that term, as if the whole of Martian and Earth society agreed it sounded stupid.

"Iscee," one of the other Breakers said. "So should we ask what the other guy looks like?"

The others laughed, and I laughed with them. "Sure, but they're looking pretty good. I tripped and fell onto Bloom's fist last night."

There was a collective 'oooh', because everyone seemed to know what I'd figured out in my short time here. If the sergeant hit you, you didn't hit back.

But that seemed to break the ice, no pun intended, and we ended up having a friendly conversation over the better-than-usual food. By the time the others went off to training fifteen minutes later, I'd made some friends. Or at least a few people who didn't actively want to give me a matching right eye, so close enough.

With my own food long finished, I glanced across the room to where the High Duke still sat with Zavier, Colby and Bloom, as well as a female Breaker whose name I didn't know. The room between us had grown a lot busier and louder than when I'd first arrived. He seemed to be focused on his own food, and I slowly got to my feet, watching to see if he'd react.

No? I quietly placed my tray on the conveyor belt that would take it to the kitchen, then sidled out the door. If anyone asked, I'd say that he hadn't specified a time, and that I was going to train-

"ISCENDRA!"

I leapt in fright, then turned around, trying to see where the voice had come from. Shandlin was nowhere in sight, but he'd been so, so loud...

"It's a new comm. system," his voice came from somewhere around the doorway. He sounded smug. "I could always see everything, but now I can talk, too. Where are you going?"

"Um..."

"Because I didn't tell you where I wanted to talk to you. And you'd better not be sneaking away."

I stood up straight. I didn't know how much he could see, but I didn't like being berated by an invisible voice. "I don't sneak. And you didn't say *when* you wanted to talk to me, so how would I know?"

"You're supposed to ask," he retorted testily.

"Fine. When do you want to talk to me? Besides now, I

mean."

There was the sound of footsteps, then Shandlin emerged from the dining room entrance, closely followed by the other four. He wasn't smiling. "Now will do."

Uh oh.

SIX
How to Make a Smoothie

I followed the High Duke to a building across the courtyard. It was the same one where I'd 'escaped' out the bathroom window, and had ended up in *his* bathroom. But this time we went to a room I hadn't visited. It was small and lined with comfortable couches. Shandlin sat in one, a round-faced teenager in a too-big chair, then gestured a hand to the other. "Sit down."

I sat, a little uncomfortable. I'd expected to be dragged before some sort of throne, but he was acting as if this was a friendly chat. Two of the other guards slouched against the wall or on the other seats, seemingly absorbed in their communicators. Bloom and Zavier vanished.

"So I understand you're a target," he said without preamble. "That redhead targeted you, didn't she? I suppose she gave you that black eye too."

I blinked at him. Where was he going with this? "You suppose wrong. But what difference does it make?"

"What do you mean?" And he had the nerve to sound offended.

I waved a hand in a roundabout gesture. "You brought me here so you could annoy the Old World, to see if they'd challenge you to get me back. They haven't, as you know. But if that was what you wanted, then does it matter if I've got a black eye, or two, or all my arms and legs broken?" I paused, my own words echoing in my ears, then hastily added, "Except to me. It matters to me."

The High Duke's eyes narrowed, and he leaned forward

in his chair. "You're acting like the Ducal Guard is some kind of dangerous fight to the death! It's not that bad. A lot of people find it exciting, and I care about the safety of the Breakers. I notice *you* seem to enjoy it well enough."

Was he serious?! My restraint forgotten, I threw my hands in the air. "Oh, so *now* you're calling us 'Breakers'! I thought that was an offensive term!"

He smirked a little. "I was just teasing that day in the gondola. Everyone calls them Breakers. It's a long and noble-"

I spoke over him. "And as for me enjoying myself? I'm trying to make the best of a bad situation! As you well know, I did *not* volunteer to be here, I don't want to stay, and I'll be out the moment you get bored or decide I'm too much trouble – if I don't kill myself first by accident! Because the Breakers *are* dangerous! They're reckless and lawless, and they steal stuff, and they solve all problems with their fists or weapons! But how can they be any better? *You* steal *people!*"

Suddenly I could sense the eyes of the other two Breakers on me, and reality seeped back in. In front of me the High Duke's mouth was half open as if in shock, and when I fell silent he finally closed it. "Are you done, Older?"

Oh help. Please don't have me executed. But I kept my chin up. "Um…yes."

"Good. Now listen to me." He paused, then stared down at his knees as an unreadable expression came over his face. Then he looked up again. "You're staying."

After several moments of waiting for further instructions, and hearing none, I shook my head in confusion. "Was that it?" Was that our 'talk'?

"Yes." Shandlin rose from his seat and headed for the door, as casually as if I hadn't just shouted out a few dangerous home truths. "So go finish your training. And if you want the Breakers to be better and safer? Then maybe *you* should show them a better way and stop trying to solve problems with *your* fists." And with that last pithy statement, he disappeared out the door.

The two Breakers followed him out, Colby throwing an

interested glance at me over his shoulder. I just sat in the comfortable chair, trying to figure out what had happened. I'd lost my temper – luckily just verbally, without throwing any more punches – and I hadn't been punished…I didn't think.

Unless he'd been planning to let me go, and I'd ruined it! That thought came to me suddenly, and my heart skipped in horror. Why couldn't I keep my mouth shut?

"Of course he wasn't going to let you go," Bloom told me in disgust ten minutes later. I'd blurted out the whole thing once she'd taken me back to training, not that she 'didn't hear the whole bloody rant' as she so nicely put it. "He's as stubborn as a wolcrox, and gets bored easily. He's not going to free you, not when you're providing such entertainment. Now staff *up*!"

I automatically lifted my weapon to block her strike. This was the first time I'd been paired with Bloom rather than another trainee, and in spite of her small size, she didn't hold back. But then I'd already known that. "Entertainment?!" I exclaimed in response to her comment. "I'm not some kind of performing pog!" Annoyed, I counter-struck then pulled back when I would have hit her shoulder.

She indicated towards the nearby building that housed the Ducal Suite, AKA the rooms I'd just been in. "Well, you're not exactly doing any guarding, are you?"

True. If a troop of rebels stormed the palace right now, I'd probably direct them straight to Shandlin's rooms.

But in spite of her words, I didn't see anything of the High Duke for the next few days. Instead I went about my training – hitting people with a variety of practice weapons, avoiding being hit back, riding those sudsing farlacs – as my eye went through fascinating shades of purple then green.

And to be honest, if I wasn't here as a prisoner, it wouldn't be so bad. It was actually kind of fun, especially now some of the other Breakers were talking to me. Some of them even called me 'Iscee' instead of 'Older'. Even Tresh, who now had *two* black eyes (because a hard blow to the nose could cause extensive bruising, ha ha!) was keeping a respectful distance. Or she wasn't still trying to trip me up, which was practically the same thing.

But one afternoon when I'd been at the palace about three weeks, I stumbled across a couple of Breakers sneakily watching a horrifying holograph. They were huddled in one corner of the bathroom, the hand-held communicator in one of their laps, and a series of images shining in the air in front of them. That was probably why they didn't notice me come in, so I stopped and watched along with them.

It was a news-vid. The holograph showed a map of Mars, highlighting two domes to the north and east of Vyce, then cut to a scene of chaos. People crying, shouting, a building ablaze. Coloured smoke, men and women in armour and holding weapons. Families rushing past, heads down and bags full of their belongings clutched under their arms. A flag with the distinctive spider-like symbol of Earth, shredded to dust in an instant as an explosive went off underneath it.

The news presenter's pleasant voice narrated the whole segment. She explained how unrest in the domes of Eser and Arparath had led to riots. Eser had overthrown their Earth-friendly ruler, and had pushed the Old Worlders out of their safe little townships, reclaiming that land for Mars. Arparath had done that second part too, but their High Duchess had led the riots. She'd blamed all that dome's social problems on the Earth territories in their midst, and the locals had been stupid enough to listen.

Suddenly the Breakers noticed me standing there. One of them, a girl, snapped the holograph shut and stared at me with wide eyes. "Tell anyone about this and we'll make you sorry," she threatened.

But I wasn't offended. I was too busy being horrified by the vid. "I won't. I don't care what you're doing, or even where you got that thing. Did they say anything about Vyce? About the Olders living here?"

The girl shook her head, studying me curiously. "We

weren't listening that long."

"Oh." That was probably a good thing, I told myself. And surely Bloom and Derry wouldn't ask for my help with their 'freedom movement' if they were planning to turn around and take my family's land? No, that wouldn't make sense. But even so I felt niggles of unease for the rest of the day, and I resolved to ask about it the first chance I had.

Later that evening I was tiredly making my way to my small room when Shandlin's voice blared from a nearby speaker. "ISCENDRA!"

I couldn't help it; I let out a shriek of fright, clutching at my chest. "Do you have to do that!?"

He snickered. "You've been summoned, Older. Bring your belongings." Then the speaker went silent.

I shot upright. My belongings – was I going to be released? Excitement made my hands shake as I quickly gathered my very few items of clothing, almost all of which were Palace property anyway. Then I made my way to the Ducal Suite.

Zavier was waiting for me at the door, and he winked as I approached. "Told you we could get you closer," he whispered.

I glanced at him in confusion. "What do you mean?"

But he didn't answer. Instead he stepped briskly forward and led me up the escalator to the second floor. Bare seconds later I was in the open area of the Ducal Suite, the part that led off to the various rooms including that couch-filled space where I'd shouted at the High Duke.

The Duke himself stood in the centre of the room, his hands in his pockets and his chin tilted back. He looked arrogant and oh so very cold in that moment, and my heart sank. It couldn't be good news.

"Good news, Older," he announced. "I've decided to let June, one of my guards, move to another city. That leaves a position open."

I frowned at him, not understanding.

"You're my new guard," Shandlin enunciated. "Congratulations."

"Your new guard?" I echoed. "But…w*hy*?"

"It's a good position, Iscee," Zavier told me encouragingly. "Safer than being a regular trainee. And we get to watch holo-vids!"

Perhaps it was *his* holo-player that had been stolen. I suddenly realised what had happened. Somehow Zavier and Bloom had talked the High Duke into giving me this position, even though I had next to no experience, and no loyalty… and I'd shouted at him mere days earlier. Getting me close to Shandlin for some unknown reason.

"I'm sure it is," I muttered. But I still felt like a deflated balloon, something that showed in my slumped shoulders. "I thought…" I didn't finish my sentence.

"What, that you were going to go home?" Shandlin shook his head, looking disgusted. "Of course not." He glanced at the small bags at my feet, and his lips tightened. "You can start out back with Zavier."

He stomped off into one of the other rooms, and then it was just me, Zavier, and the other guard, Colby. Colby studied me curiously, then disappeared after the High Duke.

"Let me show you what he meant," Zavier said finally.

I followed him to the suite's kitchen, where there was a small mountain of dishes, the sort that couldn't be auto-cleaned. Once out of the Duke's sight, I couldn't hide my disappointment. "You could have given me some warning," I said bitterly. "This was the last thing I expected."

Zavier shrugged. "You've got to roll with the punches, Iscee. But you know, this is considered an honour. No one gets offered these positions without passing their training first. And you acted disappointed. He's going to be angry with you."

I shook my head, still baffled. Shandlin made no sense – or he had something wrong with his head if he thought I'd be *happy* here, even closer to his marvellous self. "But he must know I'm not going to make a decent guard," I said anyway. "Even if I was a volunteer, I don't even know how to use the two-ender yet. How can I be any good?"

I was referring to the staves that all real Breakers carried, one end a spear-slash-gun, the other a hook. Judging by the smashed windows around the training area, they weren't that easy to aim. But it wasn't like anyone was giving me a chance to test my own abilities.

"Just wave it around and people will do what you want," he suggested. "And if they don't, then shoot them or poke them with the spear. That always works."

I shot him a look of disbelief, and he sighed. "Come on, Iscee. No one's going to give you a weapon, especially not this close to the High Duke! Just take this position as what it is, a gift. Easy work, more variety, less training." He waggled his eyebrows at me in what was probably meant to be a meaningful way, but came across as comical.

I wondered exactly what they'd said to make Shandlin want to take me on. It probably had something to do with me being the entertainment. "Fine," I agreed flatly. "It can't be any worse than being a trainee."

Wrong, I learned over the next few days. It was about the same, minus the chances for Breakers like Tresh to take shots at my face. Instead I ended up cleaning dishes a lot. You'd think a duke would have the appliances to deal with that kind of thing, but it seemed like he came up with unpleasant work for me to do that kept me out of sight.

Un-shrieking-believable, but it turned out that the personal guard were also all-round personal servants, sorting out Shandlin's suite of rooms here in the palace as well as supposedly putting our lives on the line if needed.

And with me being the newbie, within two days I'd also become the unofficial dishwasher, floor sweeper, and cleanser-cleaner of all the weird and wonderful things that belonged to the High Duke. He even had a cushion collection for some reason, all piled up in one corner in the messiest fashion, but that was not to be touched. It was a shame he didn't extend the no-touch rule to the toilets as well…

I was scrubbing at a black stain in the light grey carpet with the cleaning wand when I heard one of the others come in. They'd gone out for the day with the High Duke, while I'd been left behind as usual. But then I wasn't really a guard.

"What is this anyway?" I groused. "Seems like tar. I don't get paid enough for this."

"You don't get paid at all," Shandlin said, and when I looked up in surprise, rather than being angry he almost looked amused. "You've got a bad habit of talking before you look to see who's there, don't you?"

Grawlix. But it was the first time he'd spoken to me since I'd been 'promoted', so I kept my mouth shut. Life would be easier if he didn't hate me.

"You can finish this later," he announced. "I've got something in the kitchen for you to do."

I left the cleaning wand where it was, then followed him into the other room. There, sitting on the kitchen floor, was a big black crate with a familiar insignia on one side. My jaw dropped. "You got my crate from the forest?" I exclaimed in thrilled disbelief. "I can't believe you went and did that! I thought it was gone forever!"

Shandlin shot me a startled glance. "What are you talking about? This is *fruit*, Older. From your home town. I thought you'd recognise it."

My heart sank as I realised the truth. Of course it was fruit. It was only as a disguise that I'd put my art into one of these crates, what felt like a year ago. It had only been weeks. But I was so, *so* disappointed. Silly me. "*Ohh.*"

"You can make me a smoothie," the High Duke continued. "The best garvafruit smoothie I ever had was at an Older restaurant, but my chefs never make it as well. You *do* know how to make garvafruit smoothies, don't you Iscendra?"

I shrugged, bending down to undo the crate's latches. "Sure, but I can't make any promises to whether you'd like it. Besides, garvafruit's not in season yet- oh." The lid sprang open to reveal rows and rows of perfectly pink fruit in the specially-shaped packaging, the sort I'd seen every day growing up. I felt the back of my eyes burn with unshed tears.

"It's last season's, from the storehouses," Shandlin told

me. "That's what the advertising says, that it should be perfect for pulping."

I didn't answer, instead focusing on lifting out the trays and setting them on the nearest bench. I tapped a button, and the tray's segments flattened and tilted, sending all the fruit rolling down to one end, right into a curved indent on the bench. I'd done something like this a hundred times back at home.

There were a few minutes of silence as I went about emptying the crate, then tapped the 'finished' keys on the lid. It would be sent back to Unity along with the next mail. It was a shame I couldn't put myself inside.

But the High Duke had watched me this whole time, and finally he burst out, "Don't tell me you're upset *again*. What is it this time?"

I miss my family. That was the hard truth, so I settled for the easier one. "I thought you'd rescued my crate," I replied instead, not looking at him. "The one you had thrown off the platform the day you conscripted me. I'm disappointed, that's all."

"You should have told me what was in it, then we would have kept it," he retorted. But he still watched my face. "What was inside?"

I shrugged again. There was nothing to gain from hiding it, not now. "Art. Sketches I'd been working on for months and months. I was going to sell them in Ruges."

"Hmm." There were a few seconds of silence, then Shandlin reached over to the fruit bowl built into the bench. He picked out a garvafruit, studied it briefly, then crushed it in his fist. Deep pink juice and pulp splattered in every direction, covering the just-cleaned bench and floor, and spilling down his arm. "It's ripe, Older. Make me that smoothie…then clean this up."

Selfish, careless little beast! Lightning quick, my disappointment changed into anger, then spilled out on my tongue. "You're brave, Duke, getting an Older to make you a drink. For all you know I might poison it."

The moment the words left my mouth I regretted them, and I stood there with tense shoulders, hands clenched in fearful fists. He'd be furious at the insult, and what would he do as punishment?

But to my surprise, Shandlin was watching me with a smug sort of amusement. It reminded me a little of his cousin (only sneakier and more unpleasant) and I remembered once more why I was here – as if I could have forgotten. *This little monster shouldn't be in power – and I'll do what I can to get him out. If he doesn't have me executed first.*

"I'll make you taste it first," was all he said, and then he walked away and left me there with the splattered juice running in thick dribbles down the side of the bench. "And don't make me wait!" he shouted from the other room. "I want it within an hour."

I made him the smoothie. I didn't even spit in it, which was a wonderful sign of restraint. He did make me taste it first, and then he made Zavier and Colby taste it too, watching to see if they'd collapse in pain, start vomiting bile, turn purple…et cetera.

Zavier screwed up his face in distaste. "Too sour. You should have added sweetener."

"Garvafruit is supposed to be tangy," I told him. "You want sweet, go drink a sugar-fizz."

He shrugged and pushed the glass aside. "I don't care. Give me a good sugar-fizz any day."

"I like it," Colby said, and he winked at me. "Sour but somehow appealing, like so much from the Old World. Sound familiar, Iscee?"

"As long as it doesn't give you the trots if you have too much of it," I countered, not really flattered. Colby was cute – a lot of Breakers were – but I'd heard him talk the same way to the other girls. "Besides, that's not for you. It's for *His Grace.*" I said the last two words with my usual irony, but nobody seemed to care.

"I hope we're just talking about the smoothie," Colby said with a grin. "Otherwise, lucky guy."

Ugh. As if.

Shandlin pushed past, grabbing the smoothie jug and pouring himself some. "If it gives me the trots then you'll be the one cleaning the toilet, Iscee. You'd better hope it doesn't."

I'd almost forgotten he was there, but I didn't let him ruin my good mood. "Then I can tell my parents that I touched the throne of Vyce," I said dryly. "I just won't explain which one."

"I don't get it," Colby said.

Zavier explained, "It's an old term for a toilet. Bad joke, Iscee."

"And it'll be two years out of date when you finally use it," Shandlin said. He sipped at the smoothie, swirling it around in the glass as though it was ancient wine rather than just fruit pulp and spices. "Does this have ginger in it? I don't like ginger."

But I was caught by his previous words. "What do you mean, two years out of date?"

"One year and eleven months, then. It's a two-year contract, you know that."

I stared at him where he stood, so heedless of the destruction he caused with every word. "Are you saying that I can't even see my family even *once* in that whole two years?!"

He looked up at me, and his carelessness and arrogance exemplified everything I disliked about him and about this place. "Of course not."

"Not even by communicator?!"

Now the High Duke's dark eyes narrowed in that way that meant he was getting annoyed. "I know that you've been told how this works, *Iscendra.* If you don't want to get thrown back with the other trainees, then you do what you're told, and you don't complain. Two years, then you can see them. That's the rule."

I almost wanted to cry again, and that made me angry. So I just stood there looking at him mutinously.

"Understood?"

"I understand what you're telling me," I said in a low

voice. "But will you keep your word?"

Shandlin set the glass down hard on the side table, and stood, his slightly shorter height preventing him from evenly meeting my eyes. "Are you questioning my honour, Older?"

Of course I was! "Seems like you just do what you want, when you want. How do I know you won't just change your mind and not let me go at all, even after the two years?"

Now his dark eyes were narrow with anger, and he leaned right into my face (as much as he could, anyway). "What makes you think I'd want to keep you so long, Older? I bet that within two months you'll be back with the rest of them, directing traffic or whatever it is that they do. And do *not* question my integrity again."

I slid my eyes away, trying to show with my huddled shoulders and dipped head that I wasn't challenging him, but unable to say anything in agreement. He was like a child, just saying and doing whatever he felt like at any one time, and he didn't care about me. I might have entertained him these last few weeks by occasionally speaking too honestly, but he meant what he said. Once he grew bored, I'd say the wrong thing, and then I'd be sorry.

Finally he stepped back, picking up the dark pink glass of smoothie and tossing it on the just-cleaned carpet. "And Zavier was right: this smoothie is too sour. Clean it up, then make me a better one. And you *will* be tasting it, so don't even thinking about spitting in it."

Suds, I'd pee in it if I thought I could get away with it. *Two years with no contact!* That was un-shrieking-believable. But instead I nodded tersely, my eyes still fixed on my feet. In my peripheral vision I saw him leave, then I went and got the cleaning wand.

As I worked on the new pink stain, Zavier came up quietly beside me. "You didn't know about the two-year thing? I thought we told you on the first day."

I kept my eyes on the cleaning wand where it ran over the pink patch, leaving pale grey lines behind it. "I knew about the training period, but no one spelled out that it meant no contact. None at all! Not even for good behaviour?"

Zavier was silent a moment. "Maybe for good behaviour, for the others. But you haven't exactly been good, Iscee. And you're not like the others."

Because I was the illegally conscripted Earth citizen, here amongst the Martian-born Breakers. "He's a total grawlix," I muttered. "What did I ever do to him?" Because I'd punched him *after* he'd conscripted me, not before.

"Iscee!" Zavier snapped, his sharp tone making me jolt. "Watch your tongue!"

I'd called Shandlin worse, but I supposed that wasn't within his hearing. "Fine. Whatever."

"He puts up with a lot of trash-talk from you," Zavier continued, "but he won't put up with that sort of thing. And do *not* ever question his word. He hates it, and you'll be sorry."

I could tell by his tone that he meant to be helpful, but it didn't make any sense. "Trash-talk from me? From all four of us, I thought."

"No," Colby said from behind me. I hadn't even realised he was still in the room. "We talk to each other like that, but not to the High Duke. And you'd better be careful. Whatever interest he has in you now, it won't last. And then every half-hidden insult you've given him, it'll all come back on you."

I went cold. It was so hard to keep my mouth shut, but I'd have to… and I wouldn't question Shandlin's word, even if he was promising to turn the dome's mountain regions into cheese. "Understood."

SEVEN
Promises

◉　◉　◉

I kept my vow to be quiet and well behaved for all of three days. I did what I was told, when I was told, and tried not to think about my family or friends. I was seventeen, but I'd always lived with my parents and my two brothers. Even when I'd gone away to school I'd known I could see them easily via technology.

It was like I didn't really appreciate that freedom to see them until it was taken away. And all I could think about was that they didn't know I was safe, that they'd be worrying about me, that Alek wouldn't understand why I wasn't there anymore…

But then of course the others must have gone through the same thing, I told myself. Bloom had been a Breaker for five years, and Zavier and Colby for two and a half years each, which put this as their promoted position. Maybe each of them had months upon months of isolation, of seeing the same faces daily, but not the ones they wanted to see.

I thought of the guards' comment that Shandlin allowed trash-talk from me, but not from others. Could that really be true? I realised in sudden dismay that if people thought I was being unfairly favoured by the High Duke, then not only would they resent me, but they might think…they might think there was *something* going on.

Yuck. As if. Shandlin wasn't ugly – with those thick-lashed eyes, in a few years he might even be handsome – but he was a right little grawlix. I wouldn't touch him with a proctor rod.

Three days after the smoothie incident I was dusting bookshelves in a hallway, admiring the beautiful and extremely expensive paper books, and thinking that the High Duke must have a lot of money to throw around if he could afford so many. Just then he came into the hall behind me. I didn't look up, instead just moved out of the way to let him past, but he stopped and stood right by me.

"There's something for you in the kitchen."

I didn't look up. "You want another smoothie?" I'd finally got it right (the trick was to add a truckload of sugar, apparently) and he'd been demanding them every day since.

He made a sound of impatience. "No, not now. Just go and look, will you?"

I went, because it wasn't worth arguing with him. I always lost. And there in the kitchen, in the same place where the garvafruit crate had been, was another crate. This one was identical, right down to the plantation logo on the side. I blinked. "Fruit. Great."

"Look *inside*, Older," the High Duke said testily. He stood beside me, his arms folded, and one foot was tapping rhythmically on the smooth polished floor. "Go on."

Wondering at his tone, I bent down and undid the latches. But when the lid folded open, it revealed another crate, a red one. I froze in place. "Is this…?"

"See for yourself." But he sounded smug.

"I bet it's full of garvafruit after all," I muttered even as I tugged the second crate out of its hiding place. It was as heavy as I remembered, but I didn't want to get my hopes up. "Or rocks. Or pog intestines."

"That's disgusting," Colby said from the doorway. He came up to crouch beside me, watching curiously. "What's this?"

"It could be…" And then I opened that second, sealed lid to reveal stacks of carefully packed slides, each one representing hours of my time and invested money. But the packing had obviously been good enough to survive a hundred-metre drop. "It is! It's my sketches!"

I turned to stare at Shandlin in shocked pleasure. "You went and got them. Why?" Suddenly my heart sank. "If it's to burn them in front of me, then I swear I'll…" Punch him again? I didn't dare voice that threat.

"I'm not going to hurt them," he snapped, but he looked pleased. "Call them hostages."

"What?!"

"Hostages for your good behaviour," he explained. "You do your job without threats or spitting in my food and all that, and you can have your stuff back at the end of it." With that casual statement he came to crouch beside Colby and I, lifting one of the pieces out of its packaging. "Hey, it's a swamp-mare on a tri-wheeler. Funny."

I was so pleased I didn't even care about the 'hostage' threat. When he had *me* here, when he'd threatened my family, what were a few pictures? "There are a whole series of those," I told him. "Pogs on tri-wheelers, sheep on tri-wheelers, wolcroxes on tri-wheelers."

"Let me guess, you call it the 'tri-wheeler' series," Colby quipped.

I beamed at him. "Something like that."

The three of us moved to the table and emptied the crate, examining the stacks of carefully drawn plates. They were made of a paper-like substance – not real paper of course, because that was way too dear – then sealed in clear plasti-glass. Long lasting, simple, not too expensive. They should have been in Ruges for the opening festival, but assuming they didn't get lost in the next two years, then they'd keep just fine. There'd be other festivals.

"Do you remember that day on the gondola?" Shandlin said to me suddenly. "Where you thought I was that Felix guy, and I handed you a sketch that had fallen out of your crate."

My mouth twisted at the memory, but the usual burst of anger didn't come. "Sure. What about it?"

"It wasn't a real sketch. I saw you'd been scanned earlier, and I looked you up online." He sounded very pleased with himself, and when I looked up, I saw his face wore a matching smug expression. "So I had it printed off, then pretended you'd dropped it. But you hadn't, and you didn't even notice the difference."

My eyebrows shot up, and I stared at him for several seconds. Out of all the things that he'd done since I'd met him, that would be one of the weirdest. "Really? *Why?*"

The High Duke made a careless hand gesture. "Because I could." As if that said it all, and for him, it probably did. Just then he spotted something in the pile that caught his attention, and his head cocked to one side. He lifted up the picture to show me. "I want this one on my wall."

It was a picnic scene. A family of farlacs sat around an old-fashioned spread, each with a different expression. One was focused on its meal. Two of the littlest farlacs were fighting, and another lay on its back, studying the clouds. All of them had mismatched pupils, which had been my way of showing the slight craziness that these particular animals had in real life.

That was a great picture, if I might say so myself, and it had been one of the more time-consuming ones to create. "Eighty-five."

Shandlin arched a dark eyebrow. "You want to sell it to me, Older?"

Actually, I hadn't thought of that. "I would if I thought I could get away with it," I retorted. "But no. You said my pictures were being held hostage. There are eighty-five of them in this crate, and when I leave here I want to take all eighty-five with me. Not one less."

Colby looked at me curiously, but Shandlin rolled his eyes and let out a heavy sigh. "Come on, Older. It's just a picture, and it's not even on real paper. I could make you draw-" And then he suddenly went silent.

Hmm. "That's a dangerous silence," I said, trying to cover my unease. "What idea has popped into your head?"

"You'll see," he retorted. "Now put these all back in the crate, all eighty-five of them, or *Iscee* will be upset." Then he got up and vanished from the room.

I studied Colby quizzically, trying to see if he knew what

was going on, but he just shrugged and stood too. "I'll go help him," he said. "I'm not fond of packing. Those things are always way easier to get out than put in."

"Oh, Colby!" I whined, but he'd already left the room.

And he was right, suds it. Packing the things had been hard work, because they *were* easier to get out than put in.

Twenty minutes later I was finally slipping the last piece back into place when Shandlin came back into the room. "Put out your wrist, Iscendra."

I paused. "Is this going to hurt?"

"No! Just do it, will you?"

I did, but I was nervous, and that made my mouth go off. "You called me Iscee before. What's with the long name? Am I in trouble?"

"You're always in trouble," he said darkly. "But Iscendra's a nice name. The others call you Iscee."

I shrugged. "My friends and family call me Iscee. So I suppose you can call me Iscendra."

Shandlin scowled, and he slapped something at my wrist. "Iscee it is."

"And I'll call you 'Your Grace'," I said lightly. I studied the whatever-it-was. It looked like a thin metal bracelet, silvery and light, and it had locked into place with a single action. "Is this a shock-manacle? Another tracker?" Or heaven forbid, did he know about the Freedom Movement?!

"It's a promise-holder." He leaned forward, tapping his finger against the metal. A faint row of green lights appeared then vanished as he withdrew his hand. "It's keyed to my DNA. Once I keep my promise – which I will – I press my thumb against it for three seconds, and it opens." I was silent, and he added impatiently, "It signifies that I've given my word. It's legally binding."

So was my Earth citizenship, and he didn't care about that, did he? "Is this for the two-year thing? Or the sketch hostages?"

His dark brows furrowed. "You can't use it for two

different things! So the two-year promise. I promise that you *will* get to see your family after the full two years, or sooner, if you're good."

I perked up, since that last sentence had been promising. "How good?"

"*Really* good," he said sulkily. "Only if you actually do your job and obey me perfectly. Although I don't see what's so good about families. They either just ignore or embarrass you. Mine does."

Or try to commit treason and have you removed from your position, like his cousin Derry. I would have said that it was your family's job to embarrass or ignore you, but that they always had your back…but *his* didn't. I almost felt sorry for him. He didn't know about Derry's actions, and he didn't seem to realise how much personal information he'd given away with that careless comment.

"You can start by drawing me something that I can keep," he told me. "Something funny, like that angry pog on a tri-wheeler. I liked that one."

I knew the one he was referring to. "It was based on my pet pog, Wally. Do you have a pet?" If he did, it shouldn't be a cute fluffy pog, it should be a hairless piglet as annoying as himself.

"Pogs are smelly creatures," the High Duke said carelessly. "I don't want one, I just want a picture. You can do it for me now."

"I don't have anything to draw on."

"Colby can get you some real paper. He knows where the supplies are."

I sucked in a breath. I'd never drawn on real, tree-based paper, instead using the cheaper synthetic equivalent. "Yes, Your Grace!"

"Call me Shan." I stared at him in surprise, and he shrugged a shoulder, looking a little uncomfortable. "People call me Shan, sometimes. *You* did the other day."

That was true, but I hadn't heard anyone call him Shan. Not ever. Only Derry called him Shanny, and that was clearly meant as an insult. "Yeah, but that was an accident."

"So do it again on purpose," he said coolly. "Now stop messing around, and draw me that picture. I don't like to wait."

Yes, sir!

And so I drew him a pog on a tri-wheeler. And then a cat in a wedding dress walking down the aisle beside a duck in a top hat, and then a fish in a para-suit driving down a highway. And he watched with interest as I sketched them, and then when I'd finish he'd say, "Draw me another one."

I drew for a good two hours until my brain was low on ideas (except a piglet wearing a ducal crown: that one just kept coming back to mind even though I would *not* use it) and he finally let me go to do something else.

"You should sign them," he told me. "They might be worth something one day."

And so that was how I got back into High Duke Shandlin's good graces: through sketching animals wearing funny clothes, and through restricting my trash-talk to very, very minor things, just enough to amuse, not enough to upset… although I couldn't bring myself to call him 'Shan'.

And no matter what Colby and Zavier had said, Shandlin seemed happy enough that I was here, and surprisingly I wasn't too unhappy either. To be fair I'd still happily punch him in the gut, but it was safer here than in training camp, and most of the time I just did menial, gentle tasks. The 'spy' challenge seemed a world away, and even Zavier didn't give any further hints of what we'd once spoken about.

So far, so good.

Several weeks later we all sat in the palace's fanciest air vehicle; Bloom and Zavier in front with the driver panel, and Colby, Shandlin and I in the back. I was supposed to be drawing a picnic scene to entertain His Grace, but instead I was staring at the scenery through the clear walls.

We'd passed miles and miles of wild forest and mountain ranges, and we were coming to the edge of Vyce Dome. Soon we'd exit into the massive pressurized tube that connected this dome to the next, Rison.

Rison was just north of the Martian equator, on the edge of where the sea would be – if there had been water outside the domes. But because of how far apart these two domes were, we'd be travelling over dangerous desert for some time before entering Rison. It sounded *fascinating.*

"Close your mouth Iscee, or you'll catch flies," the High Duke told me. "Haven't you travelled between domes before?"

"I've hardly left Vyce since we arrived from Earth," I replied without taking my eyes off the view. "And then when we did leave, it was to visit Optus, and we went straight there out the exit above Unity. We didn't use the tubes."

"Humph."

I wasn't sure what that meant, so I ignored him and watched as we approached the side of the dome. We were heading towards what looked like a massive, silvery grate, big enough to fit fifty shuttles the size of our own. Our vehicle slowed briefly, and then the barrier dissipated and we shot through into the tube. But it was so enormous that it felt to me just like another dome; perhaps a slightly smaller one.

"We just left Vyce territory," Colby told me cheerfully. "These tubes are always owned equally by the domes they connect, but except for the borders like that one we just passed, no one polices them. And there's a huge shriekn' distance between Vyce and Rison. So if we crashed here, we'd be in real trouble."

I looked outside to where the tube's side flashed past so fast its colours seemed to blur. Beyond it was the orange-red soil that gave this planet its nickname, extending as far as the horizon. "Why do you sound happy about that, Colby?"

He shrugged, grinning. "Risk is fun, isn't it? That's why I'm a Breaker."

I rolled my eyes, but I couldn't entirely disagree. While I wouldn't have chosen to be here, it did have its moments of…fun. Perhaps something good was coming out of this after all. "I wonder why the two domes are so far apart?" I mused. "Surely they could have built them closer, more like the others around Vyce."

"Temperature?" Colby suggested.

"No," Shandlin cut in. "The temperature here is fine. It's to avoid Elysium Mons. You know, the volcano? If it went off, the dome could be damaged, and the dust cloud would be huge." There was a startled silence, then he added a little smugly, "You'd think you lot were never educated. The domes were built to avoid the poles, volcanoes and small basins. Of course."

"Of course," I echoed. I'd heard that somewhere before. Probably. But I found myself watching the landscape outside even more curiously. This world hadn't been tamed easily, and if not for the domes, humanity wouldn't have had a chance here.

As it was, we'd just made ourselves large, liveable spaces. But outside those spaces, the planet was still freezing, dusty and with stupidly low gravity. For all of Earth's problems, its deserts and wastelands and colossal cities, it was still much better suited for human life.

Ah, well. Our lives here might seem like they balanced on a wire, but we'd survived for aeons in terrible conditions. Like I'd said to Lanny and Aria, I'd worry when there was something to worry about. Fingers crossed.

Our trip through the tube went without issues, and about an hour later we reached yet another silvery barrier. After a short wait, the barrier was released and then we were in Rison Dome. But even from here I could see the differences compared to Vyce. The top of the dome seemed lower, and it seemed to lack the wildness of our own dome.

"Hey, it's a lot less green than Vyce, don't you think?" I commented. "I can still see red earth everywhere, even on the hillsides."

"It has less water," Shandlin replied, sounding bored. "So things don't grow on their own like they do in Vyce. But it's just another dome. Vyce is way bigger, and better too."

I didn't put much stock in that last comment, since it had come from a boy who seemed to be unpleasable. Instead I watched as the air vehicle rapidly approached a city, much like Vyce's capital, except noticeably smaller. Once in the city's centre we headed towards an enormous building made of what looked to be dozens of spires.

"There's the Rison Ducal Palace," the High Duke said in that same unimpressed tone. "My mother lived here up until she married my father."

But in spite of his tone I could see him watching me out the corner of my eye, as if waiting for my reaction. I studied the palace curiously, but couldn't make out much detail. The light down below us was strange, almost cloudy. "What's that mist?"

"The forcefield is still up," Shandlin replied. "Don't you know anything?"

"I know how to draw a pog riding a tri-wheeler," I retorted without heat. "You can't say that much."

"Anything *useful*."

Just then the driver panel flashed, sending green light across the comfortable cabin. "Welcome, High Duke Shandlin and company," a polite voice said over the intercom. "May I use visual to ascertain your identity?"

Shandlin sighed heavily. "If you must."

A bright light flashed inside the vehicle, then a moment later the mist over the spired building dissipated. The air vehicle moved through, and I looked back to see it had reappeared after our entry. Clever.

"Now why don't we have anything like that?" I murmured.

"Because we've got hundreds of dedicated guards," the High Duke replied. "You lot. Apparently you keep us safer than this kind of defence. Besides, if it came down, they'd lose everything."

I thought again of the riots in Eser and Arparath Domes, and how one government had fallen, and the other had changed methods. From the little I'd heard of Vyce, we weren't in quite the same danger, but I definitely didn't see us as safe. I didn't see *Unity* as safe.

I changed the subject. "So, we're coming to visit your family. How many cousins do you have here?"

"*I'm* coming to visit my family," Shandlin retorted. "You're just guarding me. Well, not you, Older, but the others. And I have three cousins here, but they're practically children."

"Keley won't be happy to hear you say that," Colby said. He winked at me. "She told me last time that she's very grown up."

Keley would be the next Duchess of Rison, assuming that the government wasn't overthrown first. I knew that much.

"Three cousins here?" I exclaimed. "And Derry, too. Wow, you've got a huge family."

I suddenly felt everyone's eyes on me. "How are four cousins considered a huge family?" Zavier asked from the front seat. "*I've* got seventeen."

"Seventeen!" I exploded, genuinely shocked. "How did you manage that?!"

"The old-fashioned way, I expect," Zavier said dryly. "I figure my aunts and uncles know how it works, since they did it so many times. But how many cousins do you have, Iscee?"

"Only one," Shandlin cut in. "A girl who lives on Optus."

Now I turned to stare at him, dismayed. "Since when do you know about that?!"

"I do background checks on all my personal guard," he replied coolly. "Don't think you're special, Older." But his cheeks were turning pink, belying his words.

He was embarrassed, I realised. I hadn't known he could feel that emotion. "Do I need to worry about you threatening her life if I misbehave?" I said it lightly, but behind the words was genuine fear. Why had he looked into my extended family like that?

Shandlin's dark eyes narrowed, and he looked away. "I think keeping your sketches hostage is enough, don't you? And look, we've landed."

While the air vehicle moved very quickly between domes, arriving here a mere two hours after we'd left Vyce to the southwest, it landed *slowly*. Probably trying not to squash anyone, so I could put up with that slowness. We were now inside an enormous vehicle bay, and I could see expensive machinery in every direction. Air vehicles, hovercrafts, tri-wheelers. I even spotted a bi-wheeler, which must have been an antique, or else specially made. No one rode those anymore.

But then the lights flashed once, showing we'd stopped fully, and the door opened with its tidy ramp. Bloom and Zavier got out, weapons in hand as if they'd done this a hundred times, and the High Duke followed them. Colby picked up his stave and took the rear, then glanced back at me. "Come on, Iscee."

I grabbed my precious paper sketchpad, because I still didn't have a weapon, then I trailed out onto solid ground, idly admiring the large hexagonal pavers covering this entire area. The roof had closed over us, creating a simply enormous hangar, and the light in here was artificial and bluish.

Just ahead of us was a group of half a dozen people. At a glance I could tell some of them were guards, but a girl broke away from the group. She had long, wavy auburn hair trailing down her back, and she wore a dress of the kind I hadn't seen outside historical holo-vids. It had a lace-up bodice, and actually reached her ankles. I put her age at about fifteen.

"Shan!" she cried happily. She ran up to the High Duke and threw her arms around his neck.

He made an 'urk' sound and tried to push her away. "Hi, Keley. Can you try not to choke me?"

"But that's half the fun!" she said cheerfully, finally releasing him, and I bit back a snort of laughter. "How was your trip? Did you get attacked by anyone?"

"Not this time," Shandlin started to respond, but the girl had already turned away to study the rest of us with bright eyes.

"Hi Zavier, hi Colby, hi Annabelle. Where's June?"

June was the guard I'd replaced, the one who'd moved to another city. "Who's Annabelle?" I whispered to Colby as Shandlin responded to the girl's question.

"Bloom," he whispered back, and his mouth curved into a smirk. "It's her first name, but use it at your own risk."

I glanced at the small blonde guard, trying to fit the sweet name against her rather unsweet personality. It fit her looks, but that was about it. "Understood."

"And who are you?" Keley asked. It took a moment to realise she was looking at *me*. I opened my mouth to answer, but she spoke first. "The replacement, I suppose." She glanced at Shandlin over her shoulder, her hands on her hips, and with her eyebrows very eloquently arched. "Why don't you ever pick ugly ones, Shan? Oh wait, I already know the answer."

He was turning red. He really, really was this time. But he rolled his eyes wearily as if his family wasn't exactly as embarrassing as he'd said earlier. "You're about to say that I see enough of my own ugly face each day in the mirror, so I don't need ugly guards too. Right Keley?"

"Yes!" she squealed, then burst out laughing. I revised my estimate of her age to about fourteen, maybe even younger. She linked one arm through Shandlin's, then began dragging him through the hangar towards an open hallway, talking at high speed the whole time. The four of us Breakers followed behind, and I picked up some of the others' relaxed attitudes. The weapons seemed to be for show. Perhaps that was why I'd been allowed to come too.

We'd made our way through a maze of halls when suddenly Shandlin stopped short, turning to look back over his shoulder. "Iscee, Zavier, you go with the other guards to their barracks. I'll send for you when I need you. Bloom, Colby, you come with me."

That cut off my plan to see the whole of this palace in a way that I'd never seen Vyce's, never mind that I currently lived there. But I didn't argue, instead following a few of the Rison guards into a nearby open area. I'd thought it would resemble the Breakers' quarters, but I was wrong. Where that was chaotic with colourful paint sprayed over ancient metal, these barracks were tidy blue-grey, just like the Rison guards' uniforms. Their barracks were also immaculate, and I didn't hear a hint of raised voices or even the clashing sounds of training.

But we were led past that open room too, and finally shown to a smaller room with a couple of chairs and a central holo-projector. "You can wait here," the Rison guard told us. "There are drinks and food in that dispenser there, and you can watch whatever you like on the holo-screen."

I'd been a bit disappointed before, but now my heart skipped in delight. "Can we? Thanks!"

The guard smiled at me, looking a little baffled, but left us there.

"Can I choose the station?" I asked Zavier. "'Cos this looks like the sort where you can't split screens." Old-fashioned, but still so much better than nothing.

He shrugged, but he'd already pulled out his communicator. "Whatever you like. I have to go out for a bit – you'll still be here when I come back, right?"

"I will." I'd save any escape attempt for when I thought it would actually work.

Zavier left, and it only took me thirty seconds to find the right station. I went straight for the news – not hard when there were several hundred varieties of the same thing – and then caught my breath as I saw what it was. Chaos on Mars, same as before. Chaos, and we who were meant to be *keeping order* didn't even know about it.

EIGHT
The Big Crush

I didn't know how long I watched for. Hours, maybe? I took a break to grab a drink and a spicy pot-meal from the food dispenser, then sat right back on that seat and *learned*, and anguished, and occasionally swore and waved my arms around. It didn't matter, because there was no one to see me. Zavier had vanished, and the Rison guards hadn't bothered to check on me.

Oh, the things that had been happening in the last two months! How could Earth be withdrawing their control of towns all across Mars? How could they be rewriting their treaties with Eser and Arparath, and even with Rison? And how long before they'd do the same with Vyce?

"Central to the Vyce-Old World conversation is the fate of Earth citizen Iscendra Cole, who was conscripted seven weeks ago into the Vyce Ducal Guard," the narrator told me in a pleasant, gender-neutral voice. I shot upright, stunned to hear my own name, and listened avidly. The narrator continued, "In spite of numerous attempts by the Old World to enforce centuries-old treaties, the Vyce government just isn't budging."

Then the holo-vid cut to a full-sized image of the High Duke, wearing his usual expression of cool arrogance. "This is a girl living amongst Martian natives, breathing the same air, eating the same food, and using the same transport; so why should she be subject to different laws than the locals? It's not fair."

"Not fair?!" I shouted at the holo-Shan, even as he disappeared. "You wouldn't know fairness if it bit you on the-"

"-wallet," the narrator said, finishing some sentence that I'd been shouting too loudly to hear. "Much of the unrest across Mars has been focused on this issue. Small towns and areas remain within Dome borders, but subject to Earth law, and with their citizens paying generous taxes to Earth rather than the struggling societies around them. Considering that much of that land was confiscated years ago from Martian natives as part of peace settlements, this discrepancy causes ongoing concern."

They kept talking, but I wasn't taking it in anymore. My hands tightened into fists in my lap as I pondered exactly what this could mean for me. For my family. For everyone I'd grown up with in that safe little town...even for Lanny in Ruges. Shandlin had earlier threatened to cut off exports from my family's plantation, which was bad enough. But this? This could mean we'd lose everything. All of us, and for what? Displaying the wrong symbol on our ID chips?

"Maybe we'd just end up paying taxes to Vyce instead of Earth," I said aloud. "Sure, that could work." Or maybe we'd all be shoved off our land, our bank accounts emptied, our buildings confiscated...

"That's a serious expression," Zavier's voice came from behind me. I turned to see him studying the bright holo-vid, his eyebrows raised. "I see you've been watching the news."

"Yes, I've been watching the news!" I shouted at him. "For practically the first time in seven weeks, or so they tell me! Earth *did* try to free me, but Shan just turned them down!" I spat out a few choice words. "And they're saying that Earth might lose its land within Vyce as well as the other domes!"

"Calm down, Iscee," he said patiently, taking a seat. "We always knew this might happen-"

"*I* didn't!"

"...but Vyce isn't Arparath, or Eser, or even Rison, never mind that the rulers are related. We'll make our own decisions for our own people, as it suits Vyce. There's no reason to assume the worst."

"Yet," I said darkly. "And it's not *we* who'll make the decisions. It's supposed to be the regent, isn't it? But he hasn't tried to stand up against Shandlin about the conscription thing. About *anything*."

He shrugged, suddenly looking weary. "Shandlin will have full power in two years. He's got a council running the boring stuff, but nothing can be made law without his permission." He raised his eyebrows. "Nothing *public* is going to change without Shandlin changing it."

My shoulders slumped, because I knew that was true. And for me, that was a problem.

"But if you can hold your temper for a few minutes, I've got someone to talk to you." Zavier held out his communicator. There, on its tiny surface, was an image of another dark-haired guy, although this one had the cheekbones given by age and good genes.

Derry.

"Sorry we can't go full screen," Derry's miniature image told me. I could only just hear him over the news still playing in the background. "But Shanny could come out any time, and it's better he doesn't know I'm in touch with you two."

I glanced at Zavier, whose gaze was even. He must have known, as I did, that if he was found talking to Derry like this, he might end up in serious trouble.

"What do you need?" I asked quietly. "I've been here in the personal guard for weeks now, and you've never asked for anything. I don't think I can *do* anything."

Derry's tiny face smiled at me, his dark eyes crinkling with humour. "Sure you can, lovely Iscee. You already have been."

"What have I been doing? Drawing pictures and making smoothies?"

"Distracting the High Duke," Zavier said flatly. "Keeping him entertained so he doesn't look too closely at what's going on around him. These past few months he was starting to get interested in the running of Vyce, but he dropped that the moment you were conscripted."

"Keeping him entertained?" I exclaimed. "What am I, a performing monkey?"

"You're much better-looking than that," Derry replied, still smiling. "And Shanny's never had a girlfriend before. Whatever you're doing, keep doing it."

"*I'm not his girlfriend!*" OK, that came out way too loudly. "I'm not his girlfriend," I said again, whispering this time. "Why would you think that?!"

Derry glanced up at Zavier, who shrugged. "From what my sources tell me, it wouldn't take much encouragement," Derry countered.

"Yeah," Zavier agreed. "He's got the biggest crush on you."

I felt my jaw drop in genuine shock, and for a few moments I couldn't even answer. Then I managed to choke out, "Are you crazy!? We're talking about the High Duke here, right? Shandlin? Not some other guy?"

"We'd hardly want you to distract some other guy," Derry said. He was still smiling, but now it seemed condescending, like I was some foolish but adorable child. "But it seems my cousin is so charmless that you didn't even notice."

"You're wrong," I snapped. "Not about the charm thing; about the crush. Shan doesn't think of me like that. He tells me I'm an idiot every second day, and he's never given a *hint* of that kind of interest."

"You call him Shan," Zavier pointed out. "Only Keley calls him that. For everyone else it's Shandlin or his title."

"He told me to," I argued. I'd never intended to use the nickname, but it kept slipping out. But just then a horrible possibility occurred to me. What if the High Duke *did* have a crush on me? (Ugh!) And if so, what would happen when he realised I just wasn't interested?

Sure, the first time we met I'd thought he was cute, if a bit baby-faced. That impression only lasted until he opened his mouth, and I decided he was weird, rude and unlikeable. Surely he must know that already…

"It won't be why you were conscripted," Derry said, "but

it's almost certainly why he won't give you back." I went to argue, but he continued, "But never mind the crush, or lack of. The point is, he's distracted at the moment. We need him to stay that way, just for another few months while we get things set up in the Freedom Movement. Then when we take action, there'll be nothing in the way."

My lips tightened into a thin, mutinous line, and I folded my arms in front of my chest. "I'm not an escort. I won't pretend to like him in that way, not even for the Freedom Movement. I don't even know what you're planning! And I won't do it, not even for my own freedom." I shook my head, trying to show my distaste at the idea. "Just…no."

Derry's miniature figure spread out its tiny hands placatingly. "We get it. You're not interested, but you don't have to be. Just keep doing what you're already doing, and don't actively annoy him. Is that OK?"

I hunched my shoulders, still feeling irritated. "I suppose. But not forever!"

"Not forever," he agreed. "But there's one other thing. Have you heard about the Vyce Ducal Dowry?"

I nodded. I'd seen that on the news-vids a couple of times, mention of some fabulously expensive gems that had come to Vyce from Rison along with Shandlin's mother. She'd died in the same accident that had claimed his father four years ago, but the jewels were in Shandlin's care. "Some people are saying he should sell the jewels and put the funds into solving Vyce's social issues."

"And Shanny will say that they're his family jewels, and no one can have them except him," Derry countered.

Family jewels. I bit back a giggle.

"What's so funny, Iscee?"

"It's just some Older joke," Zavier cut in, but his eyes were crinkled with laughter. *He'd* got it. "Go on, Derry."

Derry just looked confused, but he carried on. "If you find them, Iscee, you need to bring them to me. I really think they could be the game changer."

Now all humour was gone. "I don't know where they

are," I said quietly. "I've never seen them, and Shan's never mentioned their location. But even if I did know, I wouldn't take them. I told you I wouldn't steal."

"Don't think of it as theft. Think of it as balancing the scales."

I scowled at him, and finally he sighed. "Or not. I'd better go. Keep well, lovely Iscee. And Zavier – you call me later when you can."

The small screen shut off, and then it was just the two of us Breakers in that small room, still filled with the holo-news.

"He does *not* have a crush on me," I said flatly.

Zavier looked as though he would argue, but then the communicator in his hand flashed green. "Wait a moment, I'm getting a call," he cut in. "Oh. Hello, Your Grace."

Shandlin's figure shot up to fill the area in front of us, much larger than Derry's had. "You two can come now," he said moodily. "We're done."

Ah, such sweet words, I mused. How could *anyone* think he was interested in me? But we still got up and followed the Rison guards back out to the vehicle hangar, then waited beside our own air vehicle.

A few minutes later Bloom showed up. "He's following up with Colby," she told us. Her tone and expression seemed even crankier than normal.

I figured that meant he was in the bathroom, so didn't query it. But as for her expression… "You don't enjoy hanging out in palaces?" I asked, genuinely curious. After all, *she'd* got to explore, while we'd been basically left in the basement.

She scowled, her grip tightening around her two-ender. "It's that Keley," she muttered quietly enough so the nearby Rison guards couldn't hear. "She's got a head full of fluff, and seems to think that having personal guards is like having an accessory. She doesn't realise that Shandlin's life is actually in danger, and that we actually do a job."

"Do we?"

She huffed. "Well, I do. Regardless of anything else, do you know what would happen if the High Duke was injured when in our care? His uncle would go mad."

"I almost forget that he has an uncle," I admitted. But then the Regent made himself forgettable by spending most of his time off-planet, in resorts and casinos. Shandlin dying would probably stop that. "Shan acts like he's got no superior."

"I don't have any superiors," he said, coming up beside us. "That better not have been an insult."

Oops. I really needed to be more aware of my surroundings before I spoke. "Of course not. We were just saying that we have to look after you properly because otherwise your uncle will have to come back to Vyce, and you know he wouldn't like that. I almost forget you even have an uncle."

"My uncle would only care if I got murdered by rebels or something," Shandlin said casually. "Better make sure I don't get murdered, Iscee, or you'll likely be strung up by your toes for allowing it."

Eek. I was pretty sure that the rebels I'd spoken with didn't want to actually kill him, but I forced a smile even though I knew he wasn't joking.

"Now get in the air vehicle," he snapped over his shoulder. "We've waited long enough."

Yep, not exactly Prince Charming. "Crush?" I muttered under my breath. "I think not."

"What's that, Older?"

I froze mid-step. "What's what?"

Shandlin was studying me narrow-eyed from the air vehicle's entry ramp. "You said crush. What were you talking about?"

"Uh…" Oh suds, his hearing was *way* better than I'd thought. How did I fix this one?

"Derry has a crush on her," Zavier said helpfully from beside me. "I was saying that before, when we were in the barracks, but she didn't believe me."

I felt my neck and cheeks turn hot with embarrassment. Shandlin apparently having a crush was incredibly awkward. Zavier lying about Derry's 'crush' on *me* was also awkward… especially considering if anyone had the crush, it was probably me for Derry. Just a little, anyway.

"He flirts a lot," I said lamely. "He probably talks to all girls that way."

"Derry." Shandlin made a scoffing sound, then turned to take his seat inside the air vehicle. We followed him in, me still clutching that paper sketchpad, although of course I hadn't used it. "What did he say to you?" he snapped. "And when?"

"Um…" I swallowed, unable to meet his eyes. "On the first day I was conscripted, he called me lovely Iscee. You talked to him by communicator, remember?"

The High Duke seemed to relax, but I could feel his eyes still fixed on me. "You'd be smart not to take him seriously, Iscee. He's a notorious flirt."

"Yeah, I got that." Because I had. Random compliments didn't mean genuine interest. I *did* have a working brain.

"And he does talk to any girl like that," Shandlin continued emphatically. "All you need is to have all four limbs and a decent head of hair, and he'll pay you attention. Especially because you're my guard and he likes to annoy me, even though he knows you aren't allowed to date."

He was right, but I was still starting to get annoyed. I gripped my hands into the seat's armrests as the air vehicle took off with a lurch. "Well, I do have those attributes. But I'm also well aware that I can't have any relationships for the next twenty-two months. Even if I could, it wouldn't be with someone like him. I'm too smart for that."

"Good." Shandlin paused briefly, then added, "He's a wastrel, just does what he wants, spends his allowance, messes with girls, causes trouble. I hear that there are some places he's not allowed to visit anymore because of the mess he left behind."

Wastrel, eh? Sounded like Shandlin was throwing stones from that glasshouse of his, except for the bit about girls. I hadn't noticed him spend time with anyone apart from his guards and this one family visit. Besides, if Derry was a spendthrift playboy, then Shandlin was the sort of person who let his guards mistreat the general populace and who conscripted at will and who ordered people around like slaves…but who was I to complain?

"I'm sick of this conversation," he announced abruptly. "Did you finish that 'find the pog' picture I asked you for?"

"Not yet."

He huffed. "What were you doing that whole time? Gossiping with Zavier? Finish it, Older. You've got fifteen minutes."

So I set my attention to the paper sketchpad instead of the Rison scenery. It took me longer than fifteen minutes to finish the drawing, but as we were passing back through the barrier into Vyce, I was finally happy with it. I wordlessly handed it over.

Shandlin glanced at it, then tapped his finger in the corner where I'd hidden my little fluffy character behind a tree, the excited wagging of its curly tail shown in expressive marks. "Too easy. Is that it?"

There were a good thirty characters in that image, and I was annoyed that he'd found it so quickly. "There are four in total. You just found the easiest one."

"Hmm." He set himself to study the picture, and a good fifteen minutes passed before he finally said, "I can only find three. Where's the fourth?"

"I thought you wanted a challenge. Can't you find it yourself?"

Another five minutes passed, then he ordered, "Give me a clue. Maybe you just drew it badly so I can't see it."

Or maybe I'd forgotten to draw it in at all, and was trying to figure out a way to tell him that. But before I had to face that issue, a sudden blow struck the moving air vehicle, tossing it sideways sharply enough that I went flying and hit the plastic side, hard. Shandlin had been wearing his belt and had been caught in place, and when we finally righted we saw that the entire clear side of the vehicle was now bright pink.

"What the-" I murmured.

Suddenly Colby came charging in from the driver control

area, his expression uncharacteristically serious. "Out out out!" he ordered, grabbing Shandlin by one arm and dragging him from his seat even as he threw a safety cloak around Shandlin's shoulders, then pressed the override button to open the side door. "It's a bomb!"

My too-slow brain took in how Colby literally grabbed Shandlin in a gorilla-hold and then threw them both out of the door, the High Duke emitting a startled shriek along the way. *It's a bomb,* he'd said.

Suds! Suddenly I found myself reacting; throwing a safety cloak around my own shoulders and feeling it clip shut around my torso. My heart was beating so loudly it seemed to fill my hearing as I leapt out of the exit after them, and I couldn't even let myself think about how high we were, about how that safety cloak better work or I was dead…

I caught a glimpse of rocks and straggling greenery rushing up towards me – the scenery near this edge of Vyce Dome – then squeezed my eyes shut as the safety cloak suddenly expanded, almost silently releasing into a temporary glider and catching the wind. For a few seconds I just focused on breathing. I was alive, I was alive…thank you God, I was alive.

But I hadn't heard a second explosion; the sound of the real bomb going off. I tried to look over my shoulder to see if the air vehicle was OK, and if Bloom and Zavier had followed us. Surely they must be right behind! But I couldn't see anything past the cloak's enormous silver glider, although I could hear what sounded like Bloom shouting down at us…

I glanced down to see one single glider below me, round and pale blue against the rocky landscape of the Vyce mountains. It was a good thing they could hold two people, I told myself, even as I was stiff with fear and tension. I was waiting for the full explosion, for the fire and pain and metal to come raining down.

But it never did. I floated all the way to the ground, steering for the blue glider just ahead of me. It had fallen in a protective cloth dome, and the two guys who'd worn it were nowhere to be seen. The moment I touched ground I unclipped my own safety cloak's harness, then shook myself free and ran for the others. "Colby! Shan! Are you OK?"

Just then the edge of the fallen glider lifted to reveal Shandlin, its fabric casting an unhealthy blue light on his face. "Iscee!" he exclaimed, sounding relieved. "You're OK!"

"I'm fine," I said distractedly, glancing back to where the air vehicle was carefully landing in a nearby flat area. I could just make out the pink shape on its side, and it didn't look like any kind of explosive to me. It looked like something else entirely… I felt my jaw tense. "Where's Colby?"

"That's the thing," Shandlin replied, and his tone was odd. Quiet, a bit hoarse.

I turned to stare at him in surprise, and he pulled back the light cloth of the fallen glider to reveal a figure sprawled on the ground. It was Colby. His eyes were closed and his limbs oddly contorted, and a bright red trickle of blood ran from one nostril.

"He wasn't strapped on," the High Duke continued, and his voice broke. "He fell the last distance."

And that would explain Shandlin's odd tone and pale face. For a moment I couldn't breathe, and I glanced back at the nearby air vehicle, as if the other two would rush out shouting that it was all a joke, and Colby would be fine, really.

Then I saw what was on the air vehicle's side. Not a liquid explosive shot from a distance, as we'd assumed. As Colby had assumed, and had risked everything.

No, the large letters read, 'FREEDOM FROM TYRANNY!' in rough, bright pink text. It hadn't been a bomb at all; it had been a paint bomb.

A prank.

The next few hours were a mess of medics and air vehicles and tears as it became clear what had happened. 'An unknown person' had attached the explosive words as a statement, or perhaps a kind of joke. Bloom and Zavier had recognised what the thing was, since they'd had something similar happen a few months before. Or so they said.

But Colby hadn't known. He'd thought they were in danger, and he'd reacted before the other two could stop him. Shandlin said Colby had hung onto the cloak until they were ten metres from the ground, then he'd fallen. He wasn't dead, but he wasn't moving either. The medics said he'd probably wake up eventually, but he wouldn't be the same.

We returned to the Ducal Suite with one less person than we'd left with, and the mood was solemn. *Freedom from tyranny.* I couldn't push aside the similarity of the words to Derry's 'freedom movement'…and the fact Bloom and Zavier would have had perfect opportunity to attach a paint bomb to the vehicle, then quietly set it off once we'd returned to Vyce Dome. But there was no chance to challenge them on it, and I didn't know if I had the heart to.

Surely they wouldn't have meant any harm to Colby, or to any of us. Bloom had said it herself earlier: they had a real job to protect the High Duke. Even though I knew she wanted the government to change, I couldn't see her wanting to hurt the people around her. Not really.

As for me, I'd almost forgotten what I was doing here, wrapped up in the fact that I'd been taken away from my life on someone else's whim. I'd fallen into the role of entertainment-slash-resentful dogsbody, forgetting that guarding was a serious business. Colby had made jokes, but he'd never forgotten.

Shandlin was as silent as the rest of us. He'd given orders for Colby to have the best medical care, and for the culprits to be found and punished, but he hadn't requested a replacement. We went about our usual duties in silence, and I went to the kitchen to do the dishes. At this point I didn't mind the job. At least I didn't have to talk to anyone.

Footsteps sounded behind me, and I turned to see Shandlin standing in the doorway. While he never really smiled, now he looked purely sober, his eyes black in his too-pale face. "Colby might not ever walk again."

I paused, looking at the dish-box in front of me instead

of at him. "At least he's not dead. Breakers die at about one a year, and there are less than a hundred of us. That's a high mortality rate."

"Is that supposed to be my fault?" Shandlin exploded. "Maybe if Breakers weren't such shrieking idiots then they wouldn't die so easily! Colby jumped without even wearing a safety-cloak! It's like he wanted to be injured!"

He was upset, but so was I, and I didn't hold my tongue. "Are the Breakers properly trained in safety?" I retorted. "Or do you all emphasise courage over wisdom? Because I'd say you do! So Colby was brave and reckless and *stupid* because he was trying to save your life, and now he's paying the price. Not everyone would have done that."

Shandlin sucked in a deep breath, and there was a long, tense silence. "You wouldn't have. If there'd been a real bomb, then you would have let me die."

I looked away back at my dishes. "I didn't realise what was happening. But what do you expect from me? You took me away from my home without even asking, something completely illegal as well as unethical. And you don't even care! So don't ask me to risk my life for you, because it's not going to happen."

Another long silence, and then he said in a low, grim voice, "You have got to be the worst guard I have ever had. I should send you right back to the new recruits."

"Are you surprised?" My voice was brittle. I knew I'd stepped over the line now, but I was too angry to stop. "Your grand plan, the whole reason you took me in the first place, it's over. You've won. I got a message weeks ago that the Old World can't help me, and you know why?"

I didn't wait for him to answer, instead letting all those bitter words spill over. Bitter from the weeks spent here as an unpaid servant, from the hours spent watching those terrible news holo-vids.

"You won't let them help me! You want me here to prove some point, although God knows what. But they're just an organisation, Shan. They don't know me, and they value their peace treaties more than one girl. I could have been the one to fall out of that air vehicle instead of Colby, and the only people who'd mourn me would be my family! So send me back to the new recruits, I don't care. Seems like this position isn't any safer than that one anyway."

The High Duke was silent for a long while, so long I thought he'd explode or hit me or something terrible. But instead I heard him turn and stomp out of the room, and I was left there in the kitchen, shaking with adrenaline from the things I'd said.

He wouldn't have me executed, right? I didn't *think* he'd have me executed, but I knew there was no way I'd be allowed to remain in this position. I thought again of the training barracks and the rough methods, of the focus on strength and toughness and the complete lack of ethics. I didn't want to go back into that environment.

I looked at the silver bangle that I still wore on one wrist. It was a promise-holder: that if I obeyed Shandlin completely, then I could see my family after two years. Those were ridiculous terms and I'd surely breached them by now.

I left the dishes and went looking for company. I found Bloom sitting on a chair outside Shandlin's closed bedroom door, methodically polishing her double-ended stave. "What is it, Iscee?"

I stared at her, at those baby-round cheeks and those flat, emotionless eyes, and I wanted to ask, *did you set the paint bomb?* But the words wouldn't come out. So instead I answered quietly, "I think I've done it now. I've really upset him, and I don't know what he'll do."

"What did you do, punch him again?"

I frowned. "No, but I told him I wouldn't have risked my life to save his, not like Colby did. He was really angry with me."

Bloom was silent for a few moments. "Everyone knows that you wouldn't risk your life, Older, even the High Duke. I doubt he was surprised. But what do you expect me to do about it?"

I checked to see that no one was watching, then whispered, "Could you get a message to Derry? Get someone to contact Earth for me, to plead my case again on legal grounds. Anything."

She paused, running the cloth down the gleaming length of the spear tip. "I'm sorry, Iscee. I can't do that. I'm loyal to the High Duke, and I don't have any contact with Derry." Her voice was as low as mine, but she gestured minutely with her chin to the closed door behind her.

Oh. He might be listening. It sounded like something he'd do, to monitor even us four Breakers. *Three.* "Of course," I replied just as quietly. "I understand. So it's impossible?"

Bloom waved her hand subtly side to side, a gesture I only noticed because I was paying attention. *'Maybe.'* "Yes. Sorry. We don't make the rules, Iscee. We just do what we're told, when we're told."

I'd have to wait until the others could make contact. "I understand. I won't ask again."

NINE
Unrest

* * *

I was in my room, packing my few belongings into a small bag when Shandlin walked in. He didn't knock, but then I'd left the door open.

He frowned. "What are you doing?"

Wasn't it obvious? "I'm packing. I figured you'd send me back to the trainees any time now."

"Is this your response to every argument, Iscee? Thinking you'll get to leave? You're not going."

I put down the plain sleep jacket I'd been folding and turned to look at him. "What?"

He stood there still dressed in the same finery he'd worn to Rison, with his hands in his pockets and the usual absolute sense of his own power written on his face. "I've decided you're not leaving. You're a terrible guard, Iscendra Cole, but you know this wasn't about wanting another guard. It was about testing my strength against the Old World, seeing what I could get away with. It looks like they don't care about you enough to challenge me, so you'll stay here."

I'd known that already, but it didn't explain why he'd keep me *here* as a personal guard, rather than just sending me back into the dog pit. Unless Derry and Zavier were right…

"But…I'm not trained," I blurted out. "And as you just said, I'm a terrible guard. All I do is wash dishes and draw pictures, and I talk too much. I *definitely* won't risk my life for yours. What use can I possibly be?"

"You're entertaining. Besides, the toilets can always do with a clean." He lifted his chin then turned to walk out.

"But I already clean the toilets!" I called after him.

"Clean them better!" he called back, and then he was gone.

I stood in my small room, trying to figure out what had just happened. Was I the big crush...or was I the performing monkey? Because honestly, I'd prefer to be the second one.

And so I stayed. I certainly wasn't a guard anymore, and I was told to wear a simpler version of the guard's clothing (minus helmet) the few times I was allowed to go out.

Shandlin mostly ignored me, which suited me just fine, but he still seemed to delight in having me do the most menial tasks – and still creating more 'find the pog' sketches. I took revenge in always claiming there was one more pog than I'd truly drawn, although I think he picked up on that after a while.

At first being back at the palace was like being in a bubble, shut off from the outside world, but then little pieces began to filter in here and there. I managed to find active holo-vids when the others weren't in, or else looked over someone else's shoulder. They didn't try to stop me anymore.

And I saw increasing unrest. These news vids were largely from within Mars, and I had to read between the lines to get the truth. I knew Mars natives weren't allowed to openly speak against their rulers, and on the surface the stories just seemed to be making any 'rebels' sound like hewlligans and any government forces sound like the good guys. But if you looked at what they were actually describing...not so much. But that was just the local news feeds. The few that I saw from Earth were far more scathing.

They said the Vyce regent had come back to his dome because of recent rebel actions causing the death of the High Duke's personal guard (not quite true, fortunately for Colby), and I knew that was significant. Perhaps Shandlin would be bumped out of power without me even having to do anything. I didn't want him hurt (except for that punch in the gut that he was practically begging for) but I sure didn't think he should be ruling, nor his uncle.

The main topic was finances. It was now clear that Vyce was broke, regardless of how much power Shandlin liked to think it had. It was also depressed and crime-ridden. I'd already known that, but I'd known it from an outsider's point of view, from the apparent safety of Unity. And then every time the topic of money came up, the news vids would talk about Shandlin's mother's dowry.

"Idiots!" he raged the one time I saw him watching a news vid on the subject. "It was over twenty years ago, and those were my mother's personal things! They don't get to just lay a claim on them!"

Yeah, it didn't feel good when someone intruded on your personal space, did it?

But we all kept our mouths shut. Even though Shandlin's mood could be so mercurial, I didn't want to risk whatever might come if I really said the wrong thing…and I was *so* good at saying the wrong thing. Zavier and Bloom both had the 'silent guard' performance down perfectly, but then I still had to learn.

Colby hadn't yet been replaced.

Shandlin spent some time with his uncle in the business part of the palace. I didn't know what they discussed, except that when he came back, he was foul-tempered. "I'm so sick of this mess," he snapped. "I just want to get away from all these stupid, difficult people!"

"You need a holiday," Zavier ventured from his seat at the breakfast bar. I stood in the kitchen proper, making the usual garvafruit smoothies – heavy on the sugar.

"A holiday," Shandlin scoffed. "You just want to lie around on a beach somewhere."

"Sure do," Zavier agreed cheerfully. "How about you, Iscee? How does a bikini holiday sound?"

I scowled at him, knowing he'd said it to encourage Shandlin, and that annoyed me. "Good, if you'll wear the bikini."

"What do you think, Bloom?" Zavier waggled his eyebrows. "Would I suit red polka-dot, or blue frills?"

She rolled her eyes, but didn't smile. "Ugh, the images you've put in my head." Then she paused. "But perhaps getting away for a while would be a good idea. Maybe even off-world…"

Going off-world during a financial crisis!? Where were they going with this? But I could see Shandlin had been listening in, and a hopeful thought sprung to mind. "There's always Optus," I suggested, trying to sound casual. "There's a resort called Paradise which has pink sand and really great drinks. You can fly there in a couple of hours, and I hear it's cheaper to go there than some parts of Mars."

"Paradise, the resort your aunt and uncle own?" Shandlin said snarkily. "Nice try, Iscee." He paused, and as my shoulders slumped he added, "We'll go to Eden. That's on the other side of Optus, and it's *much* nicer."

Zavier cheered. Bloom looked neutral as always, and I just stood there with my hands full of sliced fruit. "Is this a real-guards-only trip, or can I come too?"

"You can come, Older." Shandlin's eyes flicked over me head-to-toe, so quickly that I would have missed it if I hadn't been paying attention. "I wouldn't want you to miss the sight of Zavier in a bikini."

I'd been feeling uncomfortable, both at how he'd looked at me, and how easily the other two Breakers seemed to manipulate him. Had they always been able to do this? Why hadn't I noticed before? But that last comment just made me laugh.

Three days later we were on Optus. The tiny man-made moon orbited Mars along with its two natural moons, and its carefully-tended artificial atmosphere meant it was summer all year round.

While part of me felt guilty over encouraging Shandlin to spend money when Vyce was in financial trouble (or realised that this would suit the Freedom Movement's purposes) the rest of me was thrilled to be here. Even if I couldn't see Aria, I was still on holiday. Whoop!

When I'd come to Optus with my family a few years earlier, we hadn't gone outside of Aria's Paradise resort. But this time we'd come out of a different exit in Vyce Dome, and we'd taken the long route to our resort, starting with a slow air tour over the whole satellite.

I'd watched in awe as we'd flown high over dozens of small, beautiful towns, complete with man-made lakes, rivers, and forests. There were even small seas for sailing, with tiny islands in whimsical shapes only seen from the air.

Then we'd come to land on this one large island, Eden. And boy was it beautiful. We stayed in a large set of rooms at the water's edge, the beach of gleaming pink and orange sand just the right temperature for bare feet.

And the High Duke had wanted to 'blend in', so he wore a wide hat and sunglasses the whole time…and we got to wear beach gear. I wasn't all that keen on the one-piece swimsuit I'd been provided, but at least it wasn't a bikini, and with a cover-up I felt just fine. It also made a nice change from the uniform I'd worn solidly for the last few months.

There wasn't that much to do here, as I'd known there wouldn't be. Bloom and Zavier, looking quite odd in civilian clothing, 'guarded' Shandlin as best they could with their limited weapons hidden in pockets and loose bags.

I trailed around after them as I was ordered, trying to spot my aunt, uncle or cousin anywhere in the hordes of underdressed, relaxed holiday-makers. Just on the very, very small chance that they'd decided to check out the competition. It was unlikely, but I couldn't help myself.

I didn't see Aria or Uncle Eliezer or Aunt Judee, who was my mother's twin. But I *did* see so many rich holiday-makers, resplendent in designer clothing and jewels, heedless of whatever was happening on the planet below. I even saw a few celebrities half-heartedly trying to hide their identities, and not quite succeeding.

"Look over there," I heard Zavier say to Bloom, sounding like a little boy in his awe. "I think that's Archi Zhang. You know, the singer from Arparath."

"Of course I know who that is," Bloom retorted, but she was craning her neck just as much as he. But then even I could recognise that perfect profile, that spiked dark-blue hair, and the distinctive tattoo down his neck and shoulder. Yup, that was Archi alright.

"I wonder if he minds fans talking to him," Zavier mused. "But he's on holiday, right? He won't want to be interrupted."

"If he didn't want to be interrupted, he should have worn a face-changer," Shandlin announced. "He's not, so he obviously wants to be recognised. I'll go and talk to him. Bloom, you come with me. You're cuter than Zavier."

He said it like a joke, but I supposed that to him, it must be true. Zavier wasn't plain, but 'cute' wasn't the right word either for someone six feet tall and covered in scars. So they went over and spoke to the slightly startled-looking singer, while Zavier stayed halfway between me and them, looking a bit longing and jealous. I just stayed where I was, because while Archi Zhang's music was decent, I didn't care to talk to him – and why would he want to talk to me?

And that was why when Derry unexpectedly appeared, I was sitting by myself.

He gave me one of those grins that made me check that all my clothing was where it ought to be, and then plopped down on the sand beside me. He wore an antique straw sunhat, loose beach trousers, and no shirt. It suited him.

"We don't have much time until my cousin comes back," he said, his tone sounding flirtatious but his words the opposite. "Pretend we're flirting."

"Fine," I muttered, feeling my cheeks heat. Was that a little disappointment I felt? "And it's just pure coincidence you're here, right?"

"Not at all." Derry smiled again, leaned in very close, then his words were low and fast; "Iscee. Well done for talking Shanny into leaving Vyce, but it's not enough. He needs to be seen behaving badly, to be seen as a poor, neglectful ruler. We need you to encourage that, to keep him here as long as you can, to make him spend as much as you can. There are casinos on the other side of the island-"

"Casinos?" I cut in, whispering hoarsely. I was genuinely shocked by the blatant request, as well as the assumption that *I* had talked him into coming. I hadn't, had I? "That's a bit much, Derry. I think he's capable of behaving badly all on his own – I don't have anything to do with it!"

Derry sighed. "You think I'm a monster for trying to make him look bad, don't you? But this is bigger than one boy being exposed for the selfish beast that he is. I don't want him hurt, I swear. But you have to realise that the sooner he's out of power, the better for you. The better for everyone. You'll be able to go right back to your home, and your family will be safe. Vyce Dome is at tipping point, and this could be the moment to change it."

I thought about that. Getting to go back home…but regardless of what Shandlin was like, I didn't want to manipulate things to be worse for him. That felt…ugly. And as I'd said, he could do that well enough himself. "Then what will happen to him?"

"Do you care?"

"I don't want him hurt either," I retorted. "Not because he doesn't deserve it, but because I'm better than that. And if there is unrest, it's going to be targeted at the Breakers, no matter what side we're really on. You know what happened to Colby, right?"

Derry looked pained. "That was a moment too slow on Bloom's part, and Colby was being heroic. Ended up alright for us, though; since he's one guard down. Two if you count you."

I scoffed. "If you can call that alright."

"Regardless, you'll be given instructions on what to do and when to do it. As Shanny's personal…oh, he's coming back. Look normal."

Indeed the High Duke had grown bored of Archi Zhang and was stomping back, sending up little puffs of coloured sand with each step. His face looked like thunder. "Derry, what are you doing here?" he asked without preamble.

"Don't say it's a coincidence that you're here when I am. You followed me, didn't you? I suppose you want to cause trouble."

Then he guessed right. My half-smile (my attempt at 'normal') froze on my face.

Derry, who'd sat even closer to me once Shandlin had come over, threw his arm around my shoulder. I shrugged it off. "Why should you get a holiday when I languish in Vyce? I was just inviting your girl here over to my beach house in her spare time. Don't begrudge me that."

"She has no spare time! Go get your own guards, and stop bothering mine."

"She's not bothered." Derry looked at me and winked. "Are you, lovely Iscee?"

"It's just Iscee," Shandlin snapped. "And you didn't come all the way to Optus just so you could ask her on a date. What are you really doing here?" We were starting to attract attention, and Shandlin finally noticed. He rolled his eyes. "Come back to my suite. There are too many people here."

I got up to go, but Derry grabbed my arm, pulling me back down. "Let's talk here, Shanny. What have you got to be ashamed of, anyway?"

"Nothing," the High Duke retorted, but his voice was lower. "Don't tell me that this is about my mother's dowry! I told you last time, those are my personal possessions, and I'm not selling them, no matter what."

Derry shrugged. "I just thought the starving people of Vyce might appreciate a bit of love from their ruler, but apparently not. So I assume the dowry's safe back in Vyce?"

"It's somewhere you can't find it. Don't mess with me on this, Derry!" Shandlin stepped closer, his expression furious. "What you're saying is starting to sound like treason. I'm the High Duke, I make the rules! And if you can't handle that…"

"Alright, alright, sorry." Derry stood, dusting the loose sand from his trousers. "Don't go on about treason, you know it's nothing like that. I'll go off and have some fun since it's pretty clear that none will be found here." He gave me another grin, one I could see was entirely artificial, then smiled at Bloom who stood silently next to Shandlin. "See you 'round, sweet Iscee, Bloomers."

Bloom turned bright pink, and Shandlin scowled. "Just go!"

Shandlin was silent almost the whole way back to the suite, not that it was a long walk. But the moment we were inside the main room he exploded. "What did I say about you talking to Derry!?"

Oh, he meant *me*. And he didn't even know what Derry had really wanted…

"You didn't say anything," I replied coolly, feeling the heat still in my cheeks. "You just said not to trust his flirting. And I don't." Especially as it was based around that nasty subject of *treason*.

"Does he have to drape himself all over you? It's sickening!" Shandlin stomped over to the drinks dispenser and tapped the button for a pressed grapefruit juice. "Besides, he only does it to annoy me." As if suddenly realising what he'd said, his expression changed and became almost rueful. "I suppose it's working. But suds, he's such a grawlix. An absolute wolcrox with no redeeming features. I can't stand him!"

Zavier had vanished into a side room and Bloom was unobtrusively cleaning her hand spear in the corner – as if it needed it – leaving me to deal with this alone. The cowards. But I was reminded of what Derry had said, that the sooner Shandlin lost power, the sooner I could leave, and so I forged ahead.

"Maybe if you didn't act so irritated then he'd stop doing it. He's like my brother Nik, not happy 'til he's got someone angry." Although unlike Derry with Shan, Nik wasn't plotting to have anyone removed from their position.

Shandlin didn't react as I thought he would. Instead he sighed heavily. "I don't trust him, and I don't want him talking to you. I know he's got another side he doesn't show to me. Who knows what he could say?"

A pang of guilt washed through me, then irritation at that guilt. No matter what Shandlin had done, or what he deserved, he wasn't as oblivious as Derry might think.

But then Bloom spoke up. "Derry's a mindless playboy with nothing to do except cause trouble. Iscee's not stupid enough to listen to anything he could say. What was he trying to do, Iscee? Get you to pop behind a bush with him?"

It was ridiculous, but I found myself blushing bright red. "No! He was just trying to be charming, that's all." And even if that had been true, there hadn't been any bushes nearby. It was a beach.

"I hope you do know better than to trust his charm," Shandlin said darkly. "He'd never be really interested in someone like you. He probably thinks you know where I've hidden the dowry or something like that."

Ouch. And that fully proved, once and for all, that the High Duke was *not* interested in me. Half amused, half annoyed, I retorted, "Way to make me feel hideous. Just because I'm not your type doesn't mean I'm not anyone's."

His jaw dropped. "That's not what I said! I meant that you're not rich or famous or even famously beautiful, and you're moody. It's off-putting."

Maybe he was right, but again, throwing stones from that glass house of his… "Well, if I'm moody, then you're just as bad, except you've got the power to back it up. No wonder we're both single."

"I'm not moody," he countered defensively. "And I could be in a relationship if I wanted to be. I'm just too young to be tied down."

"Really."

"Yes, really! Besides, I'm a High Duke. I can do what I want."

"I *know*."

"You could show a little more respect," Shandlin said sharply. "I don't know why I even keep you around."

"Entertainment value, you said," I answered flippantly.

"And to pull a middle finger to the Old World. Is it working?"

"Well, you're not entertaining me. You're annoying me. And I don't think the Old World really cares about what you're doing here, do they? Unless you're a spy."

He'd said it lightly, but I barely kept myself from jolting. Keeping my tone as normal as possible, I replied, "What, and my secret plan was to get you to pretend to be my neighbour so that you could conscript me into the Breakers, and then make me your personal toilet cleaner? I can pass back information on your bowel movements, which I'm sure will be brilliantly useful to Earth."

I heard Bloom let out a snort of laughter which was barely hidden, and Shandlin rolled his eyes. "Don't be disgusting, you know I was only teasing. And you don't *really* clean my toilets, do you? I thought the robocleaner did that."

Now I was the one to roll my eyes. "You said you wanted them cleaner."

He curled his lip. "I didn't mean it. You don't need to do that anymore."

Like suds he hadn't meant it. "Good. I won't."

"Fine."

There was a long silence where I wondered at how we'd even got to this point in conversation when we'd started with the High Duke shouting over his cousin's fake flirtation. Bloom coughed awkwardly, and Shandlin turned to her.

"Don't you have somewhere to be?"

"I'm guarding you," she replied, brow furrowed.

"Well, do it from another room. I promise to call for you if Iscee tries to kill me."

Bloom frowned, but got up to follow instructions, and then it was just me and him in the large lounge room, the couches in between us.

I studied him warily. He didn't seem angry any more, but his moods were so hard to fathom, and he could lose his temper so easily. "Why do you say things like that?"

He shrugged. "I don't know. Why are you single?"

"What?" Talk about a change of subject. "I'm a Breaker,

sort of. Dating's forbidden."

"Yeah, but before that you weren't seeing anyone. What are you, seventeen? Eighteen? Don't most girls of your age have boyfriends by now?"

I answered as impersonally as I could. "I'm seventeen. And yes, quite a few of them do. But I supposed it's just that I live in quite an isolated area – *lived* – and I don't meet a lot of boys that I didn't grow up with…and it doesn't help that I'm not rich, famous, or particularly beautiful. Oh, and moody. But I'm not on the shelf yet," I added quickly. "Ask me again when I'm forty."

"I never said you were on the shelf." Shandlin was watching me with an expression that I couldn't really read, so what he said next came as a surprise. "I never said you weren't my type, either. You're not ugly."

"Gee, thanks!"

He frowned, as if realising he'd misspoken. "What I meant was that you're actually quite attractive in your own particular way. I've always thought that. I wouldn't want you to think otherwise."

Uh oh. The conversation was going in a very unwanted direction, so I turned away, hiding my reaction by heading towards the drink dispenser. Uh oh. Uh oh. Had Derry and Zavier been right about that crush after all? And what was I supposed to do about it?

"Aren't you going to say anything to that?" Shandlin persisted when I didn't answer.

I still couldn't look at him. "What do you want me to say? Thank you? Keley said it, Derry said it. You don't choose ugly guards. You're my…boss, so whether you think I'm lovely or an absolute swamp-mare doesn't matter."

"And what if I wanted it to matter?"

I turned to see he was still watching me, those very dark eyes slightly shuttered, and suddenly the room seemed too small. "I don't get what you mean," I said. I didn't *want* to get it.

He has the biggest crush on you, Iscee.

Oh, please no. My heart leapt in my chest with panic or what might have even been excitement. I didn't know what to do. But then he took three strides across the room and suddenly he was right in front of me, grabbing my arms, and then-

…then he kissed me.

As a first kiss it was utterly awkward. I was so shocked I didn't move at all, and there was more pressure than skill. Then after a second or two the High Duke moved back and just looked at me, those dark eyelashes looking even blacker this close up. "Well?"

"Uh…"

He dropped my arms and took another step back. "Don't tell me that this is a surprise to you. I won't believe it."

"But it is a surprise," I replied, speaking through lips that felt like they belonged to another person. He'd kissed me. *Kissed* me. *Me.* No matter what the other guards had said, I hadn't believed it. Not really. "You insult me constantly. Five minutes ago you were saying that I had no redeeming qualities, the next you're acting like you're *interested.* So no, I didn't see this coming."

"Oh." At first he was taken back, then rallied. "Of course I insult you. You insult me back. We were flirting." There was a long pause. "Weren't we?"

I just stared at him. "You thought that was flirting?"

Shandlin's eyes widened, and suddenly his gaze dropped from mine, looking anywhere but at me. He turned away, flexing his hands agitatedly at his sides. "Everybody thought it was flirting, not just me. They all think you're my girlfriend. Zavier and Bloom said it. *Derry* thinks you are! That's why he keeps flirting with you, because he thinks he can take you from me."

Oh no. Oh nononononononono. I'd been set up by the others. It was worse than I'd thought, and I tried to save the situation. "He flirts with Bloom. He flirts with everyone. I think he just wants to annoy you, Shan. Anyway, he can't take what you don't even have."

"But what if I did have it?" Then I saw the High Duke's cheeks were hot red. He was blushing under that tan complexion, although he raised his eyes to meet mine again. "What if it wasn't just all rumour? I think...I think we could be good together, Iscee. I could make a few allowances for you."

I felt myself grow cold as I realised what he was saying. This, this was the exact situation that Derry had wanted me to create, and it was the exact one I'd wanted to avoid. But the choice had been taken away from me. "Allowances?"

"Yes, like...your family. I could let you visit them sometimes, although you'd have to come back home to the palace pretty quickly. You'd like that, wouldn't you?"

The last was said almost hopefully, but I'd started shaking my head. This was wrong, all wrong, and I was growing panicky and angry, and I didn't know how to deal with the situation. So as usual, my mouth made the decision for me. "The palace is not my home, Shan! It's yours, but it's my prison! Can't you see that I'm not with you by choice? You can't offer me partial freedom, then act as if I'm supposed to be happy with it!"

His eyes widened at my tone, but I couldn't stop now. "I can't believe you thought we were flirting! You insult and threaten me just like you do everyone else around you, and you've got *no* bloody idea of how we all feel! You've got to be the most selfish person I've ever met! And it's not just me who thinks that!

"Why don't you take a poll of all the Breakers, Shan? All those people who you seem to think of as yours, but who you don't even pay for the first two years? See how they like you. See how the broke, depressed people of *Vyce* like you." I lifted my chin, and my eyes were burning with unshed tears. I'd done it now, but I couldn't be sorry. "So there's my answer to your offer. *No.*"

Shandlin was silent for a long while, his dark head hanging and his hands in fists at his sides. He didn't look at me. Then finally he shook his head and stormed out the door.

TEN
Behaving Badly

◎　◎　◎

I'd been sitting in silence for several minutes, horrified by what I'd said, when Zavier came into the room. "What was that about, Iscee?"

I shook my head. My whole body was trembling: with fear, anger, or adrenaline, I didn't know. "You told him I was flirting with him?"

"Uh…not explicitly." He frowned. "Come on, Iscee. It's not like Shandlin's ugly. Some of the girls even say he's good-looking. Maybe he just needs a gentle touch."

"He's not getting any touch from me!" I shouted suddenly. "It doesn't matter what he looks like. I'm an illegal conscript, Zavier! A bloody captive! Have you forgotten that?"

"Suds, sorry, sorry." And perhaps I did see some guilt in those blue eyes. "I'd better go check on him. Just…try not to burn anything down while we're gone."

Zavier left, and I started pacing the suite, my arms wrapped tightly around myself. Oh, I'd messed up this time. I couldn't see how I could have done it differently, because I felt like I'd been backed into a corner by Zavier and Bloom and stupid, two-faced Derry, treating me as a performing monkey-crush-distraction.

Iscee can keep his attention while we take over the dome. And we'll keep her happy by promising to help her.

They'd wanted too much from me. I'd never claimed to be a perfect person, a long way from it, but I also didn't whore myself out, not even with false affection or a kiss. I didn't like lying, and I didn't steal. But they'd asked me to do all of those things. Derry had even asked me to steal the dowry if

I found it!

I'd paced into a side parlour by this time. It was filled with Shandlin's extra stuff, the things that he didn't need but had decided should come with him. There were suitcases still filled with extra clothing, shoes and hats, and for some reason his stupid cushion collection had come along too. All two dozen padded shapes were piled up on the room's plush couch.

Just then his words came back to mind; what he'd told Derry about the dowry.

Is it on Vyce?

It's somewhere you can't find it.

Shandlin had seemed so confident that it couldn't be found, not even now when there was so much focus on those jewels, and when it seemed people were actively looking. That meant it must be somewhere ridiculously well-hidden, perhaps in a safe in the palace...or perhaps it had come with him on holiday.

The dowry was said to be a collection of incredibly valuable gems. If I had them, I could hold them hostage: use them to free myself and to buy my family a new plantation somewhere safer and more beautiful, if such a place could be found. Enough money would buy silence from a thousand onlookers, and I just needed to get my family off Mars...

And so one moment I was wondering how I could stop trying to do this Derry and Bloom's way and just flee, and the next I was going through the High Duke's things, trying to find the dowry. I didn't know what it looked like or where to find it, and I knew that once I'd started looking I'd have to finish. I'd have to be gone by the time he got back.

Clothes, shoes, and random, unnecessary items I didn't have names for all went flying through the air as I searched frantically through the carefully-arranged gear. None of this was new to me since I'd helped to pack it all, but I hadn't been looking the same way then. How would it be hidden? What would it *look* like?

"Dowry, dowry, where are you?" I muttered to myself,

grabbing an ancient cushion in the shape of an Earth walrus. I squeezed its fat belly, trying to feel if there was anything inside, then in frustration dug my nails in and ripped the thing open. If there were jewels in here, I'd find them.

"What are you doing?" It was Bloom, and she was watching me neutrally from the door of the room, her miniature weapon propped at her side.

"Finding the dowry," I told her simply, still searching even as I spoke. "I've started now, so I've got to finish. It's *got* to be here."She just watched me. "Then what will you do?"

"Leave, of course. Get my family and go back to Earth. Maybe Derry can trade it for something useful." I threw aside the walrus, picking up a blue, wedge-shaped cushion – again completely useless, but for some reason Shandlin had thought it important enough to bring on holiday. "You can come too, you and Zavier. Start over."

"Where?"

"Anywhere! Somewhere you aren't a slave. Somewhere you get *paid* for your work."

"I do get paid," she told me. "You're the only one who doesn't. Besides, we've got a plan in action, you already know that, and it's a better one than just escaping." She didn't seem angry, though. "I presume this has something to do with His Grace hitting on you?"

I froze, then ripped open the new cushion. There was no time for gentleness. "You were supposed to be outside."

"I was, but it's not a surprise. He's so jealous of you with Derry that I'm surprised he didn't try it sooner."

I didn't answer, feeling somehow ashamed that it had happened, that I'd not expected it; that in a small way I'd not hated it, either. "Did you encourage him?"

"Yes," Bloom replied simply. "But in the same way we encouraged him to come to Optus. We presented the idea, he drew his own conclusions."

"You shouldn't have done it!" I shouted at her. "Now look what's happened!" I picked up the cushion again in furious disgust at her and at him. And perhaps there was a tiny part that was angry at myself, for somehow enjoying the attention. Stupid Shan, stupid me. Stupid uncle regent for leaving him alone. Stupid Derry for encouraging him!

"It's done now." As if tired of watching, Bloom stepped into the room and began replacing the items I'd thrown around. "Shandlin might not be gone long, and I don't want to have to explain this lot. I'll put you in a chokehold before I let you implicate me."

Implicate…*oh*. Suddenly deflated, I realised the mess I'd made. I picked up the wedge-shaped cushion, gently pulling it open and studying the insides. "I'll clean up and sew these things back together now. I know how to use a mend-all, and he doesn't need to know this happened."

"What made you think the dowry would be here?"

"I suppose I was being hopeful. Or desperate, more like. I just thought he'd keep it near him." I desolately picked through the soft cushion inner. "At least I used up some energy. I'll go clean this up." But as I moved my fingers through the padding, something hard hit my nail. I pulled at it in surprise, and from the inside of the wedge cushion came one, two, three pieces of plasti-glass.

Or that's what they looked like at first, they were so big and shiny. Each bigger than my thumbnail and perfectly almond-shaped, they were clear and light-refracting as if they had truly been glass. But why would anyone hide glass inside a cushion like this…?

I didn't breathe for a moment as I realised what they were.

I'd really, truly found the dowry.

"Oh suds," I murmured, so stunned I almost felt emotionless. "That finally explains the weird cushion collection." Because he was a High Duke he could pretend to have unusual tastes, but in reality it was a perfect place to hide something valuable. Not a wallet, not a safe: something that would usually be overlooked.

Enormous diamonds…in a cushion.

"Son of a swamp-mare," Bloom breathed, her eyes wide. "Let me see those."

I handed her one, and she studied it solemnly. "There have to be more of these. Three can't be the whole dowry."

"Three will be enough," I said, my heart pounding. "Enough for us, for now."

She closed her fist over the diamond. "Give me the others. I can get them to Derry."

I shook my head, suddenly possessive. "I'll look after them for now." I shoved those two into the side of my swimsuit top. The thick fabric as well as my limited curves would hide them until I could put them somewhere safer. I'd let her keep that one. "Here, help me clean up."

We hurriedly picked up each item, replacing it to its original state, and I took a little longer with the mend-all, sealing the cushion seams almost invisibly to their old state. But they felt different. It felt like Shan would just look at the cushions and *know* that he had to check them, would know that I'd stolen from him.

He didn't need it, I told myself. Besides, he stole *me*. What better did he expect? So I stomped on any qualms my conscience brought up, focusing on tidying until the room looked just like we'd left it.

Bloom and I had only just managed to escape the cushion room when the boys came back. Shandlin saw me and then his gaze skimmed right past as if I wasn't there. "Bloom, I'm going to sleep. Don't bother me."

Well, I definitely wouldn't be bothering him. Instead I went to sit in my own little room off the main complex, the two stolen jewels feeling like they were burning holes in my clothing. Bloom had the other one and there was no way she'd implicate herself, but unless I was going to return all three to their hiding place, I didn't want to have them on me.

Derry had been nearby just an hour ago, I remembered. He wouldn't have left by now, no way. So I quietly got up, taking a loose shirt-towel as if I was going swimming, then went for a hunt.

I found him in one of the many eateries scattered around the resort, sitting at the bar with a decorative drink in front of him. He was staring intently at a small screen set in the table top, and he didn't look up when I sat down next to him. After a few seconds I said, "How's your drink?"

Derry looked up with that ready-made grin, but it turned briefly into genuine shock when he saw who I was. He caught himself, turning his expression back into that smooth, playboy smile. "Couldn't keep away from me, huh? I wouldn't have thought that Shanny would let you get away like this. Especially after the talking-to he just gave me."

Now that made me curious. I hadn't even considered that Shandlin would seek out his cousin. "What did he say?"

"That I should stay away from him and all his guards if I knew what was good for me." Derry looked almost rueful. "He really hates me."

"And you go to such trouble to make him like you," I said dryly, but I couldn't keep up the joke. I was jittering in place, the jewels – now in my pocket – feeling sharp and heavy. "Can we talk somewhere privately?"

"Sweetheart, we can *talk* all you want." But he played along, getting up and strolling along beside me, and when it became clear I didn't know where I was going, he took my arm and steered me along the beach, into a different bay.

We came to a bungalow on its own, beautifully thatched with some sort of climbing greenery and flowers. The doorway slid open as we approached – it was his own room. Once we were inside, his whole demeanour changed. "We can talk openly in here; it's set to block any trackers or surveillance devices. Why did you come to find me? I'm guessing it's not because you were lonely."

"I want out."

"Of Optus? You came with Shandlin, you'll have to leave with him."

"You know what I mean. I want you to help me get away, help me and my family. I won't do this any longer. Not one single day."

Derry sat down on the nearest lounging chair, looking uncharacteristically serious. "I can't just help you leave, Iscee.

Firstly it'll make me a traitor for certain in Shandlin's eyes. Now he just dislikes me, but he'll have grounds to prosecute me then. And yes, for a member of the family he *does* need grounds. And besides, it's not cheap to uproot a whole family. Do the others know you want to do this? If you can just wait out another year or two then you'll be allowed to go, and-"

I was digging in my pocket, and finally managed to pull the contents out, holding them out to him. "Will these do?"

He blinked, stared at the diamonds, then blinked again.

I dropped them into his hand. "Bloom's got a third one. We found them- alright, I found them- hidden amongst Shandlin's things. I suppose this must be the dowry."

"Half of the dowry," Derry murmured, still staring at the jewels. "There are more than this. They were supposed to be set into a crown, but for some reason it never happened. And then after his mother died they disappeared. Where did you find them?"

I shrugged. "Doesn't matter. What can you do with them?"

And now he was smiling, a knowing close-mouthed smile that made him look a lot more like his cousin. "More than you can imagine, lovely Iscee. Thank you. This has been a wonderful help."

"I didn't do it for nothing," I warned. "I did it so you'd help me and my family escape, because I have *seriously* burned my bridges here. When will you do it?"

"I need a good month to set up an escape. Where do you want to go?"

"Anywhere not awful. Here would be fine, although I can't think that we could afford to live here for long. The Old World even. But a month is too long. I don't know how long we can keep Shandlin from noticing that the jewels have gone."

Derry nodded slowly, still staring down at the diamonds. "Mm. Two weeks, then. I might even be able to manage ten days, but we can't let anyone know that you're going. Do you know where Whirey Swamp is?"

"Of course. Why?"

"It's an evacuation spot. Obviously that's not something we want people to know, but if you get in real trouble, if your case ever seems hopeless, that's where you need to go."

"Whirey Swamp," I repeated. I remembered it was a notorious place for suicides, but this was a different type of escape we were talking about. "It's a big place. Where in the swamp?"

"Near the white cliffs. Do you know which part I mean?"

I nodded slowly, picturing the place in my mind. I'd flown over it once or twice, and I remembered because those cliffs were where people would jump into the water and have a close and personal encounter with a swamp-mare, poor souls. Honestly, if you could choose any way to go, why make it that?

"Right. White cliffs, Whirey Swamp. Thank you very much, Derry," I said briskly, "but I should go now. I'll leave these with you, and you can get the last one from Bloom in your own time."

"Mm. I will." He stood and walked me to the door, suddenly grinning again. "Will it look better or worse for you to be seen kissing me in the doorway?"

"Worse, definitely!" And I'd had one kiss already today. It was enough.

"OK. No kiss." So instead he gave me a swat on the backside as I moved past, in full view of whoever might be watching. I scowled at him over my shoulder and he grinned, giving me a thumbs up. *Play along.*

Well, I was going to escape, wasn't I? Those jewels would free me and my family, and I could put up with looking undignified in exchange. Really.

I came back to the High Duke's suite an hour later, having made a point of lying on the beach and swimming for long enough that I had an excuse for my absence. But the others barely noted my arrival. Shandlin hadn't even come out of his room the whole time, and so after a few awkward moments I just said to the room at large, "If I'm not needed here, I'm going swimming again." After all, it wasn't every day that I got to come to Optus.

"Don't," Zavier said just as I reached the doorway. "It would be better if he knew where you were."

I.e., go to your room. I studied him carefully, trying to pick up by his body language if he knew what I'd just done. "What does it matter?"

"Oh, just don't be difficult," he countered lightly, but I knew he was serious. "Go on, do some drawing or something. We can go out again when His Grace wants to. We've still got another three days."

Or so he'd thought. But that evening Shandlin announced we'd be returning the following morning; our holiday had been cut short. The whole time he didn't speak to me, he didn't look at me. He just acted sullen and self-absorbed – more so than normal, anyway. I guessed rejection didn't agree with him. If he'd wanted to hide the fact that something had happened between us, then this wasn't the way to go about it. He'd gone from casually ordering me around to not speaking to me at all, and only occasionally barking orders to the other two.

Once our private moon-shuttle arrived back in Vyce's main spaceport, we climbed out to find we were surrounded by camera drones, all bright lights and clearly filming Shandlin...and us as a result. It was only for about thirty seconds as we headed towards our waiting air vehicle, but it was strange and completely unexpected. For all of Shandlin's arrogance and drama, he mostly managed to avoid being filmed in person.

By the time we escaped to the safety of the air vehicle that would take us back to the palace, I could see the others were as shaken as I was. Bloom quickly reached over to change the vehicle's walls to 'opaque' as we took off for the palace – while we could still see the drones outside, they couldn't see us.

"What was that?" Zavier muttered.

"I don't know," Shandlin replied, his eyebrows in a low,

angry line. "But I expect we'll find out."

When we arrived at the palace we were met by a worried-looking woman in her forties. I hadn't seen her before, but judging by her excellent clothing and air of authority, she was someone important. "Your Grace," she said. "I'm terribly sorry to greet you like this, but something's happened. Your uncle has passed away."

It turned out that the regent had died of heart failure while in the middle of a meal with dignitaries from various domes and even from Earth. He'd actually been trying to do his job and fix things for Vyce, at least as much as they could be fixed, but clearly it had been too much for him. Vyce was now regentless, and Derry was fatherless. I thought of him back on Optus, how he'd been so focused on his goals, and wondered if he knew yet.

The mood over the next couple of days was glum, and Shandlin spent most of his time in his contact-chamber with Zavier or Bloom in attendance, speaking furiously to I-don't-know-who, because I wasn't allowed to be in there. I basically sat around the Ducal Suite, feeling alternately guilty over robbing him when he *really* had enough troubles of his own, and wondering where my family was, if Derry had managed to speak to them yet, when he would contact me, where we would *go*...

The High Duke finally came out after a long, intense discussion and found me sitting on the couch near the kitchen, staring blankly at the wall. "Iscee!"

I jolted. It was the first time he'd spoken to me since Optus. "Yes?"

There was a long silence. Then he said grimly, "I'm so sick of seeing you moping around. I think it's time for you to leave."

Leave? My heart jumped into my throat and I looked up at him hopefully.

That hope was squashed when he added nastily, "Don't think you're getting out of this, Older. You still stay until I say you can go. But I've decided you can visit your family after all." I jumped up, wanting to thank him or say *something*, but he held up a hand. "Go now, but you'll be wearing full Breaker armour, and you'd better be back first thing tomorrow morning. Understood?"

I nodded. One night was better than nothing, and even with the armour, maybe I could work out some way of escape. "Yes. Will I have a guard with me?"

"You *are* a guard, Iscee. Of course not." He paused. "But you've got that tracker in your arm, and we *will* be watching you."

"OK," I said meekly, but inside I was exultant.

"And I'll have that promise-holder back."

I held out my wrist, pretending not to feel awkward at his proximity as he pressed his thumb against the silvery metal. The bracelet's edge flashed green then gold, and suddenly it uncurled into a single stick. Promise kept, apparently.

I finally looked up at him, truly meeting his eyes for the first time since that awful conversation. "Thank you."

He smiled; a weird, twisted sort of smile. "Don't thank me, Iscee. Just leave."

Yes, sir!

ELEVEN
Whirey Swamp

◉ ◉ ◉

Maybe the High Duke wasn't so terrible after all, I mused as I sat in the slowly swinging gondola. The trip was a good three hours back to Unity, but I'd be home by dinner time. OK, so it was only an overnighter, and I'd had to wear the hated Breaker full armour which had been given back especially for the occasion, but yay! I was going to see my family!

I could also take the chance to update Aria, Lanny and my other friends too, to let them know I was OK. It cheered me to think that if Shandlin had relented on this matter, then perhaps he'd relent even further as time went by. Or maybe I'd have truly escaped, and it wouldn't matter anymore.

I watched the city skim by below my otherwise empty gondola cabin – the emptiness almost definitely because of that same brown uniform. No one wanted to share with a Breaker. The scenery below me was too urban and busy and chaotic, sure, but in these last few months I'd come to see a beauty in it that perhaps the Vyce locals had always noticed.

There was something about human beings cooperating to build such places, something almost magical in seeing houses and apartments and factories all so closely together, like parts of a giant machine. It might have a single ruler at its head, but the true Vyce was made up of millions of individuals, and they were what kept it running.

By the time I reached Unity I was feeling almost kind towards the High Duke. So he was completely self-absorbed, moody and controlling; but perhaps he wouldn't have been so bad if he'd been raised differently. If he'd had a few boundaries growing up, and if he'd had a decent role model, then perhaps he'd have grown up to be a good guy. As it was, it appeared he at least wasn't a complete monster.

But there was still the issue of the stolen jewels. I mused whether I could contact Derry, get him to give them back? It had only been a few days; surely he'd still have them.

My gondola came to rest in the town's last stop, only a few minutes from my family home. I took the helmet off as I got out, but a moment too late. A tiny paint bomb came flying at me, hitting me in the shoulder and spraying my armour with vivid green.

"Hey!" I shouted at nobody in particular. "It's Iscendra Cole! Who the suds did that?!"

There was silence, broken by the sound of scrambling by a nearby building. Nobody raised their hand to admit it, although I'd manage to catch the attention of all three people within earshot.

"Breakers don't even use gondolas," I muttered to myself. Ignorant vandals didn't even know that much.

"Iscendra?" A dark-skinned girl about my own age called across to me. I recognised her as Padi, someone I'd gone to school with, although we hadn't been particular friends. "They let you go."

"Hi, Padi," I said a little awkwardly, suddenly extra conscious of my Breaker uniform. I tucked the helmet under one arm as if I could hide it, then managed a smile. "No, they didn't let me go. Or just for one day, anyway. What's with the paint bombs?"

Padi didn't smile. "You're the first Breaker to show up here after the law change. I don't know who did it, but it could have been anyone."

"I'm not a Breaker." There was a long pause where she looked incredulously at my distinctive uniform, and I scrambled to correct myself. "I mean…not really, because I was illegally conscripted. The High Duke just made me wear this to be difficult, which is the same reason he won't let me go home." Then I realised what she'd said. "What law change?"

"Unity becoming part of Vyce territory," Padi cried. "How can you not know about that?"

I felt myself turn cold. Out of everything I'd seen in snatches of news vids, I hadn't seen this. They'd been talking. Just talking.

Right?

"It was finalised last night," she continued in a low voice. "We'll all be given the chance to become Mars citizens by this time next week, or else leave. They say there'll be no special treatment for us anymore. And then *you* come around here in your uniform…" Her voice trailed off, but I got the idea.

Our Earth-owned sanctuary was going to be open to all the chaos from the land outside. Our *people* would be open to it – the apparent safety of the peace treaties now gone. Not that those had helped me at all, but they'd kept this small green place safe. *Ours.*

But now there'd be visits from whoever Vyce chose to send…from the Breakers, if they could even be bothered travelling this far. And with the anti-Older sentiment I'd run across, I'd bet that they would make the effort."I'm going to see my family," I said abruptly.

I dropped the borrowed helmet and ran towards my family's plantation. I could see it even from here; the tidy walls marking the boundaries, the rows of lush green plants marching from flat ground right up the cliffside to the house, whose pillars held it up over the drop. No point using good land for building, not when it could be planted.

The many green-towers looked as full and healthy as they usually did at this time of year, but there was no one harnessed and hanging off their sides, helping the robotic fruit-pickers to select the ripe fruit and leave the unripe. When I arrived at the entry gate, it quickly scanned me then opened automatically. Unlike whoever had shot the paint bomb, this gate looked past my uniform to my DNA.

Two minutes later I was inside the house. It looked the same as always, although I couldn't hear anyone inside. "Hello?" I called. "It's Iscee. I'm home!"

A few seconds later a small, fluffy figure came charging around the corner, wagging its curly tail. It was my pog Wally, the subject of so many sketches, and he looked up at me over that fuzzy snout and yapped his odd little bark.

I reached down and picked him up for a cuddle, feeling small and scared, almost like a child again. "Mum, Dad? Hello, where is everyone…?"

Just then Mum came out into the hall and saw me standing there. She froze, then just stared. "Iscee?! What are you doing here?"

"I got a night off," I replied, trying not to react to her expression. She was white-faced and her skin seemed more lined than it had been a few months ago, but then stress would probably do that to a person. "Aren't you happy?"

"I'm happy," she whispered, not sounding that way at all. Then she ran over and put her arms around me, pog notwithstanding, and her shoulders shuddered with tears.

I hugged her back, and Wally scrambled out from between us onto the floor with an indignant yip. "It's OK, Mum," I assured her fervently, even though I wasn't at all convinced that was the case. "I heard the news about Unity becoming part of Vyce, but Padi said we'd all have the chance to apply for Mars citizenship. I'm sure they'll let us keep the plantation. Who else would run it so well?"

"Oh, *Iscee*," she murmured, then shook her head.

Just then Dad and Nik came out behind us. "Iscee?" Dad echoed. "What are you doing here?"

"Forget that," Nik snapped. "Iscee, what did you do to upset the High Duke so much?"

I froze in Mum's arms, my own falling slackly to my sides. *How did I infuriate thee? Oh, let me count the ways…*

But instead I said hoarsely, "What are you talking about? He let me come for a visit, and he's a bit of a grawlix, but I haven't been hurt…" Not recently, anyway.

But Dad was shaking his head, and Nik just stared at me with a hollow-eyed expression I hadn't seen him wear since I'd accidently mulched his favourite toy tri-wheeler.

"It's the plantation," Dad said flatly. "They've confiscated it."

For a moment I just stared at him, trying to make sense of that statement. "*Yes...*" I said finally. "But they've confiscated all Unity land, right? And you get to keep it if you become a Vyce citizen?"

Mum pulled away from me a little, shaking her head. She wiped her eyes. "Oh, Iscee, no. That's what's happened to most of Unity, from what we've heard since this morning. But not us. The High Duke has confiscated our land entirely. We have to be off it by tomorrow..." And then she broke into tears again.

"We just heard today," Dad added. He was pale and hollow-eyed just like Mum. I'd never seen him so quiet, so obviously shocked. "We've challenged them, thinking it was a mistake, but they just showed us this." Then he said, "Computer, show us the Confiscation Order."

On the nearby wall a hologram appeared, stretching from floor to ceiling. It was plain and marked with the Vyce Ducal Crest, and the text was simple.

Re: Cole plantation and greenhouses. All land is confiscated on the express order of High Duke Shandlin, and is now the property of the Vyce Ducal Government on behalf of the people of Vyce.

Then it displayed the date, and a time: *Exit required by 10 am Tuesday 14 November.*

"That's tomorrow," I breathed in horror.

"We don't know what we're going to do," Mum said rapidly. "We're trying to pull our funds together, but you know we've put it all back into this place. We don't *have* any cash available before the harvest's complete, not even to get to Aunt Judee on Optus."

"And it's just us!" Nik cut in. "Everyone else I asked gets to stay!"

My stomach felt like I'd swallowed a ball of lead, and I sank down onto the nearest chair. Wally jumped into my lap and I patted his fluffy head, but my mind was fixed on one thing. One indisputable fact. "This is my fault. He did this because of me." Whether it was because I'd turned him down, or because he'd found out about the jewels, it had to be because of me.

"That's just what I said," Nik persisted furiously. "What did you do to make him so mad, Iscee? Run over his pet pog?"

"That's enough, Nik," Dad cut in. He turned to me. "I'm sure whatever you did, it was your best. You can't expect better from someone who'd take illegal conscripts." He frowned. "Did he hurt you, Iscendra? It's not that we're not happy to see you, it's just that…"

"I'm not hurt," I answered. It was only partly true. Physically I was fine. Mentally, emotionally, I felt bruised, and I was still taking this all in. "And Nik, he doesn't have a pog. He thinks they're smelly creatures."

I looked down at Wally, who smelled like his usual mix of fur and whatever greenery he'd been rolling in. So happy, so oblivious to what was going on around him. "I'll talk to him. I'll find out what the problem is, then I'll get straight back to you."

"Iscendra," Mum said quietly. "Did something happen?"

I shrugged, shaking my head. "Maybe. But…if this can't be fixed, if the exit order stays in place, then I know a way we can get out." Derry had to help. He had the diamonds, and he'd promised. He *had to*.

And then I told them about Whirey Swamp.

I stayed for long enough to convince my family I didn't mean mass suicide, and to swear all three to secrecy. Then I got straight back on the gondola to Vyce City. I didn't want to leave, but at the same time it was so hard to stay there, with that atmosphere of grief and shock.

And I hadn't even seen Alek. Alek, my little brother who couldn't understand much outside of his daily routine, and who only wanted to play with his toy soldiers.

It was late that evening by the time I arrived back at the palace, and I went straight to the Ducal Suite.

"You're back early," Zavier began, but I cut in.

"Where is Shan?"

"In the contact-centre-"

I strode towards that room, pausing only when I realised the door was shut, and the red seal indicated it was locked. I slapped a hand against the entry panel, but it didn't open.

"Who is it?" Shandlin's voice called through the speaker.

"Iscee!" I snapped. "I know you can see me." I'd seen the surveillance he had on this very door, and knew he was just being difficult...again.

After a few seconds the door slid open. Shandlin was sitting at his too-large desk, the one he'd used so much since we'd arrived back in Vyce three days earlier. He glanced briefly up at me, then turned back to the small keypad in front of him. "Make it quick," he said, sounding bored. "I'm busy."

Bored. Not angry, not 'you stole my jewels, you horrible thief', so for a few moments I found myself just staring at him. Did he know, or didn't he? He looked just like always – perhaps a little crankier, with his dark hair partly obscuring his face as he bent over his desk. His full-body communicator booth was switched on behind him, the lights showing a call was in progress, or perhaps had just ended.

"You may notice that I didn't stay with my family overnight," I said finally.

"Accommodation a little dull after staying at the palace? I don't blame you."

My hands tightened into fists at my sides. He was taunting me, but he still didn't look up from that keypad. I pulled something out of my pocket and set it on the table in front of him with an audible *clunk*.

"It's a printout of the confiscation order you had set on my family's plantation," I told him, forcing the words out past my fear, confusion and anger. "They say it's just them. Everyone else in Unity has the chance to become Vyce citizens and to stay in their homes, but this says they have to be-"

"Out by ten in the morning," Shandlin finished flatly. "That gives them twelve hours. They'd better get packing."

I stared at him for long moments, barely breathing,

with my heart pounding double-time in my chest. "You did do this," I choked out. "*Why*? Was it because I turned you down?"

Suddenly the printout went flying across the table onto the floor, and he was finally looking at me. Oh, and he was *livid*.

"Do you really think I'm that petty, Older?" he shouted. "That I got *embarrassed* and so decided to ruin your whole family, the only thing that seems to matter to you? Or maybe there's just one more...*tiny* reason why I might have done it. And what would that be, Iscendra Cole?"

He knew about the diamonds. There was no way he didn't. I licked my lips, but words wouldn't come out.

"You've got nothing to say?" The High Duke's eyes were bright, the white showing almost all around the irises, his cheeks punctuated with hot red circles that came from fury. "No apology, Older? You don't want to explain why you stole my precious family jewels, and maybe beg for mercy?"

Family jewels. This wasn't the moment for humour, but still I let out a short, horrified laugh. "Please..."

"Please," he mimicked in a falsetto voice. "No 'sorry'? No 'I'll give them right back, Your Grace'?"

"I'm sorry," I tried to say, because I was. "I was scared, and I thought there was no choice-"

"Enough." Shandlin had one hand raised in the air, palm outwards. "No more talk. You give me back those diamonds, Older, or I'll see that your family is homeless and broke. I can do worse, too; I can conscript both your brothers to the Breakers and put them in the most dangerous places. How do you think the little one will do on those farlacs? *And* I can have your parents arrested and thrown into prison.

"And *no*," he spoke over my protests, "I do not need a reason! I can do it, because I'm the High Duke. And as you said, I do what I want. Now where are the diamonds, Iscendra?"

I was shaking, and I couldn't answer. I couldn't tell him the truth, that they were gone, and I definitely wouldn't be giving up Derry, who might now be my family's only hope of escape.

"How did you find out?" I asked in a low voice.

"Bloom told me," Shandlin replied acidly. His lips were so tight that they were white around the edges. "It's funny, I don't expect much loyalty from you, but you still managed to surprise me. I didn't think you'd do...*that*." He lifted his chin. "Can you give me those three diamonds right now?"

I shook my head. "But there are just two," I managed to say. "Bloom had the last one. She-"

"Don't blame this on Bloom!" he snapped. "Three diamonds. You've got twelve hours to get all three of them back to me, or else worse things will happen to your family than just homelessness. Is that clear?"

I just stood there. Three diamonds or two, it didn't matter. We'd lost everything anyway.

"And you know the worst part?" he said suddenly. "I was going to let you go. After what you said on Optus...I wouldn't keep you here. I was going to send you back home to your precious Unity and let you apply for citizenship, just like all the other Olders. But not anymore."

My heart plummeted to somewhere below floor level, and in that moment I would have cried. My one impulsive decision to go *against* what I knew was right – it had cost my family their home, and maybe all of our freedom. *He'd been going to let me go anyway.* I couldn't even speak.

Then the High Duke stood and moved around his desk towards me. I didn't move, not understanding as he grabbed my wrist and then slapped something thin and metallic around it. "Three diamonds. Twelve hours. Or else."

I looked down at my arm. He'd given me back the promise-holder; his sworn oath that he would follow through with that threat, and in that moment I understood that he really, really would. I nodded stiffly and left the room.

The door slid shut behind me with a gentle click, and then I was in the open area that connected all the rooms of the Ducal Suite. Zavier sat in one of the nearby chairs, an open reader on his lap, but he was watching me solemnly. "What happened, Iscee?"

I just shook my head. I couldn't voice it; it hurt too much. "Derry," I muttered. "I need to call Derry."

Zavier's eyes flickered towards that closed door, and he said dismissively, "Can't help you with that one, Older. Shandlin's probably got his contact details if you need them, but I wouldn't ask."

No. No, I wouldn't ask either.

Just then Bloom walked out of the bathroom, her hair damp as if just washed. She looked at me without a hint of surprise. "What are you doing back here?"

Suddenly my suppressed rage overtook me, and I found myself striding across the room towards her, then leaning down to grab the collar of her sleep jacket. "You lying witch!" I hissed at her. "You gave me up!"

I didn't know how it happened, but Bloom moved and then suddenly I was twisted over backwards, her arm around my throat in a chokehold. I couldn't move.

"Of course I gave you up," she spat in my ear, sounding disgusted. "When I saw you'd been tearing apart that room on Optus, then you disappeared so quickly, did you really think I wouldn't put two and two together and realise what you'd done? Did you really think I'd help a whining Older rob my employer, even if only by lack of action?" She shook her head, then suddenly shoved me away. "So get lost, and don't act like this has anything to do with me. It's all on *you*."

Lies, all lies! Or at least some of it, anyway. I was practically fizzing with rage, and for several moments I just stood there, my hands clenched at my sides. I wanted to punch her smug little face. I wanted to grab one of those paintings off the wall – never mind that they were probably eight hundred years old – and break it over her head.

But then I realised something. *I'll put you in a chokehold before I let you implicate me,* she'd said. And that was exactly what she'd done. There was no way that giving her up to Shandlin would help me now. Maybe if I got the diamonds back…

No, even that wouldn't help. I'd burned my bridges, and my family's too. I was done for.

But just then Bloom's eyes flickered down to my trousers. Just once, to where the side pocket sat on the comfortable clothing. I let my hand fall against it, then felt the slight bump of something that hadn't been there before. She'd slipped something into my pocket while she'd been choking me, I realised suddenly. Some form of help?

I stared at her, unsure whether to curse her or thank her. The same for Zavier. So instead I just took one step back, then another, then I ran for the door. I ran out through the courtyard and training area, its dark corners lit up by the fluorescent advice to 'study hard'.

I ran until I found myself at the stables, just outside the farlac stalls. Most were already shut up inside for the night, but one was still tied to the fence as though someone had forgotten to put it away after a ride. There was even a saddle hanging from a fence post, complete with straps. The farlac looked at me peacefully, chewing a mouthful of greenery from the pile in front of it, and seeming more restful here at night than I'd ever seen one during the day.

I desperately wanted to check what was in my pocket, but I knew well that the High Duke watched everything that went on here. I had to get out of the palace.

Twenty minutes later I was well away from the city centre, the farlac's white wings beating through the darkness in a noisy, frantic rhythm. I had no destination in mind; instead letting the farlac go wherever it wanted. I just made sure to keep the reins tight, steering it as high in the air as possible. Getting eaten by a swamp-mare would be the perfect end to a horrible day.

Finally we came to the city's edge, and I brought the farlac to rest on a flat paved area, the remnants of an old parking lot. It was dimly lit by the ancient streetlights in this area, but I didn't dwell on my isolation and any danger that might bring. Instead I fumbled in my pocket, pulling out a hard, round shape about the size of an old coin. It looked like a tiny communicator, no strap, and when I tapped at it, it lit up red and orange. No signal?

I tapped again, and a list of contacts shot up into the air. I recognised few of them, but then one familiar, dark-haired guy came into view. Derry.

I frantically tapped at the 'call' button. I barely waited ten seconds before the images flashed and a miniature holograph of Derry was there in front of me, a smooth grin on his face. It faltered a moment later when he saw who held the device. "Sweet Iscee, what are you doing with Bloom's communicator?"

"She gave it to me," I replied, hearing the distress in my voice and hating it. "And she gave me up to Shan about stealing the dowry! He's confiscated my parents' land, and he's making all these threats against them if I don't give all three diamonds back by tomorrow morning! Do you still have them? Do you have *Bloom's* one?"

His face creased into sympathetic lines. "Oh Iscee, Bloom only told him because he'd already guessed. She had no choice but to give you up, else we would have lost everything we'd planned. And I'm so sorry, I sold all three diamonds this morning for funds to help your family exit…just like you asked."

I had asked. But there hadn't been such imminent danger then. "Can you get them back?!"

He shook his head. "I'm sorry, they're gone." Then just as I would have cried in protest, he quickly added, "But do you really think it would make any difference now Shandlin knows what you did? That you and your family could ever be safe and comfortable in Vyce ever again?" He shook his head sadly. "No, Iscee. It was over for you the moment you took those diamonds."

"But you *told* me to!" I cried.

"Yes, but I thought you knew you'd have to leave Vyce," Derry countered. "The thing with Unity becoming a part of Vyce territory? That's been brewing for years. Decades, even. And when Shanny conscripted you, he didn't have any intention of letting you go. That's the kind of person he is. Even if you hadn't acted against him – that's how he'll see it now, Iscee – then you never would have had a normal life again." He shook his head again emphatically. "Never."

My shoulders slumped as I took in the truth of what he'd said. With or without the diamonds, life never would have gone back to normal. I'd just made it worse.

But Shan said he was going to let you go, a quiet thought popped in. I pushed it aside, because I didn't have the energy to think on what would now never happen. "Then we'll exit," I said dully. "But there's a time limit, Derry. My family's in danger now. We have to get them out tonight. All of us."

Derry seemed to be looking at something in front of him, out of range of the communicator's camera. "We can do that. I'll send someone to get them right away, the sooner the better. Will you assure them they can trust us?"

"Of course they can trust you," I answered. Just then a bright light suddenly flashed in my face, almost blinding in the darkness. I'd been recorded.

"That video will do," he told me. "Now you, Iscee. There's no time to lose. You need to leave *now*, because I'd swear on my father's freshly-dug grave that you're already being followed. My cousin is not a forgiving person."

Followed? Of course. "Seriously?" I muttered. I was so tired. I just wanted to *sit*, and not have threats of death or imprisonment made against me.

"Yes, seriously! I've known him all his life, and I promise you that's the truth. For example, when Shanny was about eight years old, another kid broke something he valued. I don't remember what it was, only that Shanny was furious, but his parents wouldn't do anything, saying it was an accident. Then three weeks after he became High Duke, the kid's father was in prison for sedition, and the kid lost everything."

Derry shook his head as if remembering that moment. "That's the least of it, Iscee. He's absolutely vile when he's been crossed, and no one's done what you did." He paused, then smiled ruefully as if to offset that awful statement. "Except me, of course. But he doesn't know about that yet."

He'd never forgive me. I didn't need him to, but I also didn't want my family's lives ruined or stolen more than they had been. "So what shall I do?"

"Hmm. The tracker on the communicator says you're not far from Whirey Swamp. Remember how I told you-"

"It's an exit point, I remember." Although going there in the dark on a farlac didn't sound like good sense.

"You can't wait 'til morning," he said again. "You understand this, right? I'll message ahead and let them know you're coming."

"But where do I go?!"

"You'll see." And then the communicator blinked once and shut off. A moment later it showed a tiny red arrow – a compass.

Suds. Whirey Swamp. But was I really in that much danger? I turned to look back towards the city, its many towers and buildings creating a blue and white light show from this distance. I could just make out the tiny red and orange lights of air vehicles still moving around at this time of night. One seemed a little larger than the others…perhaps a little closer.

I couldn't take the risk, I decided, and I had no other choice. *Whirey Swamp it is.*

The farlac seemed happy enough to move on. They didn't like man-made things, which was strange considering that they were largely man-made themselves. We sped through the night air, with me focused on that tiny arrow on the communicator, and occasionally steering when needed.

But then I saw the pale shape of the cliffs in the distance, bordered by areas of impossibly dark water. It looked completely deserted, a single tiny light on a pole the only sign of human presence. That was meant to keep air vehicles from crashing into the cliffs in the night, even if the driver had been stupid enough to turn their vehicle off auto-drive.

I brought the farlac down next to the light, then tied it to the pole. I wouldn't want it to wander off and leave me here if there'd been some kind of mistake. We now stood in scrubby, damp grass. The farlac turned its attention to a nearby gorseic bush, and I turned mine to our location.

My eyes had adjusted to the darkness and I now saw everything in shades of grey and blue. The farlac was a pale grey amongst the mottled greenery. The sky was so black, filled with billions of pinprick-sized stars. And in front of me, the massive Whirey Swamp spread out almost as far as I could see, deceptively calm and reflecting that beautiful sky like a mirror. The city lights were distant beyond it, and the space between was punctuated with sparkling red lines for the gondolas...and one bright orange spot growing larger and larger as I watched it.

I *was* being followed. Suds. I swore aloud, then began to look around me in earnest. There was nothing here to indicate any kind of exit, and I felt panic send my heart racing and my hands jittering.

Just then I noticed that Bloom's communicator seemed to be blinking with tiny bright text. I squinted, trying to make sense of it when it was moving so quickly, then held my thumb against the device. The blinking finally stilled, showing three words.

EXIT DOWN BELOW.

Below what? All that was in front of me was a long drop and somewhere that people didn't come back from...

Those thoughts ticked over very slowly, and I walked nervously to the edge of the cliffs, then unclipped my Breaker breastplate and tossed it down into the water below. It fell with barely a splash, and beneath the black water's still, almost opaque surface, something pale moved.

Exit down below? More like 'death down below!' That was a bloody dangerous location for an evacuation, and I wondered if there was a hidden entrance in the side of the cliff. I tried to lean over as if to see better, but all I could see was that black water. Black water, white shadow beneath it.

Nope. Just…nope.

But there was nowhere else to go, and I found myself standing at that cliff's edge for untold minutes, pacing away then turning back. Desperately looking for *something*. But the orange light in the distance had come closer, and was now apparent as an air vehicle. Palace issue, no doubt, and it would be here in mere minutes. I could just hear the buzzing sound of its engines approaching.

Bloody Derry. Some escape *this* was. Didn't they know I'd be tracked?

I picked up Bloom's communicator again, tapping at it in an attempt to call him back. But those words didn't change. *EXIT DOWN BELOW.*

Argh!

Jittering with panic, I walked back to the very edge, then crouched down on my hands and knees, as if the extra metre would mean I'd spot something I'd previously missed. Just then my curious farlac sidled over to the end of its tether and stepped on the back of my leg.

"Ow!" I tried to push it off, but it just lifted its leg and stepped down again, that pointy little hoof painful on my soft calf. I kicked at it, pulling away as something bright came up in the corner of my vision. The buzzing was louder and louder…

Finally I managed to scramble away from the farlac and get to my feet. Then I saw why it had reacted in such a way: both of us were bathed in white light from the air vehicle's spotlights, and it stood stock still, its eyes fixed blankly on the buzzing vehicle in front of it. Strange, because farlacs usually panicked in these kind of situations.

Just then, as if I'd called up the bad behaviour with my thoughts, the farlac reared back. Its four strong wings beat frantically, and one clipped me hard in the shoulder. I fell forward, and one foot came down over empty air.

It felt like being in slow motion as I lurched forward, trying to regain my footing, and my arms windmilling desperately as I saw the black water below me. Some noise was blaring from the air vehicle, and I let out a scream as gravity finally caught me and I tumbled over the cliff.

For a second the still water of the swamp raced up to meet me headfirst, and then the surface rippled and something white broke through and-

Aftermath

* * *

The Palace, 2 days later

The Ducal Suite was quiet. No music, no conversation. No High Duke Shandlin shouting about this or that, no sharp retort from the Older. No sound of the blender pureeing garvafruit. It almost felt empty, except for the sound of Zavier methodically sharpening the blade of his stave.

Scrape. Scrape….SCRAPE. Zavier brought the polishing block down the blade extra hard that last time, almost hoping it would get the typical reaction of 'Argh, are you trying to make my ears bleed?'

But instead the dark-haired boy just sat in his usual seat, his hands resting in his lap and a scowl on his face, but his gaze fixed blankly on something in the mid-distance.

Zavier stopped sharpening the blade. It really didn't need it, and this inaction from the High Duke was making him seriously uncomfortable. "I'm getting a drink," he announced to the silent room. There was no response, but he was relieved to escape to the nearby kitchen where Bloom sat at the large table, methodically eating her breakfast.

He ordered a berry-water from the dispenser, not wanting to risk the familiar sound of the blender, then sat next to his colleague. "Suds," he said in a low voice. "I can't stand this. It's like someone's died."

Bloom stopped with her spork halfway to her mouth, then gave him a deadpan look. "Ya think?"

Yeah, that's what he thought. And he thought that the High Duke's attachment to Iscendra Cole had been stronger than they'd imagined, or perhaps exactly what Derry had expected, because he always seemed to be a step ahead of anyone else.

And this outcome? Maybe it was what they'd expected too, but Zavier hadn't expected to feel so *bad*. To feel so sorry for the High Duke. The way he'd reacted when they'd seen the Older fall into that water... Hysterical, then catatonic. Vyce society was falling to pieces around him, but he wouldn't even answer a simple question like 'what do you want for lunch?'.

"I wish we could tell him the truth," Zavier said instead, his voice almost inaudible.

But he knew Bloom heard, because she retorted just as quietly, "And make all of this for nothing? You know better."

And he did, but he still didn't like it. And he couldn't help wondering if something, anything could be done differently...

●   ●   ●

Paradise Resort, Optus, three days after that

Aria had been waiting with bated breath ever since the news had come out with that terrible, terrible video hacked from the Ducal air vehicle. Waiting for someone to call her, for that familiar face to pop up on her communicator and say it was all a prank, ha, did we get you?

But instead things were normal, too normal, and too quiet. But she couldn't grieve, not yet. Not when she couldn't even believe it.

Iscee got eaten by a swamp-mare. Don't worry, it was probably a quick end. Yeah, millions of people have seen the video by now since someone put it online...but Iscee wouldn't have minded, right? At least her family got away, probably, even though no one's heard from them in days...

No. Just...no.

Aria ducked her head, letting her curtain of newly orange hair fall to cover her face, then focused on the bench in front of her. She scrubbed at the dark patch on the wood, even though she knew that the auto-cleaner had already done this part of the bar today. Perhaps it had run out of soap, and if she just scrubbed hard enough-

Ting. A little red and orange light flickered on her communicator where it was pinned at her collar, discreetly disguised as a hothouse flower. Aria dropped the scrubber and grabbed for the device, then turned so her back was to the almost-empty room. No image had sprung up from the little screen, although she could now hear sound.

She quickly left the bar and went to the small, quiet room out the back, then lifted it closer to her face. "Hello? Who's there?"

"ARIA?"

Argh, too loud! She pulled the communicator away a little, scrunching up her face, then gestured for the volume to turn down. "Yes. Who's this?"

"Aria, it's Aunt Bethany."

"Auntie!" She just about wept with relief. "Where are you? Are Uncle and the boys with you? Did you see-"

There was a swearword from the other end of the call that Aria wouldn't have expected her gentle aunt to use.

"Yes, I saw it. But I don't have long to talk, and this is important – and secret. You mustn't repeat what I'm about to tell you, because lives depend on it."

"I won't! I mean, I'll keep it a secret! What is it?"

So Aria listened carefully as her aunt spoke quickly and earnestly, but her spirit lifted in joy with every spoken word.

Oh my, what a secret. But oh my, what a *relief.*

Somewhere on Mars

"The fate of Vyce Dome is in the hands of a callous teenager.
YOUR fate. YOUR children, YOUR business.
If you want to ever see Vyce thrive, then vote for change.
Vote…to vote."
"Catchy."
"I thought so too. But will it be enough?"
"If enough people agree on something, change will happen. Besides, Shanny's not a contender. He's ruined himself already…and *he's* not going to change."
And if he hadn't, then they'd take the necessary steps.
Ruling wasn't for the faint-hearted.

PART TWO
Aria

TWELVE
The Visitor

Paradise Resort, Optus, 3348 AD
(two years later)

It was late morning, and the sun shone warm and gentle over the open-sided bar, just the right temperature for lounging on the beach. But then this man-made moon was covered in a thick, unnatural atmosphere, the sort that could be manipulated to ensure perfect weather all year round. Perfect beach weather, or sports weather, or lying-around-drinking weather, judging by the few people who'd come early to Paradise's Bar Four.

I parked my hoverbike out of sight behind a carefully-tended stand of trees, then climbed off onto the warm sand. It gave a little under my light sandals, spraying up to hit my bare legs as I made my way into the bar, a pleasant expression set on my face.

"Talia!"

Argh, there he was. Mr Ingbrid, red-faced drunk of the day and general pain in my neck. But I'd been doing this customer service job for six months now, and my fake smile didn't budge. "It's Aria," I corrected. "Good morning, Mr Ingbrid. How has your day been so far?"

"Aria Aria Aria, of course." He swept his arms wide in a generous gesture, knocking over a nearby vase. It sprang back up on its rounded base as if it had never fallen. "Did y' see the latest from Mars?"

Regrettably, yes. Mars's unstable political climate was the hot topic on Earth and all its colonies, and everywhere I went, there'd be a holo-vid discussing the fate of this or that dome. And by 'that' I meant Vyce.

"No politics before lunch, please," I said with a polite smile. "You know how that puts me off my food."

But Mr Ingbrid leaned forward as if I'd never spoken, his slightly bloodshot eyes fixed on my face. He was in his forties with a perfect head of hair, the sort that spoke of expensive hair thickening shots. He was rich, or else he wouldn't be here, and probably well-kept too when he was sober. That made his current insobriety even more awkward.

"This is gonna affect bus'ness, Arlia. For you. What d'ya think will happen if all the domes turn upside-down like those other ones did? Riots, gov'ment changes. Down with the dukes, then up with the dukes! 'Specially in Vyce. Tourism!"

I paused, waiting him to explain that last comment. Then when he didn't, I replied, "I figure rich people will come to visit gorgeous locations like this one, no matter who's in power. Is there anything else I can help you with?"

He blinked at me a couple of times, then his features twisted into a scowl. "You want to go away. You want to leave me, just like she did."

Oh, great. Another hostile drunk. They were few and far between – honestly we got just as many cranky celebrities who'd taken the wrong kind of happy pill – but with his comments about Vyce Dome, I wasn't feeling generous. It wasn't my favourite subject. And then his moaning about 'her'… We'd had this conversation at least twice before, and it usually ended in one way.

I reached carefully into my side pocket, then closed my fingers around the small round device that I kept just for these occasions. "I'm not leaving," I replied pleasantly. "I'm going to the next bar, to make sure everything's running well on the resort. It's my job, remember?"

"But you don't unnerstan'. She *made* me do it, you know? She *made* me sign those divorce papers, and then what happened next? She goes and blames the whole sudsn' thing on me, telling the kids that I never wann'ed to be there, that I didn't care about anything but my job…"

Oh, dear, and here came the sobbing. "And then she went and married my best friend! Just right in my face as if she didn't care about me at all, and I haven't seen the kids in five years. Five years, Arriet."

And he still couldn't even get my name right. I'd feel a lot sorrier for him if I hadn't known that the best friend was actually only an acquaintance, that there had been a good five years in between the two marriages, and that he'd actually been the one to leave his wife in the first place.

"Mm. How sad." I moved quickly, pressing the small shape against the back of his neck. There was a sharp buzzing sound like a mosquito being electrocuted, then he slumped forward onto his folded arms, his eyes still half open, but his mouth mercifully shut.

Ah, insobriety depressors. Whoever had invented these devices needed a really big pat on the back.

All resort guests gave us the right to take physical action if needed – it was a standard part of entry to Optus. After all, people who didn't have to go to work the next day, or worry about paying damages, tended to be freer with their mood-altering substances and less gentle with the furniture.

I grabbed a hover-chair from where it rested quietly against one wall, then moved it over next to him. "Get on the hover-chair, please. It'll take you back to your room where you can have a nice sleep. I've made sure you have two pillows this time."

He nodded blearily, but did as I'd asked. It was the middle of the day, but he needed sleep. I *needed* him to sleep.

Mr Ingbrid gave me a wave over his shoulder as they led him off, the sedative working as fast as it always did, but I couldn't quite hide a weary sigh as he moved out of sight. I hadn't had to use the depressor in the whole six months I'd been back on Optus after my trip away, but the moment this guy appeared it was three times in one week.

I'd push for him to be banned if I didn't know we needed the money. I knew the depressor sedatives stopped working if they were used too often, and could even have a reverse effect. By my calculations he was on his last turn.

There were only a few other guests around, and most of them were polite enough to ignore the slightly embarrassing exit of the aforementioned Mr Ingbrid. There was just one guy, part of a group that I hadn't seen before, who watched the whole scene. Did he think I couldn't tell where those reflective sunglasses were pointing? He didn't even need them since the atmosphere removed any glare from the sunlight, so it was just an affectation.

I tried to ignore him since it was my job to look unaffected by such things, but he just kept watching. He was young and lanky with short, forest-green hair, and he might have been attractive under those large shades, judging by that sharp jawline and classical profile. He sat with a single drink in front of him, still staring at me.

Did he look familiar? Maybe.

I quickly glanced down at my communicator, checking our records of all the customers staying here, and after a few seconds a name popped up.

Jank Marshal, Rison Dome.

I hid a smirk. Poor 'Jank' either had a fake name like so many celebrities used on their trips here, or else his parents hadn't liked him very much.

Just then it occurred to me that maybe there was a reason for him to stare. I walked quickly out of the area, hoping that no one would call me over for anything, then ducked into the staff bathroom hidden in a cluster of carefully sculpted bamboo.

But the mirror showed the normal me: tallish and nineteen, with lean curves and black-and-blue curls as carefully sculpted as the bamboo. I even checked my teeth – clean – and all my clothing was where it ought to be. He was probably just bad-mannered, I decided, or else had the wrong idea about what kind of place this was.

Even so, I tidied myself carefully before stepping back outside. I still had to check with the servers in section ten, since there'd been that issue with the waterworks yesterday. And two of the kitchens were behind schedule because our supply of seafood had been disrupted by a strike down in the seafarms of Arparath where we got most of our catch, and-

"Excuse me."

I jolted, shrieking in undignified surprise, and the green-haired guy from the bar smiled apologetically. "Sorry, I didn't mean to scare you. It's just…you look a lot like your cousin."

Standing up, he was as tall as I'd expected, and his voice was rough and unfamiliar. But it was his words that froze me stiff. I only had one cousin…*had* one cousin.

After several seconds of awkward silence he added, "Iscendra. She *was* your cousin, wasn't she?"

I felt my lips tighten, but with the force of my will, made myself relax again. "You obviously know that's the case, or you wouldn't have asked. And yes, our mothers were twins. How did you know Iscee?"

"It's a long story… Aria, was that your name?"

I gave a brusque nod.

"I'm Jank. Jank…Marshal."

Jank with the almost-definitely-fake name,.

"You don't have to talk if you don't want to," he said. "It's a rough subject, and I wouldn't want to make you dwell on it. But if you do want to talk…then I'd love to."

I swallowed back my sharp retort. Every time anyone brought up this subject I felt my hackles rise. Especially when a stranger from Mars was asking. "Excuse my mood," I said instead. "I've had a hard morning," – now that much harder – "but I wouldn't mind a long story if it's an interesting one. How about a drink on the house?"

I didn't trust this 'Jank', but I'd rather know what he was about, than spend the next few weeks guessing and wishing I'd asked.

"Uh…thanks. I don't know about interesting. It's a bit of a tragedy, but then you know how it ended." Jank spread his hands in front of him, palms up. His partly-hidden expression was rueful, but something about it grated on me, and my polite smile faded.

But still he followed me out of the bar to sit down under a shading group of palms, and I tapped the metal plate in the side of the tree for service. "One ora-cola, no ice, and one…"

"I'll have the same."

"Two ora-colas." I tapped the plate again to show my order was complete, then turned to Jank. "So how did you know Iscee?"

He smiled awkwardly. "Ah…we worked together."

"Oh. So you're a Breaker." I handed him the drink, neatly brought along by the servers, and he almost choked.

"What makes you think I'm a Breaker?!"

"Iscendra never had a job outside Unity besides being conscripted, if you could call that a job," I said a little scornfully. "So there was nowhere else she could have met you. And you're not an Earth citizen. Judging by your accent, you could be from Rison, like your entry details say, but more likely Vyce. You have some scarring on your neck and arms that has to have come from rough living." I shrugged, feeling rather smug at my deductions. "If you tried to cover them up, then it hasn't really worked. No offence."

Jank ducked his head, frowning. The expression didn't suit those otherwise friendly features, and he pushed his shades further up his nose. "None taken," he said, and he sounded sincere. "I consider myself lucky you haven't spat in my face then had me escorted off the resort."

"Why would I do that?"

He ventured another glance at me, those blue eyes just visible through his reflective sunglasses. "Because you figured out that I was a Breaker, and because it was my- *our* fault that Iscee died like she did. You must know that."

I took a long sip of my drink, wincing a little as the chilled liquid hit a sensitive part of my teeth. Suds, I needed to visit the dental-box again, or else get these drinks brought up to room temperature. "Your fault? By your own admission, you're just a lackey. If anyone should be getting tossed off this resort, it's that High Duke. Assuming he even *is* still a High

Duke." A horrible thought occurred. "Is he here?!"

"No!" Jank shook his head, sounding alarmed. "He… he shouldn't come on holiday when the vote's in five days. You've heard about how even though he's eighteen now and old enough to truly rule, the people are going to decide-"

"Whether they want him to, yes," I cut in. "But that's beside the point. You said it was your fault, or the Breakers' fault, that Iscee died. How so? Because I saw the video, and it looked like the farlac knocked her into the swamp. It looked like an accident."

He winced, and his head ducked away from mine again. "It was an accident," he said in a low voice. "The news and the pro-democrats made it sound like she was driven to suicide, but really it was just that the lights of the air vehicle startled the farlac. I don't know why she was there at those cliffs," and he shook his head as if it was really, truly baffling, "but she didn't seem the type to kill herself to get away from her problems."

I felt my shoulders stiffen again. "Those problems caused by the High Duke?" I retorted. "And here we come back to the real issue. You might feel some guilt because you saw her death, Jank or whoever you are. But if there's any guilt, it truly belongs to him, and he's not exactly here to apologise." I laughed, but it was without humour. "As if he would."

"You're wrong."

I snapped my head up to look at him. "Not from what I've heard."

"Then you've heard wrong. The High Duke has changed a lot in two years. He's-"

"Ended conscription, focused on cleaning up the Breakers' reputation and making Vyce a safer dome, I know," I said, echoing those many, *many* holo-vids I'd been unlucky enough to see. "But that's all just for appearances. I can't believe that someone who acted like he did – and I *know*, because I've spoken to Iscee's family and they told me all about it – would ever truly change."

Jank was silent for a long moment. "People can change,"

he said finally, his voice quiet. "They can when something horrific happens to someone they care about, and they know it's their fault. When they know that if they'd been less stubborn or less selfish, if they hadn't broken the law, then that horrific thing would never have happened. Then they can change."

"Someone they care about? Are you suggesting that the High Duke actually had a single kind thought about Iscee? I don't think he cared about anyone besides himself."

Jank let out a short laugh. "That sounds so like Iscee coming from your mouth, when you look so much like her too. Are you sure you're only cousins?"

"I know my genealogy, thank you. And answer the question."

There was a pause, then he sighed. "Yes, Aria, he had kind thoughts about her. How could he not? She was…very likeable in her own way. Good-looking, too. He had a huge crush on her." I saw his eyes widen behind those semi-opaque shades, and then flick to look at me. "That's not for public knowledge, by the way. I didn't mean to say it."

"What? The part where the High Duke had a thing for my cousin, or where you did?" I'd read between the lines, and now I was curious. Flattered on Iscee's behalf, for all the good it did her, but also curious.

His jaw dropped, and his neck reddened. "Both. Please."

"But she stole something from him," I persisted. "I heard that much, and that he was really, really angry about it. And you're saying he was still sorry that she died? I would have thought it saved him from having to punish her for theft."

"Suds no!" Jank exploded, and I finally looked up to see the sincerity in his expression. "He didn't want her dead, Aria! I swear it! I know him, after all this time I know him, and he was *not* the same person after he saw her die. He-"

Now he choked a little, almost like he was fighting tears. "I think he might have loved her in his own twisted way, in as much as someone like him could love anyone. He wanted her sorry, not dead. She'd had a tracker, and he kept watching it to see if it would move from the bottom of that swamp, but it never did."

"Oh." I didn't speak for a few seconds, trying to come up with the right thing to say at a time like this. "Well. I'm sorry for your…unhappiness. But it doesn't explain why you're here on my resort telling me about it, and with what's clearly a fake name and a hair colour meant to distract. Who are you, Jank Marshal, and did you come here just to see me because of your guilt about my cousin?"

There was a long, awkward silence. "Was it that obvious?"

"Which part?"

He sighed. "All of it, I suppose. No, I didn't come just to see you. I came for a holiday, because Optus is cheaper and closer than some parts of Mars. But I did know you'd be here, and I was…curious. I swear I didn't mean to go into…all of this."

Maybe that was true, too. Or maybe he was just a great liar. "And your real name?"

Another pause. Then he finally replied, "Zavier."

"Zavier. Right." I rose to my feet, then set my half-empty glass back on the nearby tray. It slid back into the fake tree which hid the dispenser and glass-cleaner. "If you'll excuse me, I really need to get back to work."

He looked up at me. "I understand. But even though forgiveness is impossible, and I'm not asking for it, I want you to know that I'm so, so terribly sorry."

"Forgiveness is never impossible," I said crisply, "but it's not my forgiveness to give, and that's not your apology to make. Good day."

The moment I was out of sight, I abruptly veered away from the path leading to the next section of the resort, then headed towards the back of the bar, near a mostly unused part of the beach. I stopped in front of a tall boulder, then pressed my hand against a silver square set at about chest level.

A moment later a section of the boulder swung inwards, creating a door. I stepped inside the small, otherwise-hidden weather control room, waited for the door to close after me, then lifted my communicator. I tapped in the four-key code that would change it to stealth mode, then my target's code.

The small screen flashed, then a sandy-haired holographic figure popped into view. "Cuz'! What's happening?"

"Hi, Nik. Where are your parents?"

Nik shrugged, his fair hair flopping over his eyes. That would drive me crazy, but he didn't seem to mind. "They're out of range, visiting some plantation in the middle of the jungle. They reckon it's got potential, but they left me this communicator." He shuddered. "There are spiders the size of my palm in that jungle! Can you blame me for not going with them?"

I couldn't help smiling. Nik had been fifteen when he'd had to abruptly leave Mars along with his whole family. They'd settled back into life on Earth as well as they could, and the boys seemed happy enough. But in spite of the better technology usually available on Earth, it was clear that they missed the green lushness of the New World. There were very few wild spaces remaining on Earth whatsoever. The rest of the land was covered in massive cities, farmed to the hilt, or else uninhabitable.

"No, I can't blame you," I replied. "But I wanted some advice. Since you can't give that, I'll settle for passing on some info."

His expression was instantly serious. "Are you OK? Is it about...*The Secret?*"

I rolled my eyes. "When is it not about The Secret? Yes, kind of. There's some guy from Vyce, a Breaker, staying at the resort. He just sought me out to tell me that I look like Iscee-"

And here Nik cut in with a scoffing noise...

"...and to say that he's sorry for what happened to her. He knew I was her cousin, Nik. He even tried to say that the *High Duke* was sorry."

The scoffing noise doubled in intensity, and I laughed in spite of the situation. Imagine if I told him what the guy had said about them both having a crush on her. He'd probably throw up. "But Nik, I need you to tell your parents, and to keep an eye on this communicator, because he was *definitely* hiding something."

"Do you think the High Duke sent him? That you're in danger?"

I considered the question. That was what had sent me down here, after all. "I don't think so," I replied finally. "There's no reason to believe I'm about to be kidnapped as some sort of delayed revenge against your family. He wouldn't have warned me if that was the case."

Nik's mouth straightened into a mulish line. "Yeah, but you know what they say about that High Duke. He's vicious when he's crossed."

"Mm," I agreed thoughtfully. I'd always believed that, because it was so obvious given what had happened to Iscee and her family. But could there really be any truth in what Jank/Zavier had said? Had the High Duke really felt...*gasp*... guilty?

After Iscee had fallen off that cliff, her whole extended family had been affected. Her parents and brothers had been smuggled off Mars and straight back into a busy Earth city, while my own parents, Judee and Eliezer, had been on high alert for months. They'd even had me sent back to Earth to finish my studies, thinking that with 'the resemblance' I would be in more danger than the others. Danger from a crazed, resentful teenage ruler. I'd only just come back to Optus six months ago, and I wasn't ready to flee again unless there was a really good reason.

But to Nik I said, "I'll be careful."

THIRTEEN
Illusions

*   *   *

That night I spent some time looking up Zavier's records. He'd arrived with two others, both apparently also from Rison, Mars. One was a short, Asian woman with glossy black hair, age twenty-five, going by the name of Amber Lee. The other was a narrow-faced man called Jermaine Elsewich. Now that had to be a fake name, although at least in his picture he still had natural-looking brown hair. His age was listed as twenty-seven.

I hadn't seen either of them around the resort, but with thousands of guests, that was no surprise. The fact that Zavier had even seen me…that meant he'd been looking for me.

Hmmm. And he said he'd had a thing for Iscee…

I stood in front of my bathroom mirror, the gentle lights casting a flattering glow over my naturally tanned skin. The black and blue hair wasn't so natural, but it wasn't the only thing that stopped me from looking like Iscee. We might have had almost identical features, but Iscee had been a tomboy, lean as a racehorse with wild brown hair. She'd never worn makeup, and her clothing had been adequate rather than beautiful. She just hadn't cared.

As for me, I enjoyed messing around with my appearance to perfect my eyebrows or my lips, and I was a size bigger than she had been. With my carefully applied makeup and clothing, I'd thought the difference was distinct. But perhaps that was a matter of opinion, and DNA couldn't be so easily hidden.

I slept well enough in spite of the weird interaction, then went about my regular workday. But I couldn't stop thinking about the Breaker and about what he'd said about Iscee…and about the Duke.

He'd wanted her sorry, not dead…. He kept watching for her tracker to move from the bottom of the swamp, but it never did…

A twinge of grief or anger shot through me at those thoughts, but instead of feeding it, I took a deep, calming breath. Life was short (more so for some than others) and it could be difficult, but I knew something that Iscee hadn't. Being angry all the time might feel like it made you strong, but really it was like was feeding yourself a slow, steady dose of poison.

I used to be angry in the past, easily offended, but time and even trouble had changed me. At some point I'd just decided not to carry grudges anymore, and I was so much more relaxed. Holding grudges, even legitimate ones, didn't improve my life at all. They just tied me to the trouble and the pain, and stopped me from really leaving it behind.

Well, that was my deep musing for the day. Back to work, back to my rounds of all the bars, making sure everything was working as it should. After a while I got caught up in the hundred small, fixable problems enough to forget that bigger problem – the one with green hair.

But then that afternoon, when I returned to Bar Four, there he was again. Zavier/Jank Marshal, sitting on a side bench and with his mirrored sunglasses directed right at my face. I smiled politely and he gave me a rueful little wave, then looked away.

But when I glanced back again a few minutes later, he was still staring. Just…staring. While it was nice that he was focusing on my *face* rather than other body parts like some other guests did, it was becoming a little uncomfortable.

Finally I went over to him. "Do you need something?"

"Ah. Sorry, I was staring again, wasn't I? It's just that you really *do* look like…like her."

"Our mothers were twins," I replied briskly, not for the first time. "But in colouring and body type we're not at all alike." That was what hair dye and chocolate were for.

"Yes, but your *face…*" He saw the expression on mine and sighed. "I'm so sorry. I've been remarkably rude, again. Can I make it up to you by buying you lunch?"

"I don't know. Will it involve a long, soul-cleansing conversation about your employer and my dead cousin?"

He flinched when I said 'dead', but shook his head. "Nothing about Iscee, I promise. You can tell me about life here on Optus. It sounds like a dream."

I looked around the room, but no one was watching us. And I still…*still* didn't trust this guy, but in truth? I wanted to talk, and even about Iscee. So I sat down next to him and talked.

We chatted about my life and his, about how the best part of the resort was its peacefulness, but also how I wanted to experience life outside but wasn't sure how to go about it. We talked about how he felt trapped in his position – but then he'd cut that part short, saying that it might not be for much longer anyway. It seemed that the Ducal Guard's time in Vyce was limited.

In four days there would be a Dome-wide vote over whether to continue with the same ruling system or whether Vyce Dome would become a democracy like so many of its neighbours. If the second option was chosen, then Jank-Zavier would lose his job. But since the decision would be made by every Vyce citizen *voting*…it sounded to me like they'd already made their choice.

"What do you think will happen?" I asked curiously. "Do you think the High Duke will be voted in or out?"

He shrugged pensively. "I've no idea. He's been far more responsible these past two years, but the issue remains that even if he was a good ruler, his heir might not be, or his heir's heir. You can't guarantee the future."

"You can't guarantee it with democracy either, but I suppose we'll give it our best try," I commented. "At least that way we could get rid of any democratic leader if we didn't like them. Do you like the High Duke?"

Jank-Zavier let out a short, startled laugh. "Uh…

interesting question, Aria. I suppose in some ways I can't stand him, but in others I feel compelled to take care of him. He doesn't have any family worth mentioning, no one who could hold him accountable for his actions. He thought... well, that the *Breakers* were his family. Or as close as anyone could be, anyway."

"But he conscripted them!" I blurted out, shocked. "How was that supposed to work?"

He shrugged. "He was clueless, but he's a lot better than he used to be. You know there's no conscription anymore, hasn't been since...well. And Breakers now have a maximum of six days' work in an eight-day period, and no more than 50 hours per week. Pay's gone up, too." He frowned. "Although we did lose a lot of people once conscription ended, we also gained some when he tightened the rules on Breaker code of conduct."

Those weren't great hours, but hardly slave labour. I probably worked more than that on the resort. "That's not too bad. What did it used to be like?"

He scowled. "Different. Do you want to meet him?"

"What?"

"The High Duke," he enunciated. "Do you want to meet him?"

"You said he wasn't here."

Jank-Zavier looked awkward, as much as I could tell under those sunglasses he still wore. "Um... he's not. It was a stupid question, forget I even asked."

I studied him suspiciously. "OK... Look, I have to go. But you can tell the High Duke...wherever he is...that I forgive him. Assuming he needs or wants my forgiveness. Maybe Iscee's family would have lost their land anyway, since most of the Olders on Mars have, and maybe he couldn't have changed that. Although I still think he's a bit of a grawlix, and he'll have to work through any guilt on his own."

He let out a short laugh, but nodded. "I hear you."

I put out my hand to shake his. "In case I don't see you again, I wish you all the best."

He looked down at my hand as if I'd offered him a spider (what, did I have Optus germs or something?) and then reluctantly shook it, pulling his hand away almost immediately. And while that would usually be rude and weird, there was a change in his face that happened when we touched.

No, not a change of expression, but a strange, shifting surface change, almost like his skin and features shimmered. It lasted only an instant, but it caught my attention.

That wasn't normal, but I did know what it *could* be. One particular device for one particular purpose. All the rich, secretive people were using those devices now, even though they were barely legal.

So quicker than Jank-Zavier could react, I lifted my hand and touched his lightly stubbled cheek. He pulled away, but it was too late. I'd already felt smooth skin, and the touch made his face briefly distort even further.

I stepped back, belligerently setting both hands on my hips. "You're wearing a face changer, aren't you?!"

"Aria…"

"I can't believe this!" I turned away briefly, almost laughing at the shock of it. Sometimes surprise made me act in inappropriate ways. "Don't tell me you got that on a Breaker's salary, because I won't believe it. Who are you really, Jank-Zavier Marshal?"

He looked at me solemnly, the expression not sitting quite right on those features, and I realised that this was why some of his expressions had seemed awkward; why he'd worn the sunglasses. Face changers were never really effective with the eyes, because they moved around too much.

But then he reached up behind his ear, pressing the small disc I knew would be there, and the person before me changed.

In an instant I was looking at an entirely different person from the neck up: with similar classical bones but a squarer, smooth-skinned jaw, and with black eyebrows barely visible above those shades. His hair changed from forest green to darkest brown.

I reached up to pull off his sunglasses, and his eyes had changed too. Now they were larger, almost black, with thick eyelashes like a girl's. Younger than the false face, a little better-looking.

I knew this face. I'd seen it on a thousand holo-vids, and in other places, although not looking so grown up.

"I'm sorry," the High Duke said.

I just stared at him, shaking my head in disbelief. Then I really did start laughing: not just because it was inappropriate and I couldn't seem to help myself, but because it was so, so remarkably ironic. And he had no idea...

"Sorry for what?" I asked when I could finally speak again. "Sorry for lying to me repeatedly when I asked you if you were here? Sorry for giving me a false name, twice? Sorry for trying to get sympathy by pretending to be somebody else? Or sorry for that horrible green hair you inflicted on the world?"

His jaw tightened, but those dark eyes didn't leave my face. "For all of that, even though the part about sympathy isn't true. I thought that if you knew I was here, you'd kick me out. You wouldn't want to speak to me. And I was...selfish, again. I wanted to see you."

Back when I thought he was someone else, I'd accidently asked his opinion about himself. Good grief. "Because I look like Iscee," I prompted, half-sarcastically. "Who you had a big crush on, is that right?"

His cheeks turned red, but he didn't lower his eyes from mine. "Yes. I had a huge crush on her, even though I acted like a little monster and she couldn't stand me. And then she died."

He'd forgotten to mention the part about her stealing his mother's dowry: the catalyst to her family's land being confiscated and every other ugly thing that had happened afterward.

"Her family told me everything they knew," I said instead. "You *were* a little monster. You're a bit bigger now."

A lot bigger, in fact. They'd described a boy. This was a young man – a tall, lanky young man who'd achieved his adult height, but would probably fill out over the next few years. "Are you wearing a voice changer?"

The High Duke shook his head. "I was injured last year in an attempted assassination, and my throat is still healing. I guess you didn't hear about that up here on Optus." He watched me curiously, that new face so very different from the other... But those faint scars on the neck *hadn't* gone away. Interesting. "But how would you know how my voice sounds? I haven't given an interview in years."

I shrugged. "It made sense that you'd changed your voice if you'd changed your face."

"Of course." He looked away, something in the mid-distance seeming easier to look at than me. "I suppose your forgiveness doesn't apply now that you know who I am."

"Maybe it doesn't," I said honestly. It was a lot easier to forgive some random Breaker, another minion like Iscee had been, rather than the supervillain himself. "You say you've changed, but did you give the Coles their land back? Did you do everything you could to make up for what you did to all of them, not just Iscee?"

He was quiet for a while. "Iscee is dead, Aria, and all over a few stupid rocks. Surely that's worse than losing...*land*."

"Yes, but not giving it back is adding insult to injury," I retorted. "And did you just call those diamonds 'stupid rocks'?"

"They *are* stupid! They're not worth dying over."

Wow. Just...wow. "So you've forgiven her for stealing from you?" I asked, genuinely curious.

He nodded brusquely. "Of course. It was my fault she was driven to that in the first place."

I pondered his words for a few moments. He really seemed serious, and I struggled to reconcile this repentant young man in front of me with the stories of vicious, vengeful Shandlin. So I pushed back my fear and confusion, and took refuge in false confidence. Then I asked that question that just kept nagging me. "Yeah, it was your fault," I agreed lightly. "She made her own choices, but that was definitely your fault. Um…did you really mean what you said about loving her?"

The High Duke scoffed. "I didn't know how to love anyone. But in my own way I did care for her – not that it matters now."

Interesting. He looked so miserable that I actually felt sorry for him, so I didn't point out the obvious truth that if you cared for someone, you didn't do what he'd done. But what could I say now? "Well, I suppose justice has been done, if you're looking for an eye for an eye. The vote's in four days. You're just about to lose everything, aren't you?"

"Probably. But Iscee is still dead, isn't she? Justice won't be done until I fall right into a swamp-mare's mouth."

I sighed heavily. "Please don't do that. Guilt only takes you so far. But if you really want to make up for it, you can promise me one thing."

"Anything."

I rolled my eyes. "Don't say that, or I might hold you to it! No, I want you to promise that if you get to stay High Duke, then all the families from Unity will get their land back, even if they didn't become Vyce citizens." A surprising number of people had chosen to leave Mars rather than give up the apparent safety of Earth citizenship. "Oh, and a posthumous pardon for Iscee."

"I had her pardoned eighteen months ago. As for the rest, I've applied for a bill to have the land returned on the condition that taxes are paid to Vyce rather than Old World." He shrugged, looking away. "Even if they aren't Vyce citizens."

Now that surprised me – the first part, anyway. "That seems fair. Now like I said, I have to get back to work. I think it would be better if you put that fake face back on. The real Zavier isn't here, I presume? Did he give permission for you to use his identity?"

The High Duke looked at me suspiciously. "His face, but not his identity, so I messed up there. But how did you know there was a real Zavier?"

My heart skipped in sudden panic, but I rolled my eyes. "I was making an assumption, and you've just confirmed I was right. Please stop acting as if you're suddenly going to catch me out and I'm suddenly going to admit that I'm really Iscee, then pull off my own face changer. I'm sorry, but life's just not that tidy. You *saw* what happened to her."

He still looked unconvinced, so I turned and lifted the heavy mass of my hair to reveal my ears. "See? No face-changer. It's just me."

I felt the gentle touch of his hand against the back of my ear, and then he sighed, closing his eyes briefly. "Just wishful thinking. I'm sorry, Aria."

"I'm sorry too," I told him. And in a way, I was.

I couldn't stop thinking about what had happened, and Judee finally noticed my mood change during her visit the next day. "What's the problem?"

Should I tell her? "Just someone from Iscee's past wanting to talk," I said finally. "It's a bit draining." And confusing, and scary, and even more confusing. The High Duke wasn't what I'd expected. Not at all. And if he wasn't lying, then maybe some *other* assumptions were wrong too, and then my whole worldview would need to change...

"Ah, must be the trio from Vyce. Are they giving you trouble?" she asked sharply. "They're not due to leave until tomorrow, but I can ask them to go earlier if you need me to." She lowered her voice. "*You* can leave, if you feel you need to."

Giving me trouble? I bit back hysterical laughter. "Thank you, Judee, but it wouldn't help business to turn customers away, even...difficult ones. No, I can manage another day. And I'm definitely not ready to go, not when I just got here. It's all just talk, anyway."

But it wasn't all just talk. The very next morning I received a holo-message, one of the kinds only available on the resort for guests to talk to each other. The video was blank, probably because the face-changers stopped it working properly. "I promise this is the last time I'll ask," came the High Duke's altered voice; "but could I see you one more time before I go? It'll be brief, I promise."

Wow, that was two 'I promises'. He must really want me to believe him, I mused.

I stood there with one hand on my communicator, fear warring with curiosity, and perhaps even sympathy. The High Duke was the whole reason for The Secret. Sure, he might be far more attractive now, and even elicit a little compassion with that show of grief for Iscee, but if it wasn't for him, then none of this would have happened. The last two years would have looked very, very different.

I shouldn't go. I should let him leave along with his two friends who were probably his guards, and never see him again. Maybe I should even make that call on the communicator; vanish to the other side of Optus or even Earth until he disappeared again.

But somehow I found myself lifting my hand to that holo-message, and tapping on the 'send reply' panel. "I'll meet you at Bar Four."

The reply came almost immediately. "We're leaving in half an hour. Can you come to my bungalow?"

I hesitated a moment, then shrugged. Bungalow, bar, what did it matter? I replied in the affirmative. Sure, I'd meet him. But I still made a quick communicator call to Judee, then another to the Earth family. If I didn't contact them again within an hour, they should panic.

Then I headed for the bungalow. And vain girl that I was, I couldn't help myself checking my reflection in the mirror as I went. It was best to look *good* when meeting one's nemesis, again.

Ten minutes later my hoverbike pulled up outside the generous bungalow assigned to 'Jank Marshal'. It was middle-of-the-range for what we offered here on Paradise, with tropical flowers winding their way up the walls and onto the roof, and it was right at the beach front. (But then so was everything; since the beach had been designed around the resort.)

Over the back of the bungalow was a small, private space shuttle, the sort that could make it all the way back to Mars, although probably not to Earth. Most moderate payers didn't have *those*.

A narrow-faced young man was sitting on a chair outside the front door, leaning back as if relaxed, but with a subtle tension to his posture that told me he had to be a guard. I couldn't remember his name except that it was something stupid, so probably fake. When he saw me he sprang upright, then called in through the open door, "She's here."

"Great!" the High Duke called back. "Tell her to come in!"

The guard nodded towards the door. "He says to-"

"Come in?" I cut in wryly. "Yes, I heard." But I found myself pausing at the threshold. Somehow being on his territory – even though it was *my* resort – felt a little risky.

"Go on," the guard told me sardonically. "He doesn't bite."

My pride stung, I lifted my chin and stepped inside. He was standing inside the bungalow's entry parlour, dressed as if to leave, and almost vibrating with some unrecognisable emotion. Or perhaps he'd just taken one of those energy pills so popular with some of our guests.

"I thought you wouldn't come," he said.

Geez, try not to look so needy. "I just came to hear what you wanted to say. You said it would be brief."

"Of course, of course. I have something to show you. You'll want to see this."

"Okay…" I followed him across the room to a table in the middle of the parlour. It was designed to look like mother-of-pearl set into glass, all very pretty, but that wasn't what he was showing me. No, there were two thin slides sitting side by side in the middle of the table – printouts full of fine text almost like shopping receipts. I looked at them, then up at him. "What are these?"

Behind me I heard the door open and close again,

admitting the guard, and I saw someone else short and dark-haired in the corner of my eye. The hairs on the back of my neck began to prickle.

"Sample A and sample B," the High Duke said cheerfully, tapping at the nearest slide. "Look at the results at the end. See?"

I studied the information. All I could see were symbols and numbers and things that didn't make any sense to me, and at the end: *samples match.* "I don't understand." But I was getting a bad feeling about this…

"I think you do, Iscee. You just still think you can lie your way out of this." And now he was actually grinning, hands rubbing together as if in ecstasy. "You horrible, terrible, *awful* person. I can't believe you let me think you were dead! You let *everyone* think you were dead."

Uh oh. Just….*no.* Fear flooded me and my heart skipped a beat in my chest, then began beating double-time to make up for it.

Iscee. He'd called me Iscee. "I'm not Iscee. I'm Aria Mav-"

"Don't even bother lying," he cut in, a wide grin splitting his face. He was *beaming..* "Look. Look at this." And then he waved his hand over the two slides on the table, and the text changed. Instead of 'Sample A' and 'Sample B', it now read, 'Iscendra Cole' and 'Aria Mavick'. *Samples match.* "DNA doesn't lie, Iscee, so you don't need to either. These tests show that you're Iscee. *Iscendra.*"

Ah, suds suds suds suds suds suds suds *suds!* He was clearly convinced, and it was going to take a lot to get him to think otherwise. But in spite of the harsh words his tone was actually *happy,* and I shook my head in horrified dismay, looking around behind me to the two waiting guards. One of them was the small Asian woman I'd seen in the customer records, but she had a face as expressionless as a mannequin. "Please tell me he doesn't actually think I'm my cousin."

The male guard shrugged. The woman stared at me blankly, but didn't answer.

"Sure do," the High Duke said cheerfully from behind me.

"I accidently got one of your hairs yesterday when I touched your neck. And of course we already had your details on record from when you were conscripted, so there it is. You're not dead. You're not dead!"

No, no, this was terrible. I felt coldness run through my whole body even as I shook my head. Fear, panic. Two years worth of The Secret, just to end up at this point. "*I'm* not dead. Iscee is."

"What, are you going to say they messed up the samples? I was suspicious after you knew some details that no one else should have, and I had the test run twice, Iscee. I know it's you. I don't blame you for trying to hide your identity, but the game's up. Time to tell me how you faked getting swallowed by that swamp-mare – it was a hologram, right? And you must have had that tracker removed and left at the bottom of the swamp…"

I was still shaking my head. "You want to know if someone was so desperate to get away from you that they faked being eaten alive? That makes you feel better?"

"Yes! Yes, *sooo* much better."

There was a long silence, then finally I sat down on the nearest chair, feeling very solemn. He was still smiling, but that smile faded in reaction to my expression. "DNA does sometimes lie, Your Grace, because no matter what those tests say, I'm not Iscendra Cole. I'm Aria Mavick." Then I told the story that was part of The Secret, but that I'd rarely had to mention. "We're twins."

FOURTEEN
Twins

◎   ◎   ◎

"Oh really?" The High Duke sat down opposite me, his arms sprawled over the padded sides of the chair. "You and Iscendra are twins, and your mothers are twins too? Please, tell me more."

He obviously hadn't believed a word I'd said, but I carried on anyway. "Judee Mavick had just got married, but she couldn't have children because of an injury, so her sister Bethany donated an egg. But it split after it was fertilised, and the sisters decided to take one embryo each." I stretched my palms out in front of me, my expression as serious as the grave. "Cousins, but twins. Same DNA. Different people."

"Gross," the male guard muttered, but the High Duke was shaking his head. His smile had now faded completely, replaced by uncertainty.

"No. No, that's not right. I suppose it's possible…but you *are* Iscee. You have to be!" He turned to his guards. "She looks like her, doesn't she?"

The male guard shrugged again, and the woman raised an eyebrow. "She's fatter."

"Barely!" I snapped. Iscee had been lean, without any spare flesh. "And I prefer curvier, thanks very much." I turned to the guards. "Please tell me you two haven't been encouraging him with this."

"His Grace makes up his own mind," the woman replied stolidly.

"They're not stupid, and neither am I," the High Duke said in a low voice. He was obviously growing angry with my answers. "You know too much to be Aria. You knew that she- *you* had stolen from me, and I never said that! You know too much about *us*." He turned to the woman, suddenly scowling. "Oh, turn off that face-changer, Bloom! You don't need it anymore."

She lifted one hand to her ear, then her face flickered and a moment later it was slightly different. Rounder cheeks, different eyes. Fair-haired. She glanced at me, holding my gaze without any expression.

I blinked, startled. There'd already been one face-changer, why not two? Then I turned back to the High Duke. "Knowing things about you is pretty normal, Your Grace. You're a hugely public figure, especially at the moment. But look at this." I lifted my wrist, showing my communicator that also doubled as a 'hold everything' device. "Show me Aria and Iscee."

A holographic image of two girls popped into the air. They were both in their early teens; one with wild brown hair trailing from a ponytail down her back, and the other with a short, spiked orange crop. But their faces and bodies were almost identical.

"This is us," I told him. "We look like twins, right? Because genetically we are."

I finally saw uncertainty in his expression, but he still was shaking his head. "No. No, that can't be right. You've *got* to be Iscee. Come on, admit it. I don't want to hurt you, I just need to *know*."

Crazy to think that after everything that happened to Iscee and her family, after how The Secret affected *me*, I still felt sorry for him. He seemed so sincere, so desperate, and I wanted to say something that would make him feel better. As he'd said, I didn't think he wanted to hurt me. But The Secret existed for a reason, and I couldn't breach it on a whim.

So even though it was hard, and it was the last thing he wanted to hear, I stuck with my course and rose to my feet. "I'm sorry, Your Grace. I'm not Iscee, and I think it's time for me to go." I indicated to the shuttle visible through the large windows. "And you too. Haven't you got a speech to deliver?"

He'd stood as I did, and now he was between me and the door, and he wore the most agitated, crestfallen expression I thought I'd ever seen. I moved to step around him, and he reached out with one hand towards me as if to strike me. I couldn't help raising a hand defensively in front of my face.

The High Duke's eyes widened, and his hands fell as his expression turned to pure shock. "I wasn't going to hit you," he said in dismay. "Surely you aren't *scared* of me?"

Yes. It had been a visceral reaction, and I couldn't help myself. But... "No," I replied quickly.

"Yes you are," he countered. He took a step back from me, shaking his head once more. "Is that what this is all about? You're afraid of me?"

I wavered between agreeing and running for it, then settled on 'fake confidence'. "Do I have a reason to be afraid?"

"Of course not!" he replied, just as the woman, Bloom, said, "Your Grace, we have to leave."

He swore under his breath, turning away to look at her, and I took my chance. I ducked past him and dashed for the door, but the male guard stepped in front of it, a smirk on his face.

A sudden wave of fear-driven anger washed over me. "Get out of my way!" I ordered him, my hands in tight fists at my sides.

"Or what?" the guard taunted.

"Iscee...Aria..." the High Duke said from behind me, but I didn't turn around.

"Or I'll see that you're sorry," I snapped.

"That sounds like a threat," I heard Bloom say from just behind me. Then I felt something touch my arm, and *zzt-*

Suds! A stunner!

And then the darkness rushed in.

I blinked, and light pricked at my eyes. A few moments later the room came into focus, but its dimensions were all wrong: stretching over me in long silver curves. One of the walls was right by my face. I tried to reach out for it but couldn't move;

could only look and wonder where on earth I was. In the background I could hear a conversation, the voices seeming far too loud. They made my head hurt, and I scrunched my eyes shut again.

"They've moved the date of the vote forward by a day – Derry's work, no doubt. I'll have to go straight from the ship to the speaking platform if I don't want to lose before I've even started."

"Are you sure bringing the girl along was a good idea?" This was a female voice, one that began to click in my memory. *"You said you weren't going to conscript anymore."*

"This isn't a conscription," the first, male voice said irritably. *"It's a temporary kidnapping."*

As if that was better?

"Besides, it was your idea, Bloom. Oh, she's awake."

She being me. I finally took control of my heavy-limbed body and rolled over to stare at the approaching figure. It was male, tall with an almost pretty face and very dark hair, and the memory of everything that had happened came rushing back in along with my limited sense of movement. I tried to throw myself off the bunk (to what? Strangle Shandlin?) but ended up on the floor instead, fuming helplessly.

"You won't be able to move properly yet," he said redundantly. "The stunner said it would take at least ten minutes from waking."

Which meant that they'd either set the stunner too high, or else used a cheap brand that was knock-out or nothing. No gentle sedatives like I'd used on Mr Ingbrid a few days earlier. When I could finally speak, I bellowed, "I cannot *believe* you just kidnapped me. What do you think you're doing?"

"Helping you up," Shandlin replied.

He reached over as if to hoist me up by the armpits, and I tried to do what he so sorely deserved – punch him in the gut. But my hands were weak and instead I flopped forward into a sort of headbutt, smacking his nose hard with my forehead.

Ouch.

"Argh! What did you do that for?"

"What did *I* do it for? Why did *you* do this, you crazy

person?" My voice was coming out with less force than I intended, but I carried on. "Do you really need to drug and kidnap girls in order to hold their attention? Barring the ones you pay, of course."

The High Duke had the good grace to look sheepish, rubbing his reddened nose. "I'm sorry. Really, really sorry. I panicked after Bloom stunned you, and then we had to leave. She said- I mean, I thought that if you came along, we could talk some more and maybe make sense of all of this, but...I suppose that was a bad idea."

"What did you just say?"

"It was a bad idea," he repeated. "Because now I've basically kidnapped you, and just when I was telling you how sorry I was for mistreating Iscee. Whether you're Iscee or Aria, it doesn't matter. You deserve to be treated with respect."

I just stared at him for several long moments. "I actually meant the part where you apologised. Who are you and what have you done with the High Duke?"

He scowled, looking much more like the old, cranky pictures of himself. "What, because I apologised? I do that. Sometimes."

I didn't answer, or I would have said that the Shandlin I knew never apologised to anyone for anything. Instead I focused on sitting upright. "Alright, Mr High Duke. You've accidently kidnapped me now. What's your plan, to drag me on holo-vid and tell everyone that I faked my death? That all that bad reputation wasn't earned? Because if you want to look like a sound ruler who should be left in charge of a whole dome, that's not the way to do it."

Shandlin winced, and a rueful half-smile came over his face. He sat down on a nearby chair fixed to the small ship's carpeted floor. His nose wasn't going to bleed, disappointingly, although it was glowing a lovely shade of red. Good luck hiding *that* before his big speech.

"You wouldn't believe the gossip after you left," he said, his tone a little distant as if deep in memory. "Suds, it was vicious. I suppose that if you came back from the dead-"

"I'm Aria!"

"Or if *Iscee* was shown to be alive, then it might help my cause," he finished. "But probably not, because I can't take back how I'd behaved beforehand. Whether Iscee is around or not, I can't fix that. I can't take it back." He looked at me, one eyebrow raised. "You wouldn't want to say you were here voluntarily, would you?"

"Do I want to say that I came voluntarily?" I crossed my arms, finally feeling a little better, although inside I was a mess of fury and leftover stunner and even some inappropriate amusement. To think that after all this time he'd come to *my* resort… and apologised, *after* kidnapping me. "Not going to happen. You'll be lucky if I don't kick up a fuss and ruin your reputation even further – or what's left of it. I can see the articles – 'big fat grawlix of a High Duke has awkward obsession with dead girl.'"

Shandlin let out a sound of disbelief. "Did you just call me a big fat grawlix?!"

"Maybe not fat," I amended. Then to the guard snickering in the background, I added, "And you're an accessory to a grawlix, so you can just stop laughing, whatever-your-name-is."

"It's Jermaine," the guard told me, his laugh gone although the smirk was still there. "Jermaine Elsewich. Remember that name."

"Suds," I muttered under my breath. "I thought that was a fake name." Poor guy. Cursed with a silly name from birth – so of course he had to end up annoying.

Just then the other guard, Bloom, walked over from the front of the shuttle. She studied me coolly then turned to the High Duke. "We'll be back in Vyce in about an hour. We're just passing Phobos."

Phobos was the smaller of the New World's moons: an ugly, misshapen lump that circled far too closely to the planet's surface. A few hundred years ago attempts had been made to adjust its course. They'd failed, and the Mars domes still argued over who ought to pay the bill to try again. But for now, it was a good marker for when we were nearly back on the surface.

The High Duke still didn't answer, and she repeated herself. "Your Grace, we're-"

"I heard you, Bloom," he cut in, sounding rather odd. "I'll just need…a few more minutes here."

"To convince me to support your cause?" I folded my arms militantly. "Go ahead. Impress me."

He didn't answer, just looked at me with those big dark eyes for several seconds. Then he held up his wrist, pushing the sleeve back a little to display a thin silver band. "I've worn this since two weeks after Iscee…disappeared, from the day I finally realised it had been my fault. Just mine. It symbolises a promise to myself."

I was silent, and he continued, "That I would never again cause grief to anyone, not if I could help it. And since that date, I've done my best to keep that promise."

I'd sat there silently, shocked by what he was saying, and perhaps a little touched. But it seemed he was waiting for a response, and finally I said, "Until today, when you had a girl stunned and kidnapped. Is that it?"

The High Duke froze, then slowly lowered his wrist, a humourless half smile on his face. "Until today. I messed up, again. Even if you are Iscee, or you aren't, I've screwed up. And if we turn the shuttle around now, I'll miss my speech. Once we arrive in Vyce and we've refuelled, I'll have someone return you immediately to Optus. I will also give you whatever compensation is within my means to give."

I studied his face, his body language, and while I wasn't always the best judge of people, I would swear that he was telling the truth. "Anything, eh? You should be careful with statements like that."

He just looked at me. "Within reason."

Now how far could I take this…? "You might lose everything after this speech," I said bluntly. "Do you have anything that's *yours*, that you can give?"

He barked out a laugh. "Well, I've got my family jewels. My mother's dowry. Do you want one?"

Family jewels. I swallowed back a laugh, but some of it still escaped out of my nose in an unappealing snort.

"What's so funny? Do you not believe me?"

"Maybe," I replied, not because I didn't believe him, but because I didn't want to explain the joke. "What are you offering?"

The High Duke paused. "A diamond. Say…Grandfather."

"That's an odd name for a gem."

"Yes, it is." But he didn't elaborate. "Do you want it?"

A diamond was a diamond! "Sure. You give me the grandfather diamond, and I won't press charges. I'll call it an unplanned holiday."

The High Duke sighed. "Very well. But you'll have to wait until after my speech."

"I can wait." I'd be interested to see the real Vyce, after all the news of the last two years.

"Anything else you'd like?" he asked sardonically. "My firstborn child, perhaps?"

"How about just a call to let my parents know where I am?"

I was directed to a small alcove in the very back of the ship, and a few minutes later I was staring at Judee's concerned face, rather pixelated considering that this should have been a top-of-the-line shuttle. "Where are you, sweetie? What's going on?"

"I've actually taken a quick trip to the surface," I told her, "but I'll be back by tonight. Sorry about the short notice."

"Tonight?" Her eyes widened. "It was that High Duke, wasn't it? Did he hurt you? Are you safe…*Aria*?"

"Yes, I'm safe," I replied, because I really felt like I was. Forget The Secret. I didn't think I was in danger. "I'll tell you about it later, and I'll let you know when I've got to Vyce, and again when I'm on my way back. You know what to do if I don't make contact."

"Hmmm…" Judee sounded unconvinced, and I couldn't

blame her.

"I'm fine, really. Don't worry about me – unless I don't show up by tomorrow morning, in which case I'm…" *in a dungeon?* "…crashed into Phobos," I improvised. "But that won't happen, so I'll see you then, alright?"

Whatever Judee's answer would have been was blanked out, and now the screen was just black. "Hey," I exclaimed. "The contact screen's down."

Shandlin moved over towards the screen, studying it with a frown. "Huh. Did you manage to say what you needed to?"

"I think so-"

Floomph.

There should have been sound, but there was nothing except a bright light and a sudden sense of wrongness. I was thrown backwards into the small space, the seat's auto-belt locking around my torso and holding my neck into place, and then I could only watch in horror as the front half of the ship broke away and spun off sideways.

Or maybe it was me who was spinning sideways, the shock of it making me breathless, and then a crash-suit's mask locked down over my face and I could breathe again – perhaps not the shock after all. And then infinite moments later I was flying free of the ship, a big, brown expanse rushing up into my vision…

Oof. The landing was hard even though I was now wearing a crash-suit, and my neck jolted sharply enough to make me wonder if it was broken. I skidded across the rocky surface, bouncing lightly in the low gravity until finally I'd hit enough big rocks to stop me moving, and then I just lay where I'd stopped, paralysed by the shock of it.

I'd actually crashed into Phobos. Just me, because I couldn't see anything else, anyone else…

Except there was someone else, clad in a pale crash-suit like mine, and spiralling towards the surface of the moon at a speed that made me cringe. They disappeared over the horizon line, and I finally managed to push myself to my feet, scrambling to follow.

Phobos had only one eighth the gravity of Earth and Mars's domes, and running was like finding that I'd had wings strapped to my shoulders, with every step high and slow. My breath was harsh in my own ears, recycled by the small unit built into the mask, and I uttered the same prayer over and over. *Please let them be alive... Please let them be alive...*

It didn't matter who it was, I vowed. Once we were safe, once we were out of this, I'd tell the truth. I'd tell everything, because secrets were useless to dead men – or women, for that matter. I just needed to find whoever it was, make sure they were safe, and then we'd both need to make sure that we reached the nearest manned station before we could find the other two. There was one around here somewhere, right?

They'd have seen us fall, they'd be tracking us. They'd be even finding the other two from the ship even now, I told myself. There were four of us but I'd only seen one, so logically the other two in their suits had just been flung in the other direction. They'd be fine, right?

There were a lot of other directions, and most didn't point to land. And where they landed wouldn't matter if they weren't in one piece...

I shook off that ugly thought. Funny how the prospect of imminent death could put everything into perspective: it was hard to hate someone when they might have been blown into bits.

I reached the fallen figure, but was unable to slow down fast enough so ended up accidentally kicking them. The body slumped, twitched a little, and while I couldn't tell through the reflective mask who was inside, the long, lanky body type could only belong to the High Duke.

"Shan!" I shouted, shaking him. "Are you alright?"

Obviously not, and he twitched a little more but didn't try to get up, didn't try to speak. It was dead silent out here, and all I could hear was the sound of my own harsh, panicked breaths. But all wasn't lost. We were on a hill, and in the distance I could see a small grey blob stuck to the chocolate-brown surface of the moon like a barnacle on the hull of an ancient ship.

A station. A beacon of hope, more like. Even if there was no one there, there'd certainly be a way to contact others, medical supplies…

I grabbed Shandlin under the arms and began dragging him towards the station, but luckily for him the low gravity kept him from scraping the ground. The station was disappointingly small close up, its low door barely as high as my head. I slapped my free hand onto the metal disk that you always saw in bunkers like this, and after a few seconds it registered, the door sliding open to show a dimly lit, sparse interior.

Once inside I closed the door, noting the instructions in the three main languages: *WARNING: low oxygen environment! Do not remove breathing apparatus until inside inner compartment of station. Disregarding this warning may cause death or brain damage.*

Inner compartment… I spotted yet another door to my left, this one even set further into the ground. The roof of the station might look small, but it seemed the bulk of it was underground.

But the second door's metal plate didn't register my hand inside its protective glove, and I knew I couldn't take it off without risking losing my own air. The seal around my neck wasn't secure enough in this one-size-fits-all crash-suit.

I was beginning to despair when suddenly the inner door slid open to reveal a man standing there, dressed in a one-piece engineer's suit and with a small breather-mask over his lower face. He looked stunned to see us, but I was so happy I could have cried.

FIFTEEN
The Secret

The engineer's name was Harry, and he was stationed here on Phobos until the next changeover in three weeks, monitoring the technology that kept the moon from crashing into the planet below. There were supposed to be two engineers here, but the other had left early.

"His wife had a baby," Harry told me in disgust, "so he thinks he has to head off a month before he's supposed to, and the replacement hasn't come yet. What if something happened to me, I ask you?"

He'd noticed the crash (or explosion, as he'd called it) but thought there couldn't possibly be any survivors. I thought of Bloom and Jermaine, and with every word he spoke, my hopes for them shrivelled.

"I've already sent a report through," he told me. "Mars will send marshals and medics out within a couple of hours if they're not already on the way. Good thing our lad here's awake, right?"

Awake, yes, but completely befuddled. From what we could tell with Harry's simple scanner, Shandlin had hit his head hard as he'd been ejected. He also had a badly broken arm, but compared to what could have happened he'd got off lightly. After all, his trajectory had made his fall a lot longer and harder than mine.

The High Duke had lain there on the makeshift bed (translation: floor) while we ran the scanner over him and put on a temporary splint, and had only flinched slightly at the pain. And then he'd looked at me. "Iscee!" he'd cried, sounding woozy but delighted. "I didn't know you had blue hair. It looks funny."

Were we going to go through this again? "Call me Aria. And I happen to think it's pretty, thank you."

"It is pretty," he agreed. "You are pretty. Put on a bit of weight, though." Talk about a back-handed compliment. I turned him over perhaps a little too roughly, and he frowned. "Ugh, my head hurts. What are we doing here?"

"We had an accident," I told him. "We had to stop here, but we'll be back in a couple of hours. You've missed your speech, though."

"Speech?" There were several long, slow seconds and then finally I saw it dawn on him, what was supposed to happen today. "*My speech*. Oh, no. I've missed it. How could I have missed it?"

"I'm sorry you've missed it, but the shuttle-"

He swore, trying to sit up and failing. Clearly he was back to his old self. "Did you make me miss the speech, Iscee? Don't you know how important this is to me?"

"I didn't make you-"

"Where's Bloom?" he cut in, his voice slurred. "I need to talk to Bloom, now!"

And it was that last part which made me respond so much more gently than I would have otherwise. "I didn't stop the shuttle, Shan. It exploded. Bloom is...Bloom isn't available right now."

"Exploded...?" He lay there blinking, two vertical frown lines forming between his eyebrows. I could almost see his thoughts coming together, but not quite connecting. "I don't understand. Why would the shuttle explode? We had it checked before we left."

I busied myself with cleaning my fingernails – short and practical, with a coat of pink sparkly lacquer that wasn't quite standing up to stress. "I don't know. They're going to send people out to take a look."

"OK. Where's Bloom? And the other one, er..."

"Jermaine Elsewich," I finished for him. Because like the guy had said, I wouldn't be forgetting that name.

"That's right. He was new, wasn't he? Where are they, Iscee?"

This time I didn't bother correcting my name – there were more important things to worry about. "The safety system sent you and I towards Phobos. I don't know where the other two went."

Now I saw as the implications of my words sank in, and the High Duke's face fell. "You mean they could be dead."

"Possibly." Probably.

There was a long silence, and when I finally looked at him I saw that his eyes were bright with tears. It wasn't an expression I'd ever seen on him, nor even expected to see. Whatever my opinion had been of that humourless guard, she was still a person, and she had mattered to him. "I'm really sorry," I told him gently. "I know she was a good friend."

"A good friend?" Shandlin wiped his hand over his reddened eyes. "She was a traitor, a double agent working with my cousin to bring down my rule. She wasn't my friend at all." I was stunned into silence, and he mused, "It's funny that even though I knew I couldn't trust her, I still care that she might be gone. She'd been my guard since I was thirteen, did you know that? That's a long time."

Finally I managed to choke out a few words. "You knew she was a traitor?!"

"Yeah." He sighed. "Took me a long time to figure it out, though. She had this way of making suggestions, when I didn't even realise she was doing it, but I'd listen. Sometimes it was *bad* advice. So, so bad." He cut his eyes to me. "Like challenging the Old World by illegally conscripting one of their citizens. I did that, and look where we are."

He'd known Bloom was a traitor. And *she'd* suggested Iscee's conscription? Wow. Just…wow. "But…if you knew she was a double agent, then why did you just leave her there? Why didn't you fire her?"

He shrugged dully. "What's that saying; keep your friends close, and your enemies closer? By the time I figured it out, it seemed just easier to let her stay and ignore everything she said. At least it gave me an idea of what she and Derry wanted." He looked straight at me. "She didn't want me to come to Optus looking for Aria. She thought that was a bad idea, so naturally I did it. Why wouldn't she want me to come to Optus, Aria?"

I could have said, 'to avoid putting stress on a family that had suffered enough', but I didn't. Instead I looked away, and he sighed again, this time in a long, heavy exhale. "Even with what's just happened – I wish you'd just tell me the truth."

I knew he meant about Iscee/Aria. "I *have* told you. I've told you twenty times!"

"Yes, but..." Shandlin paused, and he closed his eyes briefly as if in pain. "...I can't let it go, and I can't shake the feeling that you're lying."

"You mean you want me to be lying."

"I do," he allowed. "Especially now." Then he was silent, sprawled there on the floor with one arm half outstretched. The silver promise-holder showed at his wrist, and I couldn't take my eyes off it.

Could people really change that much? Could our perceptions have been skewed right from the start anyway?

"You promised you'd never purposely cause anyone grief again," I said slowly, my eyes still fixed on that bright metallic band. "But what if someone really, really wronged you? Wouldn't you still want revenge?"

"I'd want justice," Shandlin said thoughtfully. "But I've decided to let the courts decide how people should be punished."

"Iscee stole from you." That was what had set off the worst of this drama, wasn't it?

"I had her illegally conscripted," he shot back. "And anyway, she's been pardoned. I said that before."

"How pardoned?"

"Fully and completely," he said, and now he was looking right at me, his almost black eyes fixed on my face. "And her family too, not that they did anything wrong. There'll be no revenge from me, no causing further grief. I'll do what I can to make up for my mistakes. I swear it." He paused, lifting up his wrist to show me the bracelet. "I'll get another one of these. I'll make it a public oath-"

"Oh, shut up," I cut in, half amused, half exasperated. "If you say it, I'll believe it. Your word should be enough."

The High Duke went very still. "Enough for Iscee?"

I sighed, and in that moment something inside me broke. Like a tie, a bondage that kept the real me hidden. It was a lie, and I'd lived it for two years. "Enough for me, yes."

Several seconds went by, and I could see in his motionless posture that he was taking in what I'd said. Then his mouth curved into a wide, wide smile. "I knew it!" he crowed. "I knew it, I knew it, I knew it!" He tried to sit up, then fell back again, a twisted expression of pain on his face. But it didn't hold him back. He grabbed for my hand from his prone position. "Iscee," he said. "Iscee. Iscee, I thought you were dead. I've been drowning in guilt all this time, and now I don't have to anymore. You're not dead."

"Drowning in guilt, huh?" I tugged lightly at my hand, but he had a tight grip on it, and it didn't seem worth the fight. People were *dead,* but I wasn't. "Guilt can be useful if it makes you change your behaviour. Maybe it was worth it. You *are* going to keep your promises, aren't you?"

Shandlin scowled, once again looking very much like his usual self. "When do I not keep my promises? Bloom always said-" But then as if realising what he'd said, his face crumpled and he turned away.

Bloom was gone, probably. And if there was any time for me to reveal my identity – not that hiding it seemed to have worked for long once he'd come here to Optus – then it was now. There were bigger things to worry about than one girl who'd faked her death, apparently.

And as for Shandlin drowning in guilt? That made me feel good. Not because I wanted him to suffer forever and ever, but because it showed that he *knew* he'd been wrong. That seemed to validate how my family and I had felt these past years, how hard it had been, how much I'd hated and feared him. And that meant that now, now I was safe. My family was safe, and he'd promised to return their land. And you know what? I believed him.

He'd been lying there on the floor with his hand still gripping mine tightly, but his eyes were still closed. I could see something bright trickle out from under those dark lashes – a tear – and that made something burn in the back of my own eyes and throat. I hadn't always liked Bloom, but I cared that she was gone. Almost definitely gone, that was.

I hadn't even *known* Jermaine – and I hadn't liked him much either – but I still found I cared that he was gone too. Dead was dead. And perhaps Shan had also lost his dome to his older cousin who might or might not be a better ruler, if only the people of Vyce would choose to vote him in.

But then the High Duke's stiff shoulders seemed to relax and his hand loosened around my fingers, and I realised he'd fallen asleep.

"I've been so scared of you all this time," I murmured. "Of what you would do if you found me or my family. But maybe I hadn't needed to be. What if you'd caught us two years ago, Shan? What would you have done?"

His fingers squeezed around mine again, just once, and I realised in surprise that he'd heard me. "Why do we always end up like this, Iscee?" he mumbled, sounding half asleep.

"Like what?" Pondering the other's motives?

"Survivors." Then the High Duke let out a heavy sigh, followed by a snore. Now he was definitely sleeping.

Survivors. What had he meant by that?

But then I remembered a similar situation two years ago when our air vehicle had been paint bombed while still high above the ground. Another Breaker, Colby, had mistaken it for a real bomb, and the three of us had leapt out of the vehicle, apparently to safety. But only Shandlin and I had walked away from that accident.

Bloom had been there too, I remembered. And the real Zavier. But they hadn't jumped...and I still didn't know if they'd planted that paint bomb or not. Either way, Bloom wouldn't be telling me the answer.

Just then Harry walked back into the room. "Help's coming from Mars, love. Only thirty minutes, tops. Shall we wake up your boy there?"

I blinked at him. I'd told him who Shandlin was, but he didn't seem to have really understood. "No, that's fine," I replied instead. "We'll wait."

Harry shrugged then left, and I looked down again and realised what a picture we must have made: me sitting right next to the sleeping young man, our hands loosely clasped. Good grief. I got up, using the movement as an excuse to pull my hand away. But he frowned again in his sleep, and I couldn't help feeling guilty.

Now I was the one scowling. I shook my head, then went off to find Harry.

Shandlin slept until the medics and marshals arrived in their shuttles. Then he slept again once they'd sedated him, because he'd got quite upset when someone had inadvertently described the shuttle's destruction within his hearing. It had been shattered, with the back half sent spiralling towards Phobos, and the front going just about everywhere else. They were looking for body parts, not survivors.

I was treated for minor cuts and bruises in the bay of the small ship, the medic scanning the chip in my wrist to confirm my identity. "Miz Aria Mavick," he said aloud. "You've been a lucky, lucky girl. Not even a broken arm like His Grace there. A pressure bandage on your bruised ribs, and you should be just fine."

I mumbled agreement. The truth was, I didn't know why we'd survived and the others hadn't. Could such things truly be pure coincidence? I was more inclined to believe it had happened for a higher purpose, although I didn't yet know what.

Living another day. That was a high enough purpose for me, I decided.

The medic patched me up then moved away. I could

have got up, could have spoken to the marshals or pilot, but I couldn't be bothered. Instead I leaned back on my bench, resting against the wall of the new shuttle taking us back to Vyce Dome.

"He called you Aria," Shandlin said quietly. "How did you change your ID chip?"

I turned to look at him. He now wore one arm in a cast, as well as a silvery skull plate over half his head like an old football helmet, and his dark hair stuck out from underneath it. It looked a bit silly, but it was supposed to help his fractured skull heal. "I didn't realise you were awake."

"The chip," he persisted. "Did you swap it with your cousin, or did they reset yours?"

"Both, kind of," I replied finally. "After they smuggled me off Mars, we both went to stay on Earth again. I had a false chip inserted over my real one, but with Aria's details. Aria's carrying completely made up details." I shrugged a shoulder, half-smiling. "She thinks of all this as an adventure. I think she'll almost be disappointed to be plain old Aria Mavick again."

Shan was still studying me intently. "And are you disappointed to be Iscendra Cole again?"

Was I? After the escape, I would have given almost anything to go back to normal. To be safe, to be home. Of course I'd blamed the High Duke, because it had been his fault. Eventually I'd decided that holding a grudge was hard work, but I was still happy to be myself again, fully and completely. "Nope. I'll keep the hair, though." And perhaps the tidily arched eyebrows too. I'd become used to being so groomed, I'd feel like a wild girl if I went back to my old, untamed self.

"It looks nice." He let out a heavy, sleepy sigh. "D'you really look that much like your cousin? It seems weird."

"As children we were almost identical, except that her hair was fairer. Now I'm half a head taller, and anyone who really knows us wouldn't be fooled." I shrugged again. "Not that it matters anymore."

"Why doesn't it matter anymore?"

I looked across at him quizzically. "Because you were the one we were supposed to be tricking, and now you know."

"Oh." Shandlin looked terribly sad for a moment. "You lost two years of your life because of me, Iscee. Living a lie."

"Yes, I know." Hearing him say it aloud didn't help at all. In fact, it made me feel rather cranky. "But I'm alive, and the lie's over."

"And your poor family, being uprooted like that. Suds, they must hate me."

"Oh, they do." I had to admit that one. "They've never really settled back on Earth, and they've been scared for me all this time. I'll have to let them know things have changed, but they might not believe it at first." I paused. "And if you ever meet my brother Nik, cover your face. And your gut. And your knees." Nik had been quite detailed in regards to what he'd do to the High Duke should they ever meet. "Er… and maybe wear some kind of protective cup."

"What!?" Shandlin's eyebrows shot up. "I was thinking I could apologise to your parents in person when I give the land back. Maybe I shouldn't do that after all."

"Maybe you should reimburse them for the lost income and the costs of leaving," I suggested. "If you can. Money covers over all kinds of wrongs. Were you really going to set me free?"

He turned his head towards me, frowning. Perhaps he was confused at the sudden change of subject, so I elaborated, "Two years ago when we'd come home from Optus, before you knew about me stealing the jewels. You said you were going to let me go from the Breakers, but then when Bloom told you what I'd done, you changed your mind."

"Oh." His eyes dropped from mine to stare at his arm in that cast. "Yes, I *was* going to let you go. I'd conscripted you as a stunt, then kept you because…well, I'd thought we had something between us, and I was a stupid, difficult little grawlix, as you'd said. Then when I realised we hadn't had anything at all and that you couldn't stand me, I was horrified.

I wanted you as far away from me as possible. Sending you home seemed like a good idea."

"Until you decided to confiscate the plantation instead," I supplied helpfully. But I was fascinated by what he'd said about his reasons for keeping me on. Had he really been that clueless, that easily influenced?

Well, I'd been clueless enough not to notice his interest, I acknowledged. Hindsight was a wonderful thing. And hindsight also told me that at the time, I wouldn't have said we had *nothing* between us. Just irritation, anger and perhaps a tiny little unwilling attraction...

"Until I did that," he agreed, sounding disgruntled. "I suppose you can get revenge by hiring me as a toilet cleaner or something once I've officially lost my position. You saved my life, did you know that? The marshal said that because I came to the back of the shuttle to talk to you, I didn't take the full force of the blast. And now I've missed my speech, but chances are I would have lost the Dome anyway. Maybe. You know I wasn't very popular."

"I know that you *weren't* very popular," I countered. "But the news made things look much better over the last couple of years. Was it really just guilt that made you change so much?"

He shrugged, then managed to struggle to an upright position. He didn't look much better that way. Forget the skull plate looking a bit silly – it looked ridiculous. "Guilt, and I finally got some good advice. After you…disappeared, Zavier told me that if I wanted to keep my position, then I needed to make some changes."

My eyebrows shot up. "Zavier! He was-" But then I quickly shut my mouth. I still didn't want to incriminate the ones who'd helped me leave, even though I was pretty sure Derry had purposely scared me into staying silent for so long. "Zavier," I finished instead.

"Zavier was Zavier," Shandlin agreed sardonically. "But he was also quite useful. A good friend, in the end. But you know what?"

"What?"

"Even if I'm not High Duke anymore, then I can still give you Grandfather, if you want him."

"The diamond?" I queried. "Why do you call it 'him'?" I couldn't hold back a smile. "Is it something to do with them being the, er, *family jewels*?"

Shandlin shook his head. "You smirked. You smirk every time you hear that phrase. What's the problem with it?"

But I couldn't tell him. "Um…look it up, it's an Older saying. So…what about the names…"

And now he laughed aloud. "That's the fun part. You know why they're called the family jewels, why they belong to me personally rather than to Vyce?"

"I was hoping you'd tell me."

"Because they're made from the compressed ashes of my ancestors," he said simply. "Grandfather and his parents, and a couple of his uncles. He wanted the jewels made into a coronet to be worn by the future High Dukes of Rison, but of course that never happened, since they came to Vyce along with my mother. Apparently Grandmother thought the idea was horrible and refused to take part, but you can understand why we don't exactly shout about their origins."

My jaw dropped. "You're joking. Surely that's not even possible."

"Oh, but it is possible, although most people think that keeping their dead relatives on their person is creepy. Humans have been making artificial diamonds for millenia, although it's rarer to have them made in such a way. Did you notice the slight orange tint to them?"

I shook my head.

"It's only very slight, but it shows that they're impure." He let out a short laugh. "If I had them on me now I'd show you, but you'll have to wait until we get back to Vyce for that, sorry. What did you do with the two you stole?"

There were a few moments of silence while I considered my crime versus hiding the one that had helped me. But I hadn't just taken jewels; I'd taken *bodies*. Oh, suds.

"I'm so sorry," I blurted out. "I never should have taken

them."

"I drove you to it," he said impatiently. "Now where-"

"No," I cut in. "I'll take responsibility for my own actions, thank you. You've managed to do that, so I can too. I *knew* I shouldn't take things that didn't belong to me, and it didn't matter who you were or what you'd done. I chose to take them even though I was going against my conscience, and you can't stop me from being sorry, alright?"

He blinked a couple of times. "Alright...so where are they?"

"I gave them to someone in exchange for getting me and my family out of Vyce."

"Was it Derry?" My eyes widened, and he continued, "Because I can't think who else it would have been, or who else you would have had contact with. *He* didn't even know what the diamonds were, though. I didn't want anyone to know."

I couldn't blame him for that. I could only think of how I'd stuffed them into my bikini top while smuggling them away. Someone's dead family members...yuck.

Yuckyuckyuckyuck *yuck.*

Just then one of the marshals came back with a communicator for Shandlin. It was the Vyce Council, telling him how pleased they were that he'd survived (!) and that the vote would be delayed until he was able to deliver his speech. I decided it was good news. Whether or not Shandlin remained in power should be up to the people of Vyce, not up to a mechanical fault that stopped him from having his fair say.

But then after he finished his conversation with the council, the marshals explained that it hadn't been a mechanical fault after all. They'd figured that out even before they'd reached Phobos, because the whole thing had been filmed since we'd been within scanning distance of the moon.

They confirmed that an explosion of that kind didn't come around by accident. Someone had done it to us – or to Shandlin, more likely, since no one really knew or cared about me – and it was only by pure luck that he'd been talking to me at the back of the shuttle rather than sitting in his usual seat at the front. If he'd gone to the front he'd have been just like the guards. Dead, dead, dead.

"So you did save my life," Shandlin murmured, his face pale and his eyes hollow. "Or that would have been me too."

"If you hadn't brought me on the ship, then you wouldn't have been talking to me," I pointed out reasonably, but inside I felt queasy. To the marshals I said, "Are you *sure* they're dead? What if they're in crash-suits, floating off somewhere and waiting to be picked up?"

The two of them in their matching uniforms exchanged glances, then one said, "We found pieces, ma'am. They've been identified as belonging to one Jermaine Elsewich, and an arm belonging to one Annabel Bloom. No one could survive that."

The High Duke lurched to his feet and rushed off to the rubbish compactor, where we could hear him vomiting up his lunch. I couldn't blame him. I felt sick myself thinking about it, and I hadn't even had a head injury.

Things were quiet after that, and we'd almost reached the surface of Mars on our silent journey when the news came through. The late Jermaine Elsewich had made a pre-suicide holo-vid, and had uploaded it online. There he was, sitting in civilian uniform at just the right distance from the camera to show his surroundings in what I recognised as the Ducal Palace.

"I've made this choice," he said, his eyes bulging a little with zealous fervour. "I will kill the High Duke and destroy the evil of the Ducal Dome once and for all. Even though it will cost me my life, I will know that people just like me will have the freedom to run Vyce-"

At which point Shandlin ordered it turned off. I couldn't blame him for that either. He'd hardly known the guard, but to spend time in close quarters with a man who tried to kill him?

I wondered at the vid, at its very clear and well posed

angle. Had Jermaine just been a skilled cam-user, or had he had help?

We arrived in Vyce, going directly from the medic shuttle to a waiting car, almost like a replica of the last time I'd come here from Optus. This time there wasn't a crowd of cameras waiting to tell us the Regent had died, just a couple of hover-cams that flashed at us a couple of times and then sped off for something else more interesting. But what could be more interesting than this?

Into the silence Shandlin said, "I've got to give my speech directly on arriving at the palace. I hope you can understand not being taken straight back – I'll see who I can get to help you…"

"I'm not in a hurry," I replied honestly. At this point all I wanted to do was rest, and not have to *think*.

But as advised, once we arrived back at the very familiar complex Shandlin was taken away, and I managed to find someone to let me send a message back to Judee again. She deserved to know I was alright, but I didn't give a set date for my return. A couple of days, I told her, and she accepted that.

I slept for about an hour, but then the painkiller for my bruised everything began to wear off, and besides, my head was buzzing too much to sleep further. All that had happened, all that Shandlin had said, it wasn't what I'd expected. It wasn't what I'd been *told*.

I wandered over to the Breaker barracks, but didn't spot any familiar faces. After two years, everyone I'd trained with would have moved on. But I made a point of asking the nearest person anyway; a sturdy teenager in the usual Breaker brown armour. "Is Zavier here?"

"Zavier who?"

"Uh…tall, blond, scarred. He's one of the High Duke's personal guards."

The Breaker shook his head. "Dunno. Ask Bloom, or maybe Jermaine."

I blinked at him, stunned. "You haven't heard the news today?"

"What news?" The Breaker looked me up and down. "Hey, aren't you that-"

"Never mind," I cut in. I wasn't interested in explaining who I was, and I *certainly* wasn't interested in explaining what had happened to Bloom and Jermaine. I turned and walked away, wondering who I could talk to to get some answers, and where I could go. I'd rather talk to Zavier, but if not him, Derry would do. But I didn't know how to get in contact with either one. And in the end, I could only think of one place where they might be.

And that was why I went back to the Whirey Swamp.

SIXTEEN
Family Jewels

On my last visit to Whirey Swamp I'd found the secret entrance to the impressively named 'rebel headquarters' quite by accident, and it had been one of the most frightening experiences of my life. But this time when I stood at the edge of the cliff I made a point of looking for what I knew was down there.

I could make it out under the still dark water: the vague pale outline of a massive cyborg swamp-mare, centuries old and still in place. They'd built a fence up here, a nice tall one all along the cliff's edge, and I wondered if that had anything to do with my disappearance two years earlier. Probably, but they still hadn't worked out that the swamp-mare wasn't even real.

"It doesn't *really* eat people," I told myself, but my heart beat double-time. Still, I took that last step forward, then leapt off the cliff, right into the water.

This time the cyborg didn't register quickly enough to keep me from getting wet, and when I finally slid out the other end of the padded tunnel that started in its wide-open mouth, I landed on the floor in a pile of sodden clothing.

A young man that I vaguely recognised from last time wandered up to me and handed me a towel. "We didn't see you 'til you'd hit the water," he told me casually. "You'll want to be more careful next time; there are real swamp-mares in this area."

Yes, I did know that, I thought crossly. "I'm not planning to do it again. I want to speak to Derry."

"If he's here, he's in the vid-bunker. You can find him

yourself."

And this underground complex was the centre of the bid for democracy in Vyce? It seemed unnecessary now, since the same people who ran the place also had a public platform for their politics – secrecy no longer required. But this time the place felt empty. My steps echoed as I walked down the plain underground halls, well-lit with an almost daylight feel, and found the vid-bunker after a few wrong turns. My family and I had spent two weeks here back when we'd left, trying to find the right time to sneak out the other exits and make our way off Mars.

Derry wasn't in that small room with its many seats and large screen, but someone else was. Someone tall and blond, with a very familiar face. This, however, looked like the real Zavier. He glanced up to see who'd come in, smiled at me blankly, and then did a double-take once he saw past the black-and-blue hair and change of clothes. "No way! Iscee?"

"In the flesh," I said dryly, but I was just as curious. Shandlin had said that Zavier told him how to behave better, but it was clear Zavier hadn't told Shandlin anything about *me*. "What are you doing here?"

"What am I doing here? What are *you* doing here?"

"Ran into Shan on Optus, he recognised me, I came back with him," I said simply, leaving out a lot of information in the middle. "Oh, and we crashed into Phobos on the way, but you might have heard about that already."

"Crashed…" His face fell. "So is it true that Bloom is…"

"It would be a miracle if she wasn't."

There were several long moments of awkward silence, and then he said, "Suds. I can't believe she's gone."

I sat down next to him. "I know. She was so tough…but it happened so fast, and it wouldn't matter how tough she was. She wouldn't have…suffered." That was a relief for me too. For all of our past problems, I didn't want Bloom to have died in such a way.

Another few minutes passed, then Zavier cleared his throat. "Well, I'm glad to see that you're not hurt. And the

High Duke?"

"Alive. Zavier, I do have a question for you, if you're alright to answer?" He'd known Bloom a lot longer than I had, and presumably Jermaine too. Right now he sat with his brow drawn low over his eyes, looking unhappy and thoughtful rather than showing any obvious signs of grief.

He gestured a hand towards me. "Go ahead."

I checked that we were alone, then lowered my voice. "Where do your loyalties lie? Because here you are, but Shan told me that you helped him…and yet you never said that I was alive, not once in that whole time."

"Well, that wasn't my place to tell, was it? It was about your safety, and he was so angry and upset at first that I didn't dare say it. I thought that once he got over the initial shock of being tricked, he might try to come after you." He shrugged. "He still could change his mind, I suppose, once he's got used to the idea of you being alive. He might be angry again."

"He promised he wouldn't seek any revenge," I countered, suddenly worried. "He said the theft didn't matter, and that he'd driven me to it, and he promised to give my family their plantation back. Do you really think he'll go back on that?"

"The High Duke said all that?" Zavier's eyebrows shot up. "No, he won't go back on his word. He's still the same that way. If he said it, he'll do it."

"Oh." I felt my whole body sag with relief. "I thought that was the case, but I didn't know him for long, not really. But Zavier…I have to know. Two years ago, right before it all went very nasty, Shan told me he'd thought we were flirting. He'd said that *you* thought I was his girlfriend. That was obviously not true! What did you say to him to give him such a stupid idea?"

Zavier went silent for several moments, and his mouth twisted in an unhappy smile. "Maybe a better question would be, what did I not say to him? Iscee…back then, we thought it would be a good idea for him to be distracted by you. I guess you'll remember that.

"And so Derry and b-*Bloom* used to say things to him,

talking about the, um, *tension* between the two of you, or that girls like you were mean to people you liked, or even…that you were enjoying yourself here, but you were too stubborn to admit it, so no one better say anything." He finished with a sheepish shrug.

My jaw had dropped lower with every word he'd said, and I snapped it audibly shut. My face felt like it was frozen. After all this time, to be told all such information? I felt like I'd been stabbed in the back. "You said all that wolcrox excrement, Zavier? You said that to Shan!?"

"No, no, *I* didn't say it," he hastily corrected. "The others did, but I didn't…I didn't correct them, so I let him think it too." He hung his head. "I owe you a real apology, Iscee. We shouldn't have used you like that. He might even have let you go much earlier, if we'd not encouraged him."

"I'll say you owe me a shrieking apology!" I shook my head. "That explains so much! Argh! I can't *believe* you all, Zavier! To imply that I was happy here, when you knew exactly how I was feeling? To tell him I *liked* him?"

Zavier inched away from me, holding both hands up to cover his face. "Please don't hit me. Or if you must, then hit me in the shoulder or something. But Iscee…weren't you enjoying yourself just a little? Because you made a good Breaker for someone who was miserable!"

I sucked in a deep breath, but held back the words that wanted to come pouring out. In my heart I knew he was right. Perhaps if I hadn't been an illegal conscript, if I'd chosen to join at a time when the Breakers were better than they'd been two years ago, then perhaps I *would* have enjoyed myself… just a little.

So I changed the subject. "You said that at first you didn't tell Shan I was alive, because you thought he might come after me. Was that the whole reason?"

Zavier lowered his hands, looking relieved. "No, it wasn't. I didn't tell him because…well, after your fake death he became a better person, that's all I can say. He was more careful, and he made better judgements. I didn't want to lose that. See, Iscee, I think that what we needed isn't necessarily a new government, but a new *way* of governing. More accountability, you know? And the High Duke could be part of that."

"And yet you're down here?" I gestured at our surroundings.

He smiled hesitantly. "I've got my fingers in a lot of pies, and I still do sympathise with some of this cause. Some of it, but-" Just then footsteps echoed in the hall, and he said more loudly, "They're playing a repeat of the speech while people are voting. Do you want to hear it?"

Shandlin's speech. He'd already given it while I'd been sleeping, hard as that was to believe. But now there he was on that big screen, the silver fracture helmet having been removed for the purposes of the speech, although his arm cast was visible. Clearly he wasn't going for the sympathy vote – or else didn't want people thinking he'd been brain-damaged. He'd brushed his hair and was probably wearing a bit of makeup too, but I could still see the tiredness and the shock from recent events.

"...freedom and democracy," Shandlin was saying, "the freedom for everyone to play a part in the rules that govern their lives, to be safe and happy and prosperous. But do we really need to remove the hereditary rulers in order to achieve this?

"I'll start by saying that if any system of government gives one person all power and no accountability, then it is flawed, whether that person gained power by inheritance or by election, or by strength. When I was young, no one held me accountable. I made my own decisions based on what I wanted, and I didn't think about anyone else, and very few people told me to behave otherwise. There were no boundaries on what I could or couldn't do, and I was a very poor ruler. I hurt people, some in ways that can never be corrected."

He paused. "I was also twelve years old when my father died and made me High Duke of Vyce Dome. Yes, my uncle was regent, but he lacked interest in reining me in. What kind of system allows a twelve-year-old child to have any control over the lives of others, let alone a whole dome?

"But I'm not twelve any more, and I'm no longer careless and irresponsible. I am now careful of those around me and fully aware of how much Vyce needs good leadership. I listen to good advice – have listened to it ever since a notable event two years ago, actually – and I believe that I have made some excellent changes towards the future of Vyce, towards making it beautiful, safe and prosperous." He quickly ran through some of the things that he'd told me, outlining what he also planned to do in the future.

"But here's our problem, Vyce. Even if I become a perfect person and a perfect High Duke and I stay in power, there's no guarantee that my heir, or my heir's heir, won't become the same or worse than I had been. So this is what I propose. Shared power, shared between a High Duke and an elected council of twenty-four, one from each district of the Dome. All decisions will need a majority vote of seventy percent, and the High Duke's vote should hold only 40 percent of the power…"

Shandlin's speech carried on in the same way, and my jaw dropped. "Do you think he means it?"

Zavier nodded. "I know he does, and take a look at the vote statistics. People have been listening, and it seems he's more popular than he thought. Looks like Vyce might still be a Ducal Dome after all."

Down the bottom of the screen there was a percentage table flickering and changing as people put their votes in, but the result was clear. More than half wanted to retain Shandlin as ruler, and I wasn't sure how I felt about that. With the proposed changes, it might just work…

If that wasn't surprising enough, what Shandlin said last took the cake. He looked directly at the screen and said, "This is for Iscee, if she's listening. I made a promise to you to get your family their land back regardless of what happens today, and I meant it. You know I can follow through with this."

But how could he, if he hadn't been voted in? I realised a

moment later what he'd meant – that he would sell the family jewels, disgustingly beautiful things that they were. Wow.

"So he knows you're alive," Zavier said in amazement, shaking his head. "He's not going to be happy that I didn't tell him."

"He might not know that you knew," I advised, still staring at the screen. They'd changed from Shandlin's speech to another, the leader of the move for democracy. It was an unfamiliar man, and while I listened in some interest, I had to ask. "I thought Derry was the face for democracy."

Zavier shook his head. "Nah, he didn't want people to think he was trying to sneak into power using the back door, so to speak. He-"

Just then quiet footsteps sounded behind us, and we turned to see the man himself standing in the doorway. He looked much the same as when I'd last seen him, although he wore a dark green business suit, complete with high collar, and had his hair neatly brushed. "Please finish, Zavier," he said mildly. "I wouldn't want to interrupt your conversation."

The guard looked flustered. "Sir Derry. I was just saying that you were taking a back seat in this vote so that no one would misinterpret your motives in trying to get the High Duke out of power."

Derry's eyebrows rose. "Ah, and yet it looks like all the work of the last few years might have been for nothing. Can the people of Vyce be so easily fooled by a pretty speech? It seems that they can."

And he'd know all about pretty speeches, of course. He hadn't acknowledged me yet, but perhaps he didn't recognise me. While we'd spoken a few times via holo-vid, we hadn't met in person since I'd originally left Vyce. "Hello, Derry."

"Iscendra." He came over to me and took both of my hands, staring intently into my eyes. "I heard about the crash – what a miracle you survived. And to be forced to come back like that? Shocking."

I stepped away, uncomfortable with his boldness. Even though he was right about how I was forced to come back, the things he'd told me earlier made me less than trusting. Besides, he'd heard about the crash a lot sooner than most – he'd even known that I was on the shuttle, and few had known that. But probably Bloom would have told him that I'd been taken, right?

"It's not so bad," I said lightly. "It seems that Shan carried a lot of guilt over my fake death. He's been quite kind."

"Of course he has," Derry said in disgust. "He's good at lying, or don't you remember that from when he first visited you? He'll not do you any harm now, not when his position is so precarious."

"You said that I couldn't tell who I was, because he'd surely come after me and my family. You told me he was dangerous and vicious, and that he'd surely make me suffer. You scared the suds out of me, Derry! But he's apologised, and he's said he'll get us back our land. Things aren't exactly what you've made them out to be, are they?"

"And you believed him?" Derry shook his head in disbelief. "I didn't try to scare you, I just told you the truth. Just wait until he feels secure again, and then you'll see what he's really like. Can't you see that, sweet Iscee?"

He could have been right, but the picture he painted was so different from my experience of the last few days, and even from Zavier had just told me. I was less naïve than I'd been two years ago, and I wouldn't take Derry's words as complete truth without some solid evidence.

"Just Iscee, please," I said, gritting my teeth in irritation. "Or Aria, if you must."

"Iscee-Aria, then. Will you still work with me? I hadn't accounted for this situation, but we can make use of it. Shanny's still sweet on you, isn't he? We can use that to-"

I held up one hand, palm outwards, and feeling quite irritated. "Derry. Please." While Derry claimed I was in danger from Shandlin even now, he still seemed happy enough to try to use the High Duke's apparent fondness for me. That in itself made me trust him even less.

He finally stopped talking. Zavier had slipped out of the

room, and now it was just the two of us.

"I know that this really matters to you," I continued, "but I'm tired of lies and subterfuge of any kind. I almost died today, and so did Shan. Bloom's gone, although you must already know that. Unless you'd had a little something to do with the explosion?"

The last was said as a challenge, and he looked startled, almost smiling. I could see no sign of grief for the girl he'd known for so many years. "The explosion, me? Of course not. That was the work of a sick mind, and you know that for all of my desire to reform Vyce, I'd never hurt my cousin. He's not evil, he's just not the best choice to rule."

"Then who is the best choice, Derry?"

His lips curved in a smile that didn't reach his eyes. "I thought that the people of Vyce would be smart enough to see, but they're not. They're like sheep, just following the direction of the one in front of them, and you're acting like the rest, so easily taken in. Don't you see what Shandlin is really like? Don't you remember what he said to you when he found you'd taken the diamonds? He threatened to kill you."

Of course I remembered. But he hadn't threatened to kill me, just punish me horribly. (Still scary, but not quite as bad.) And he'd known for years that my family had escaped Mars, and they'd not been pursued. "Why didn't you warn me that he was coming to my resort?" I asked instead. "Surely Bloom would have mentioned it."

"I didn't know until right before it happened," Derry replied smoothly. "Bloom thought he was going to his usual place in the south of Optus, but he changed plans at the last minute."

Bloom. Oh, *Bloom*. And he barely looked affected at her death. "She's dead, unless she just decided to leave her arm behind," I told him again, trying to gain some reaction. "Maybe you didn't hear me properly before."

"Yes, of course. What a terrible tragedy." He barely paused. "But you know that we have to move now unless Shanny is to be High Duke permanently. Lovely Iscee, I need you to-"

"Don't you dare say seduce him," I cut in sharply. "It was disgusting when he was sixteen, and it's disgusting now."

"I wouldn't say that. No, I just need you to be his friend, his confidante," Derry murmured, gazing at me with sincere dark eyes.

He shared his cousin's colouring, but past that I didn't really see any resemblance anymore. I also didn't find him attractive like I used to – in the two years since he'd sneaked me out of Vyce, my tastes had clearly changed. Now I saw him again in person rather than by communicator he seemed very ordinary, like a side character trying to play the part of a hero.

"I'll give you further instructions when you need them, but-"

"No. No more instructions," I told him, shaking my head firmly. "In fact I don't want to be part of this anymore. Whatever Shan was before, he's not now. I don't want to play kingmaker anymore, and I don't want to manipulate anyone. The people have decided, Derry. Just let their choice stand. And if you're so desperate for power, why don't you apply to become a councillor?"

For a moment a terrible, furious expression passed over his face, but then it was gone. "A councillor, me? I want true democracy, not this weak version of it. But if you're determined to break away then I won't hold you back. Just do one last thing for me. Remember, I helped you escape when no one else could or would. I did that for you, Iscendra. Me, not anyone else."

Actually it had been via Bloom. "What do you need?" I asked, deciding that I wouldn't obey blindly. I'd judge the request, and if I decided it was reasonable then I'd do it. But after seeing Shandlin again, seeing how he'd changed – and more so, what he'd thought of *me* – I couldn't do anything further to hurt him. I was moving on.

Derry didn't answer at first, watching me assessingly. "The darker hair suits you. I always thought it would."

"Thanks. What did you need?"

He let out a short, self-depreciating laugh. "I see you're rather less enamoured of me than you used to be. Must you be so harsh with me after all this time?"

"I was never enamoured of you," I replied, carefully gentling my tone into something more respectful. "At least not more than a little at the very beginning. But I didn't mean to be harsh. I'm just tired of lying all the time. I want to be myself again."

"Well, that's put me in my place," he replied softly. "So I won't hold obligations over your head. I'll just ask you to do this one thing. Take my cousin back his family jewels."

My eyebrows shot up. "The diamonds? You still have them?"

"Both right here." He pulled a small cloth purse out of his pocket, then tipped the contents into his palm. The jewels were as large and tacky-looking as I remembered, although now I could see the faint orange tint that told their unpleasant origins. They were also set into small clear balls only slightly larger than themselves.

"I've got them in protective casing, so Shanny will have to get that removed. But I've felt guilty all these years over encouraging you to take the things, so I went and bought them back a few months ago. I've decided that it isn't right for me to keep them any longer, no matter what happens now." Derry slipped them back into the cloth wallet and handed it to me.

I took it, feeling shocked in the most pleasant way. "That's so kind... Shan never would have known."

He met my eyes with his dark ones. "But I would have known. You don't have to like me, but I won't have you thinking I'm dishonest."

So perhaps he was like Shandlin in that way. "I don't think that," I replied. "I won't. Thank you, Derry."

His gaze skated away from mine. "You're welcome, sweet Iscee. But do me a favour, and return them to him in private. Do you mind?"

So he felt guilty that he'd had them, and wasn't sure how Shandlin would react. "Of course I'll do that. If I don't see you again, I wish you all the best with whatever the future may bring. Keep your integrity, no matter what else comes your way."

"My integrity, eh?" He gave me a poetic bow. "An unusual farewell, but then I also wish you to keep your integrity, no matter what may come. Do you need a ride back to the city?"

I shook my head. "I left a farlac tied at the top of the cliff."

"Then you know the way back. Just be careful that nobody sees you. Just because you've lost interest in the cause, doesn't mean others haven't."

He had to say that just when I was almost starting to like him again. "Understood."

The way back out of the base was winding and long. It led to the quiet landing strip a good half hour's walk from the cliff top, so I had to struggle my way through the dense brush until I reached that same spot again. My farlac was still there, but it wasn't alone any longer. There was a small air vehicle parked next to it, and not far from them both was a tall, dark-haired young man. He was trying to climb up the high wire fence edging the cliff, but was clearly hampered by his broken arm.

I came out into the open and just watched him in silence for a few moments while he swore and struggled to climb the fence. I couldn't tell if I was more amused or disturbed by the fact that he was here; that he'd clearly worked out that this wasn't a suicide spot after all. "Victory a bit much for you, Shan? Trying to end it all?"

The High Duke almost fell off the fence, not that he was more than a foot off the ground, and his shock turned to annoyance. "Me trying to end it all? Can't you trust me for one moment, girl? I told you I'd have you taken back to Optus, but instead you come here?"

He seemed genuinely hurt, and I sighed. "I wasn't trying to leave, I swear. I just wanted to talk to someone, and I thought I'd find them here."

His tight expression relaxed a little, but not completely. "And did you find Derry here?"

It looked like Shan wasn't so naïve after all. "I spoke to who I wanted to speak to," I replied instead. "And I don't need to talk to them anymore. Congratulations on your victory, by the way. I guess you were more popular than you realised."

"Not with everybody," he said sourly. "Or there wouldn't be some sort of secret base around here made by people who hate me. Should I be worried about bombs landing on my head?"

Shandlin's words were harsh, but his tone was becoming lighter. I moved forward, taking his cast-free arm and steering him back to the air vehicle. "You should be more worried about coming out alone, to somewhere you might not have friends, right after you've survived a skull-cracking shuttle crash. How did you manage to get away?"

He shrugged. "I just said I was going to use the bathroom, then I left. No one stopped me."

"Just as easy as that. Huh. How did you guess I'd come here?"

Shan's cranky expression changed to one of guilt. "Um… there might be a tracker attached to your bandages. Not my idea, I promise! But when I came out of the speaking room and finally had a minute to myself, no one knew where you were. I just wanted to…" He paused, and I cocked my head to the side, waiting for him to complete his sentence. "…to say goodbye," he finished finally.

That gave me an unexpected warm feeling inside, only slightly offset by knowing about the tracker in one of my many bandages. "I told you I was coming back. After I've finally come all this way to Mars I find I don't want to leave just yet."

"Of course. Good." He nodded, moving back into the air vehicle. "Do you want to ride with me? I can send someone to pick up the farlac."

It seemed happy enough grazing on the fluffy lichen growing from the cliff top, and I decided that another ride on the thing wasn't worth disturbing its peace. "Sure."

"I heard your speech," I said once we were inside and moving. It was an auto-driven air vehicle, so it was just the two of us. "It was good."

"Thanks." He paused. "Did you hear the part about you?"

I grinned. "Where you swore to return my land to my family? I did. I'll hold you to that, by the way."

"Of course you will. I've already spoken to the standing council. We've voted that all Earth citizens whose land was confiscated can apply to have it back again, although they'll have to pay tax to Vyce now and follow local laws. They won't have to become Mars citizens. Your plantation is there for the taking, if you want it."

My family home. My heart skipped, and on impulse I put my hand on his. "Thank you so much, Shan. Perhaps you aren't such a grawlix after all."

He laughed, as he was meant to, but his cheeks flushed a little. "Perhaps you aren't a horrible witch after all, either." Now that made me laugh, and he added, "Although…"

"What?"

"Not that I'm jealous, and I know it's none of my business, but…is there something going on between you and my cousin?"

"Derry? Not at all," I said firmly. "Besides the fact that he told me that you'd harm me if I ever came back to Vyce, he's simply not my type."

Shandlin swore. "So that's why you wouldn't admit who you were. You know I'd never hurt you, right?"

I paused. "I do now, although I wasn't so sure at the time. Besides, Derry used to pretend to flirt with me just because it worked you up, because you were so possessive of your Breakers. Even if he was my type, I wasn't stupid enough to fall for it." Even though Derry *was* good-looking, his looks didn't appeal to me any longer. He had too much ambition and duplicity.

Shan seemed to accept that, although he watched my face carefully. "I was possessive of some Breakers more than others, if you remember, even if some couldn't guard to save their lives. I wasn't like that with everyone."

Now came a question I'd long wondered about. "Not even with Bloom?"

"Ugh, no. That would be like…trying to kiss my sister. Just wrong – God rest her soul." He frowned. "No, I seemed to prefer the ones that would run off screaming, then rob me and try to flee the planet. It seems I didn't have good taste in personal guards."

Now I was the one blushing. "Maybe you shouldn't try to date your personal guards," I retorted. "But speaking of robbery, I have something for you." I pulled out the small wallet that held the two plastic-encased jewels. "It's the last two diamonds from your mother's dowry. They're your family's – your family, whatever – and you should have them."

He took the wallet in amazement. "You had them all this time?"

"No! Not at all! Der-" I realised that I was giving up my source, and clamped my mouth shut. "I mean, someone got them back for me just now. I didn't know where they were."

"Derry had them," Shandlin said dryly, not fooled for a moment. "I'd guessed he had something to do with your escape. The jewels were to be traded to pay your way, I suppose?"

I nodded guiltily. "I'd probably have been able to leave without them anyway. I'm-"

"Don't say you're sorry," he cut in. "Whatever you did, it's more than made up by what I'd pushed you into."

"It's not about you, it's about my integrity. I chose-"

"I know, I know! And I chose to behave like a little monster and try to control everyone around me, but I'd really love to not talk about the past anymore." His voice gentled. "Can we just start over? From this moment, pretend that none of the rest of it happened. Maybe we could even be friends."

I looked away, feeling somehow lighter. Mutual forgiveness was like taking off a heavy backpack you didn't even know you'd been wearing, and I liked the feeling. "In between you making important rulings for the future of the Dome, of course."

"And in between you using sedatives on unhappy customers. Maybe we could even have dinner sometime."

Was he asking me out? How very…normal of him, even if misplaced. I found myself smiling. "Maybe we could. But just as friends," I said quickly. There was too much history between us for anything else.

There was a pause. "Just as friends," Shandlin agreed.

"And I could draw you a find-the-pog sketch, just for old times' sake."

He laughed. "What, and tell me that there's one more to find than there actually is? And then you can sneakily draw the last one in when I look away."

"You'd noticed that?!"

"I did, but I liked the fact that you'd even try it, so I didn't say anything."

Huh, and here I'd thought I'd been getting one over him.

"Are you planning to stay on Optus, then?" he asked.

"I'm not sure. You can't live on permanent holiday, and I get tired of tending to other people's. But I'll have to talk to my family. I think they'd really like to come back here once they know it's safe. They miss the plantation, because Earth's just not the same."

As I'd been speaking, Shandlin had tipped the contents of the small wallet into his hand, and his face lost colour as he saw the plastic surrounding the two gems. In a voice like stone he ordered, "Open the window, NOW!"

I didn't know what to do, so I just obeyed, and he tossed the whole handful right out into the depths of the swamp below, slamming the window shut even as he pressed the 'accelerate button on the air vehicle's console. The vehicle rocketed forward, and I turned to stare at where the gems had vanished under the dark water, the pale splash mark rapidly disappearing as we sped away. "Why-"

The explosion rocked our vehicle even from this distance,

sending gobs of slime and greenery slapping into the vehicle's hard hull. It shook a little and then righted itself, and Shandlin and I stared at each other white-faced. "What was that?" I asked hoarsely, although I already could have guessed.

"Plasti-bomb," he replied, tone clipped. "They're set to register the heat of a hand, or sometimes a particular set of DNA. In this case, mine. I had them made illegal three years ago when they first came up. They look far too much like toys, and once they explode you can't find the remnants of them."

"Oh suds," I moaned, the implications of that beginning to sink in. Shan had slowed the vehicle, turning it so we could see what had been left behind. The black water where the gems had fallen was still rocking madly from the force of the explosion, and off to the side of the cliff was an enormous white body like a stout crocodile with an oversized head and huge front flippers.

A full grown swamp-mare, and it was quite dead. And if it could have killed a two-tonne swamp-mare the size of an ancient bus, then it really could have killed us. "Do you think there's any chance he didn't know?"

He knew who I meant. "Not when Derry was the one to introduce them as weapons in the first place," Shan answered, his face still white. "He's never used them, and the rebels never have either. But I guess he gave up on trying to distance himself from them after all."

And I guessed that Derry hadn't had a soft spot for me whatsoever, as he'd even made a point of asking me to hand the jewels over in private. "I suppose he might have had something to do with that shuttle after all," I said numbly. "But you've got to stop travelling with me, Shan. Three explosions, all with me in your vehicle. I'm starting to think I'm bad luck."

Shandlin gave me a long look, then finally rolled his eyes. "Oh, shut it, Older. It's not you, it's me choosing my guards badly. Now let's get back to the palace before the dome collapses on our heads, or something equally awful."

We went.

SEVENTEEN
Piglet

Late that evening I was back in my suite of rooms in Paradise Resort, lying on the couch in the entry parlour. I felt weary and thoughtful, but wasn't quite ready to go to bed yet. So much had happened, and it had done more than just bruise me a little. My worldview had been changed, and I didn't think it would ever change back.

I was also in the middle of a holo-call with the real Aria for the first time in two years. Her semi-transparent form sat half buried in the table in front of me, complete with pink and white plaits and a delicate tattoo scrolling along her left cheekbone. (I'd bet her parents hadn't approved *that* one.)

She was also raging like a bee-stung wolcrox. "I can't believe that grawlix tried to blow you up again!" she ranted. "Twice in one day, Iscee! And here we thought it was that beast of a High Duke the whole time, but it was really his cousin! My mind is blown, Iz, and in the worst possible way!"

I blinked a little as if it would reduce her intensity. It didn't. "I don't think Derry was really trying to blow me up, Aria. He was aiming for Shan, but I just happened to be there."

The event with the jewel-bombs had gone very, very public, even though my name had been left out of it. Shan had been enveloped in a crowd of people the moment we'd arrived back at the palace from Whirey Swamp, and I'd quietly been shuttled back to Optus, still using Aria's name. No one had stopped me, and I was glad. What a day it had been.

"Oh, so we're calling him Shan now, are we? A bit friendly considering what he put you through!"

"I thought you just agreed it was Derry's fault," I countered, feeling my cheeks warm.

After the news about Derry's true nature had come out, several double-agents had stepped forward. They'd said that Derry had been trying to have Shandlin ousted from power since the day he'd become High Duke, having seen that as an opportunity for change. And while Shan was absolutely right to take responsibility for his actions, it seemed to me that he'd been strongly influenced by the people around him…so they had to take responsibility for that, too.

"And that's his name," I added. "Everyone calls him Shan."

"No, they don't. You told me all about it, and it's just you and that girl cousin of his. I remember you told me that in the two years you were *hiding*."

I scowled. "Focusing on the minors, are we? Aria, the whole world has changed. I can come home. *You* can come home."

There was a silence. "Yeah," Aria replied finally, her tone pensive. "That's what you say, but are you sure it's true? Absolutely, one hundred percent, would-stake-your-life-on-it sure?"

That was the same question my parents had raised when I'd spoken to them earlier. *So the High Duke says you're safe,* they'd said. *And of course we want to come home. But after what he did, can you really believe him?*

So I said the same thing I'd said to them. "I already have, because I was in Vyce with him. And I've staked my family's safety on it too, and you know what that means to me. But what you do is up to you, Aria. You can stay where you are, or come back to Optus. Don't you want to use your real name again?"

She pouted. "Maybe. I kind of like being Agnes Merric. It has a nice ring to it."

More like she didn't know about the possible compensation for the whole family, because if she did, she'd be much keener to retake her true identity. And personally I thought the name Aria was *far* nicer, but then I'd been using it for two years.

Just then I tried to suppress a yawn, but it made its way out anyway. "I love talking to you, but I need to go to bed, OK?"

"OK, but one last thing," Aria said quickly. "Because you're going back to boring old Unity-"

"That's not definite!" I cut in. "And it's not boring; it's peaceful and pretty. Not like that plasti-metal box you live in." My cousin was currently studying in one of the biggest Earth cities – a monstrosity of noise, tiny apartments in massive buildings and half a billion people. And even worse…she liked it.

Aria made a scoffing noise. "My apartment might be a box, but I live in the most exciting place I've ever visited. Before you called, I was about to go to a skating rink in the roof of my building."

"Skating doesn't sound that fun."

"It's anti-gravity," she said triumphantly. "There are magnets in the boots, and you can go straight up walls and even upside-down."

"Sounds like a good way to land on your head."

"Sounds like you've got boring in your old age," she teased. "You need to do something fun. Why not get a tattoo? I think a nice flame design on your jawbone would look perfect."

"I'm not boring," I argued. "I kept the black and blue hair, didn't I? And there's no way I'm getting a tattoo on my jaw. That'd look like a beard from a distance, and tattoos aren't easy to remove."

Also, my parents would spontaneously combust when they saw it. They hadn't made many rules while growing up – *don't hit people, Iscendra. Don't curse. And no facial tattoos!* – but 'no facial tattoos' was the only one I'd managed to keep.

Aria scrunched up her face in a way that made me wonder if she'd tried to remove her own, but had failed. "Fine, not your jaw. But you've got to do something to commemorate your awesome time being *me*! I sent you a little something last week, but I guess you haven't got it yet. But when you do, I want you to swear you'll use it."

I rolled my eyes. "I'm not agreeing to something when I don't even know what it is."

"Don't be boring!" She huffed out a sigh. "I have to go, but just…think about it, OK?"

"Fine, I'll think about it. Now go and enjoy your weird skating, and try not to fall on your head."

We ended the call on a good note, and I hauled myself towards the cleanser-room, my mind churning. I was exhausted emotionally as well as physically, but I couldn't stop thinking about what had happened today.

Shan was being hailed a hero in the news-vids, and half a dozen Freedom Movement activists had been revealed from within his staff and yes…another Breaker or two. Even Zavier had voluntarily come clean, but I wondered if Shan had already known about him. I wondered too if Zavier would tell everything he knew. I hoped he would, because in spite of everything, I liked him.

Derry was nowhere to be found. A warrant was out for his arrest for attempted murder of both the High Duke and I, (the first one counting as treason) and also for being an accomplice to Bloom's murder. Fair enough, although to me it seemed too little, too late.

Bloom had made her choices, although I doubted she'd intended to end up in pieces orbiting Mars. I still didn't understand why Derry had been so careless with her life. He'd treated her with casual flirtation just as he had me, but then perhaps that was the answer right there. He'd almost killed me, too – although if I'd died in the air vehicle, it seemed the plan was for me to carry the blame rather than Jermaine. 'Disgruntled ex-guard kills herself and High Duke'…

It had been very, very close.

I shut my eyes under the cleanser, feeling it switch from 'clean' to 'dry'. The cleanser-cycles here on Optus were much shorter than on Vyce due to all the water being shipped in, but that wouldn't be a factor in my choice to move home. While I'd told Aria that my move wasn't definite, it became more so with every passing minute.

I wanted to go home. I wanted to go back to beautiful green Unity, whether or not I had to become a Vyce citizen to do so. I thought that my family would do the same, but they'd need to feel truly safe first, and I couldn't blame them.

When I came back out of the cleanser-room, comfortably clothed in my nightwear, I spotted something in the entry parlour that I hadn't noticed previously. It was a small parcel the size of my palm, and marked with an interworld stamp showing it had come from Earth. The sender's details read, *MIZ AGNES MERRIC, PACIFIKA CITY.*

In spite of my tiredness, I felt my mouth curve in a smile. Here was Aria's gift – the sort I was supposed to agree to use before even knowing what it was.

Yeah, right.

I opened the parcel to find a thin silver shape along with a set of written instructions. *Painless tattoo pen*, it read. *For the artist in you.*

Now I laughed aloud. "Nice try, Aria." Although maybe she had a point about commemorating this time, I mused as I walked back to my room. Maybe I should draw something small and easily hidden, but meaningful. A cartoon pog, perhaps?

Just then the doorbell sounded. *"Miz Mavick?"*

I didn't recognise the voice, but it could have been any one of Paradise's thirty staff. As far as they knew, I was still Aria Mavick, and they'd only come to me if there was something important.

"Door open," I called, and I heard the automated door slide open in response. "Just a moment, I'm coming out."

I sat the tattoo pen next to my bed, then after a brief check my clothing was correct, came out into my small parlour, a pleasant smile fixed to my face. A couple of times guests had followed our staff into our back rooms, and so I'd learned to always look professional. Even my nightwear was discreet and formal enough to pass as daywear...yet another reason to move back to Unity.

There was a man standing in the doorway. He was somewhere in his thirties, with smooth skin and regular features, but I didn't recognise him at all. He stepped inside, and I kept my fixed smile but internally was cursing myself. I really, *really* needed to check who was there before letting them in! "Can I help you, sir?"

"Sure," he said in a vaguely familiar voice. "Just a moment."

Then he stepped aside and in came a short girl in a hooded top. Even with the shadow cast by that hood and the dim lighting, I recognised her immediately. No one else had that combination of baby-face and emotionlessness.

"Bloom?" I exclaimed in disbelief.

She raised her hand as if in greeting. *Zzt.* There was a sound like a mosquito whizzing past my ear, and suddenly my shoulder itched. I looked down to see a tiny, spiked orange shape sticking through my clothing. It was a dart, the sort hunters would use for bringing down wild animals.

"You've got to be shriekn' kidding me," I said in dismay. "I'm not for target practice, you two! And Bloom..."

But now I could feel the numbness rushing down from my shoulder throughout my body until it hit a barrier somewhere around my ribs, where the bandaging remained from the shuttle explosion. The shock had made me freeze more than the dart, and even once I realised who'd come to visit me, I managed to fake partial paralysis, falling to my knees with a clunk on the carpeted floor.

Ouch.

"Nice to see you're not dead," I said weakly, reaching up to tug out the dart and flick it aside. "And here I'd felt so bad that you were gone. How did you manage to fake losing your arm? And who's your friend?"

"Shut up, Iscee," the man said, lifting his jacket to show the small but effective stunner hidden beneath, and I finally identified the man's voice. It was Derry.

Suds.

"You're going to help us get out of here," he told me, "or I swear I'll post plasti-bombs to every member of your family. A nice toy soldier for Alek, perhaps?"

It seemed that Shan wasn't the only one to find a face-changer. But Derry's threat made me turn cold, then hot with fury, although I did my best not to show it. "That won't be necessary," I replied calmly. "What do you need?"

Derry-in-disguise paused, a cruel smile curving that disguised mouth, and he moved a little closer. "Nice to hear that you're asking what I need, rather than turning me down flat like you did earlier. What I need, sweet Iscee, is for you to order an interworld shuttle for yourself and your two friends. Do that now."

"I can hardly move," I lied, still holding my body limply. "You'll have to bring me the communicator."

"Can't you do it from anywhere in the room?"

I shook my head. "This isn't a guest room. The services aren't as good in here."

"You answered the door verbally."

"It's not the same thing. It only works for internal commands, not external. I need the communicator to call a shuttle." I held my breath as I waited for his response. Would he believe me?

Derry studied me with narrowed eyes, then gestured with his chin towards the silent Bloom. "Go get it for her."

The small woman's expression barely changed. "I don't know where it is."

"Over by the entryway. It's a round disc," I told her. "How did you two get here, anyway? Seems like half of Mars is looking for you."

"Same way we left everyone thinking Bloom was dead and Jermaine was behind the shuttle bomb," Derry said arrogantly. "By being very clever."

No, if he was very clever, he'd have made it past Optus already and wouldn't need to threaten me.

"Bloom's uncle works for a meat factory, and he'd cloned

a few body parts for his family in case they ever needed replacements," he told me. "She just took one of her spare arms and left it hidden in the shuttle. Then she told Jermaine she was going to the bathroom, but actually she left the shuttle then set off the explosive from a distance. She was wearing a crash-suit the whole time."

Almost all meat was grown in a lab, although there were a few pest species on both planets that could be hunted for food. But the idea of growing *human* meat for any reason…yuck.

"Clever," I said flatly. "So very, very clever. But I can't see how I'm going to walk you to a shuttle when I can't even move. Did you think that one through?"

"I can't find the communicator," Bloom said from the other side of the room. "There's only an empty socket."

"I might have left it in one of the resort bars," I said, weaving in place as though I was about to fall over. "There's another one in the bedroom right by the bed."

"For shriek's sake, just hurry up," Derry snapped, and I saw a flicker of annoyance go over Bloom's face as she left the room. Her pace didn't speed up at all, I noted.

He'd moved closer to me by this time, and I knew I only had a few moments before she came back. "So I guess this was about revenge," I murmured. "Your precious democracy isn't going to take off the way you thought it would, so killing was your alternative."

"I don't care about *democracy*," Derry spat, and his false face flickered awkwardly at the expression beneath it. "I care about power. My father was born two minutes after Shanny's, did you know that? Two minutes, and I would have been the heir. I would have been the High Duke, and I wouldn't have given a crack about whether the people got a vote. Do you understand?"

I did understand. It seemed Derry never cared about the people; he cared about himself. Of course. Too ordinary, too easy. *He* wanted to rule, and it had seemed that the Freedom Movement had been a roundabout way to achieve that –

until Shan actually started doing a decent job and ruined everything for him. But if Shan had died on the shuttle, then the vote never would have happened. And who was Shan's heir? Derry, because his father had died two years ago.

"I didn't know that your fathers were so close," I replied gently, still swaying where I knelt. Just then my slack hand brushed over something spiky on the carpet – the dart I'd so carelessly dropped earlier. My heart racing, I closed my fingers over it.

"They weren't close, they didn't care a jot for each other. But timing, the timing was so- what are you doing?"

"What?"

"With your hand?" he asked sharply. "What are you doing?"

My eyes widened, and I shifted my gaze to a spot beyond his shoulder. "What's that!?"

And Derry clearly wasn't as smart as he thought he was, because he still turned, just for a moment, and that moment was enough for me to lunge towards him and jam the dart hard into his thigh.

"Argh!"

He howled and we both reached for his stunner at the same time. But the dart had made me clumsy and I punched it instead, sending it skidding out of his grasp to whack him in the face before it fell to the floor. He screeched again and turned towards it, but his movements were slowing and I grabbed him around the shoulders, trying to pull him back.

Somehow we both ended up on the floor in a desperate scramble for the weapon, made slower by whatever drug was even now coursing through both our bodies. But he was bigger and stronger than me, and he pushed me away with one hand and reached for the stunner with the other. As I saw his fingers close around the stunner's grip I knew that this could be life or death…so I bit him as hard as I could on the closest place I could reach, which was his forearm.

"*AAAAARGGHHH!*"

Ah, that was more like it. Derry's grip on the stunner

relaxed and somehow I managed to get it instead. I fumbled to hold it the right way, and I could hear footsteps rushing up behind me, so I turned and pulled the trigger.

Bloom jolted back then fell to the floor, a patch of red rapidly widening over her collarbone.

Oops. Maybe it hadn't been a stunner after all.

Beside me Derry had stopped moving, and I struggled my way into a sitting position, aiming the weapon towards him the whole time. His false eyes were half open, tracking my movements, but his body appeared to have gone slack.

I gave him a prod with my free hand. "Hands in the air, or I'll shoot you too," I told him. My own voice sounded vague and cheerful in spite of the situation, like there'd been more than just numbing agent in that dart.

"Stupid girl," he slurred, his lips barely moving. "Whahfhsugg."

Or that was what it sounded like to me, anyway. "You're the stupid one," I told him cheerfully. "Now if you'll excuse me, I'll just call security." I paused. "Security!"

I had lied to them earlier, of course. I didn't need my communicator to request things on the resort. I could ask for anything, from anywhere in these rooms. Nice, right?

Nice. Nice. Everything was nice. The way Derry and Bloom just lay there was nice. The manacles I kept in my closet for this type of situation were most effective…and also nice. The way a compression patch stopped the bleeding on Bloom's chest was nice, and the fact she was still breathing was nice. "I'm glad you're not dead," I told her unconscious form. "I think prison would be better, hmm?"

She didn't respond.

I moved back to Derry, checking that he was also breathing, and felt my way around his neck. I found the face-changer tab stuck behind his left ear. I pulled it away and his false face vanished, revealing his usual features, plus a very reddened, swollen nose. A trickle of blood was running out of one nostril, perhaps from where the stunner had hit him. "You look horrible," I told him happily. "Like a Derry-pig with that nose."

Then I noticed that the orange dart was still buried in his leg, deeply enough that removing it would probably hurt. It might also explain why he'd been hit so hard by the drug, when I was just cheerful from my smaller dose. So very, very cheerful. "I think I'm high. What was in that dart?"

"Ngghnn."

"Alright then. But seriously, what was in it?"

I sat down on a nearby chair with the lethal 'stunner' in one hand, studying my handiwork. Maybe I wasn't such a bad guard after all, I mused. In fact, I was a rather excellent one. I'd have to tell Shan about this. And Zavier. And Nik, and Lanny, and Aria. I needed to commemorate this moment of awesomeness. The bite mark reddening on Derry's arm was impressive, but it would heal, unfortunately.

Then I remembered that slim silver pen Aria had sent me. Could I do it...?

Yes, I decided. Yes, I could.

EIGHTEEN
The Apology

⊚　⊚　⊚

Ten minutes later security *still* hadn't arrived, but I'd used up all the ink in the tattoo pen and disposed of it in the waste compactor.

Just then there was a holler at the door. "Older! Are you alright?"

That sounded like…but it couldn't be. I stumbled my way to the surveillance cam for the front door and squinted at it in disbelief. Half a dozen Breakers in full uniform stood outside the door, staves and all.

But perhaps I'd been silent too long, because the next thing I heard was, "We're coming in!"

"No!"

Too late. There was a crash at the door and the whole building shook, then suddenly the door was open and the room was full of brown uniforms.

"Where's the threat!?" the lead Breaker shouted. She was a redhead with faded scarring on her neck, and she held her stave like she'd happily gut someone with it.

My jaw dropped, and in that moment even the buzz from the dart wasn't enough. "Tresh?"

Her stave lowered, and she gave me a friendly nod. "Hey, Older. Where is that scummy grawlix?"

"If you mean Derry rather than some other scummy grawlix, then he's over there." I pointed towards his slumped figure. Considering it was in the middle of the floor next to Bloom, it was strange she'd had to ask. "What the suds are you all doing here? I called for resort security, not Breakers!" And as per tradition, they'd broken something. The door.

"Security? Was that some kind of drone thing? 'Cos we shot a couple down as we arrived, just outside this building. They looked threatening."

I choked a little. "They're security drones, of course they're meant to be threatening!"

She shrugged, seeming unbothered. "Oh. Sorry 'bout that. We'd followed Derry here, and- hey, is that Bloom?"

One of the male Breakers whistled, poking at Bloom's fallen form with his stave. "Thought she was in pieces around Mars. Huh."

"She's good at faking," I told him, "because she organised the shuttle explosion along with Derry." There were exclamations of shock and disgust, and I added, "But that is a real wound on her chest. From this…thing." I held up the stunner I'd been carrying around since I'd wrestled it from Derry.

The Breakers all 'ooohed' in unison. "Didn't think you were one for illegal weapons, Older," Tresh said with eyebrows raised. "But alright then."

"It's not mine," I said hastily, but I didn't give it back either. In this moment I felt like mine were the safest hands for whatever-it-was. "Uh…so what now?"

"We'll take this worthless one back to Vyce," Tresh began to say. But just then there was a burst of laughter from the Breakers surrounding the still-shackled Derry. They'd turned him over, exposing the lovely artwork on his face. And it *was* lovely. An Iscendra Cole original, in fact.

"What's this thing on his cheek?" Tresh asked, grinning.

"I have no idea," I replied with dignity. "A bruise, maybe?"

"Looks like a piglet," one of the others said with a laugh. "Wonder how long *that'll* take to wash off. Ha."

It would never wash off. Ha, ha, *ha*. But I smiled politely. "Good question. Would you mind getting those two out of my room? I was about to go to bed when they barged in." Or I'd let them in. Same thing.

Tresh shrugged. "Sure. We'll see you back at the palace,

right?"

"I'm not a Breaker anymore."

"We know *that*. But we'll see you."

I didn't argue, because I didn't know the answer. But they were unloading the two would-be murderers from my floor when my communicator went off. The call came straight through to audio-only.

"Iscee!" came Shan's panicked voice. "I've heard Derry's on his way to Optus! He might be in disguise-"

"I appreciate the warning," I interrupted, "but it's about fifteen minutes too late." I switched on the visual function and turned it to the scene of the two traitors being carried out, and for several seconds Shan was dead silent.

Then he said, "Is that *Bloom*?!"

"Yep. The good news is that she's alive, just. The bad news is that she's even more of a traitor than you already thought, since she and Derry both set off that bomb in the shuttle."

"Oh." There was another long silence, then, "Well, I suppose I should be glad she's not dead. Maybe. I'm glad *you're* not dead."

"Me too." I gave him a quick rundown of what had happened, and when I got to the bit about the tattoo pen, he interrupted.

"Please, I have got to see this. A piglet?"

I called out for the Breakers to stop moving, and shuffled my still-partially-sedated way towards where Derry lay. His eyes were still half-open, and the tattoo looked just as I'd intended it. It was an ugly little cartoon piglet scrawled from his chin, up his cheek to his forehead. The piglet was stretching upwards for a ducal coronet held just out of its reach, and had a shadow of stubble on its chubby face.

In case the picture still wasn't clear enough, I'd carefully written 'Desperate Derry' on the piglet's belly. The whole thing was drawn in bold black lines, because the pen was too cheap to do any colours. I'd have to tell Aria off for not sending a multi-coloured option.

I heard Shan gasp, and then he laughed. He laughed, and

laughed, and I laughed too until my chest hurt. We were still laughing when everyone finally left, probably from the shock as much as anything else.

Finally I managed to stop enough to say, "Did I tell you that I bit him, too?"

"Bit him?" And now that set Shan off again, and when he finally calmed down he had tears of laughter in his eyes. "Bite marks and piglets, what a fitting punishment. I think I love you, Iscendra Cole."

My breath stopped, and I didn't even mind that he'd used my full name. "Careful," I said lightly. "I might think you mean that."

Suddenly he wasn't laughing anymore either, but his gaze was fixed on mine through the small viewing screen. "I did mean it, you know. I don't just think I love you. I do. I always have, really."

I was dumbstruck. "You said that before, but I hadn't really thought you meant it."

"I did. I really do, especially now." He paused, looking a little anxious, and I found I liked that uncertainty on him. It meant he wasn't being an arrogant so-and-so. "Do you mind? Or do you still hate me and think I'm a big fat grawlix?"

"Well," I said slowly, "I'm still kind of sedated, but I can honestly say that I don't think you're a big fat grawlix anymore, or even really just a grawlix. And I don't hate you anymore either." I paused, reflecting on my words. "You're really good-looking now too. I'm not sure how that happened."

Shan sputtered what might have been a laugh. "Uh... thank you?"

"But here's the thing," I continued carefully. "Yesterday you thought I was dead, and I thought I had to hide from you. Even now we know what Derry and Bloom did, we still made our own choices two years ago, and most of them weren't good. I can't see how we can really...*love*...when there's all that between us."

He tried to say something, and I spoke over him. "Besides,

you're a High Duke, even if you pretend you're not. You want to be one of the Breakers, one of the family, but you'll have to marry some High Duchess in the end, just like your father did. And I'll be on a plantation somewhere, sketching cartoons and picking garvafruit." That thought made me feel strangely tearful.

He was silent for a long while. Then he said, "It's a new day, Iscee. I don't have to do what my father did, and you don't have to do what your parents did. But I see what you're saying. There's too much history between us, and until yesterday I did think you were dead. That's got to be affecting my thinking. But maybe we could be friends anyway?"

I considered the question. "Maybe you should get my parents their land back, and see about some kind of compensation for them and the other families to help them come back to Vyce. And maybe you should focus on putting together your new government."

"Oh." Shan's face fell. "I suppose I should do all those things."

"And," I continued, "maybe you should holo-call me some time. Just for a friendly chat."

His disappointed expression lifted again. "Maybe I should."

We ended the call, but I found myself smiling just a little.

Unity, Vyce Dome
Six months later

"Are the cinnarolls ready?" my mother queried over my shoulder. "And what about the drinks? Iscee, I don't know how to use this new blender, and we're running out of garvafruit."

"Wewwy."

"What? Oh Iscendra, don't talk while you're eating!"

I swallowed my mouthful of cinnaroll, unbothered by her

frantic tone. Mum always got like this when we had company. "They're ready. I can put them on the table now."

"I'll do it." A long arm reached over me, picking up the warm tray and whisking it over my head.

I tried to grab the tray back. "Don't let Nik do it, he'll eat half of them before they get to the table!"

My brother lifted the tray out of my reach. In the last two years he'd grown even further, and I'd now need a stepladder to match his height. "I'll take one to Alek in his room," he told our mother, "then the rest to the table." Then in contrast to his lovely speech, he stuck his tongue out at me.

I was about to stick mine back, then realised Mum was watching, so sighed dramatically instead. "Oh Nikolai, don't be so childish." To my unimpressed mother I said, "I'll sort the drinks."

"Thank you – but don't put too much sweetener into the smoothies. Garvafruit should always be a bit tart."

She left the room, and I found myself pausing halfway to the blender. I had made all these ultra-sweet smoothies on the High Duke's instruction, and even though so much time had passed, it seemed that my tastes had changed accordingly. How odd.

Ten minutes later I carried the keg of drink out to the busy living area, setting it down next to the dozen or so other drinks with a sigh of relief. I was promptly joined by two of my favourite people in all the worlds, Lanny and Aria.

"You were carrying that yourself," Lanny said disapprovingly. "It looks heavy. You should have asked me to help."

"You're a guest. And I could handle it."

"Good old Iscee," Aria said, slipping her arm through mine. "Tough enough for anything, except accepting help." She paused, looking thoughtful. "Or getting a tattoo."

"Or a piercing," Lanny added. "She was too cowardly for that." He himself sported a brand-new gold bar through his eyebrow, which Aria had earlier admired.

"Or getting criticism about those sketches of hers," Aria

countered. "Never mind that they're selling so well at your dad's shop, Lanny."

I sighed. "Anything else you two want to insult me about? My hair? My dress?" I spread out the puffed hem of my skirt, which I'd bought especially for this occasion. (OK, so Aria had hauled me around the shops and made me buy it especially for this occasion. Same thing.)

"No need to get huffy," my cousin said with mock dignity. "We're just saying that you seem so tough in some things, but we know the truth. You're as soft as…" She paused, seeming stuck for comparison, then spotted something across the room. "…as your pet pog's fluffy tail, and we love you for it."

"It's true," Lanny agreed solemnly. "You're squishy on the inside, Unshakeable Iscee. The fern proves it." He pointed across the room to the welcome-home gift he'd brought; an enormous green fern in a shiny red pot. He'd already told me that it was the very same fern I'd rescued from Vyce Central Station once upon a time – he'd shoved it in a pot, and it had put down roots then proceeded to grow quite happily.

I'd found that quite touching for some reason. This living thing had through no fault of its own been taken out of its element, but had thrived anyway. Lovely.

Hmm. On second thoughts, perhaps I *did* know why that touched me. But I didn't want to cry in public or they'd tease me forever, so instead I replied to his earlier comment. "Everyone's squishy on the inside, Lanny, even you. Shall I get a knife and prove it?"

He stepped back. "Ugh. I take it back – you *are* tough. That was scary Iz, even for you."

"I told you that you were the scary cousin," Aria said happily. "Isn't she, Lanny?"

"That she is, Aria. I've always known it."

I scowled at the two of them. "Remind me why I invited you here again?"

"Because you love us," my cousin told me, slipping her arm around Lanny's waist in a rather friendly gesture. "Now did you invite your boyfriend today? I told you we want to meet him."

I turned away, pretending to busy myself with pouring a drink. The smoothie was just the right shade of dark pink, but I knew it would be a touch tart for my tastes. "You know I don't have a boyfriend, unlike *you*. Getting cosy with my best friend, are you?"

"Well, he is rather fantastic," Aria replied unashamedly. "And he has the best hair." Lanny looked pleased with that, and she added, "But stop changing the subject. Is he coming?"

"Yeah," Lanny piped up. "If you've been having long holo-calls with the guy every single day, then we want to meet him. We have to know if he's good enough for you."

"He's definitely not," Aria told him. "Think of everything he did. Just 'cos Iscee's forgiven him and he's given everyone compensation and paid for them to come back to Vyce, doesn't mean he's good enough for her." She glanced at me under her lashes, a cheeky smile curving her mouth. "But he's hot now, so that makes it OK, right Iscee?"

I could feel my face burning by this point, and I burst out, "I am not dating the High Duke, OK? We're just friends!" In spite of Shan's declaration of love that day, he hadn't mentioned it again since.

"Friends who talk every single day. Friends who each think the other one is *hot*," Aria teased.

By this time I could feel a number of eyes on me, not just from the terrible two in front of me. How had I not known Aria and Lanny would be such a terrifying duo?

So I didn't bother arguing that Shan and I spoke only every second day...mostly. And I definitely didn't make any comment on Shan's looks, which had only grown more attractive now he'd healed up from his injuries. Instead when the doorbell went off, I ran to get it.

"Go on, abandon your guests," I heard Lanny shout after me, then his and Aria's laughter.

Suds. Those two – I'd have to separate them at once, I decided, because the combination of people who knew all my secrets *and* weren't afraid of me was just too dangerous.

Except the way they were acting, perhaps it might be too late to separate them…

But when I got to the door and saw the two men waiting behind the one-way clear pane, my heart leapt a little in my chest. Even if the face and the horrible green hair of the first one had been unfamiliar, I would have still recognised that tall, lanky figure immediately. I tapped the 'open' button, but instead of letting them in, stepped outside and set one hand against the first man's chest as if to hold him back. "What are you doing here?"

The High Duke reached up to the face-changer tab I knew was behind his ear, and a moment later his borrowed face flickered and changed. Then it was just Shan, complete with nicely styled dark hair, big black-lashed eyes, and an uncertain expression on his handsome face. "You told me to come, remember? We've talked about this for ages."

"Not today," I whined. "*Tomorrow.*" Suds – any day but today would have been alright.

"I'm sure you said it was today," Zavier said from behind Shan. Both men wore street clothes, but I knew Zavier's hand-stave would be tucked under that jacket somewhere. After all the attempts on Shan's life, I couldn't blame him for his caution. "It's the twentieth. Remember?"

I blinked at him. Had I said that? But it didn't really matter, because they were here now. I scrubbed a hand over my face, never mind the makeup that Aria had carefully applied. "Argh. You could be right. I'm sorry."

"Is it so bad?" Shan queried, still looking uncertain. As always, uncertainty suited him better than the arrogance he often wore. "I mean, your family knew I would be coming by. You said you warned them, so if we're here now rather than tomorrow…I'm busy then, you see. There's a council meeting that I can't miss."

"Oh." I paused, considering our options. It was so strange having the two of them here, but at the same time nice. It was just *today*… "We've got some visitors," I said instead. "A sort of welcome home, since my family's officially taken back the plantation now."

Shan shrugged a broad shoulder. "Anyone I know?"

"Uh…my cousin, and a few others." Or maybe more than a few.

Behind Shan, Zavier perked up visibly. "Aria's here? Can we stay?"

They'd 'met' via holo-call a few weeks earlier, and the guard had seemed quite taken with her. Must have been the tattoo. But he didn't wait for my permission. Instead he stepped around both of us, then headed inside. "I'll just wait in here," he called back to us, then disappeared around a corner before I could tell him that he'd have some competition for Aria's attention.

Shan huffed out a laugh. "Some guard he is. Shall I call him back, Iscee?"

I sighed. "No, don't bother. It may as well be today – except that I didn't *actually* warn my family you were coming. I meant that I was going to warn them at the last minute, so they didn't have a chance to make a fuss about it."

"Oh." There was a long silence where I'd swear I saw panic in Shan's expression. Then he steeled himself. "So… should I have worn a cup?"

I would have laughed, except he was quite serious. "If Nik tries to punch you, then I'll punch him right back. But I don't think there'll be a problem. While he's not a big fan of yours, he seems to admire the Breakers, at least as they are now." Just then the door beeped, indicating it had been open for too long. "Will you come in, Shan?"

"In a moment," he said, his gaze searching mine. "Iscee, are you happy to be back here?"

"Of course," I replied in surprise. "I've told you that before. I love Vyce, and I love Unity."

He smiled crookedly. "You've said that, but it was always by holo-call, and I can't always catch people's expressions correctly. After how much I've messed up in the past, I wanted to see it face-to-face. I had to know that you hadn't just felt pressured to come back for some reason."

I rolled my eyes. "Don't be paranoid, Shan. If I was unhappy, I would have said so."

"Yes, but-"

"Iscendra, who's this?"

I looked over my shoulder to see my mother, who must have come in response to the beeping door. But she was watching with raised eyebrows, and I realised my body must be blocking her full view of Shandlin. I also realised in that moment that the two of us were standing very close...and I still had my hand on his chest.

I felt my cheeks heat, then dropped my hand. "Uh... Mum. Maybe you could go get Dad and Nik?"

"Here," Dad said cheerfully as he stepped into sight. "Who's that blond young man who's being so friendly with Aria, Iscee? He said you'd need to talk to us."

That Zavier. I hadn't decided whether he was a traitor, or just using initiative. "Uh..."

"Iz," Nik said from behind my dad. "What's going on? Some guy said you needed to talk to us."

Lanny had called me unshakeable, and he and Aria had mocked my apparent toughness. But in this moment I couldn't even utter a word. I wet my lips. "Uh..."

Then Shan put his hand on my arm, moving me aside just a little, and stepped around me into sight. "Mister and Miz Cole. I'm the High Duke of Vyce, and I'm here to make an apology."

That had been the plan the whole time; the thing that Shan had argued for in so many of our conversations. It hadn't been enough for him to give back the things that had been taken. He wanted my family to know face-to-face how much he regretted what he'd done.

But they might not accept your apology, I'd told him over and over. *It might not go well. Nik might kick you in the family jewels. Really, he might do it.*

And so on. But even though Shan now knew 'family jewels' meant something quite different to Olders, for some reason that apology had been really important to him. So finally I'd given in and agreed for him to come to visit... tomorrow, after I'd warned my family about their impending visitor.

Oops.

But all things considered, it could have gone worse. My parents looked stunned for a moment, but they listened as Shan spoke about exactly how he'd hurt them by conscripting me, and then by the flow-on effect from our escape from Vyce. Then he told them how sorry he was, and that he could never really make up for it, but he was going to try.

And then my parents had exchanged a glance, and my father had said, "You're right that you can't change the past, Your Grace. But you're right to try to make amends, and we'd be right to let that past go. There's nothing to be gained by holding a grudge now." But he looked at me thoughtfully while he said it.

But then Nik stepped forward. He was only seventeen, but he had the height and broad shoulders of someone who would always need specially-made shirts. He also wore a very unfriendly scowl. "I suppose you'd kick us off Mars again if I called you a worthless, scum-sucking grawlix."

"Nik!" Mum scolded, but Shan just raised his eyebrows.

"I might have been a grawlix once, but I'm not now. And this is the only apology you'll get from me. You insult me in future, and you'll get what you deserve." Suddenly the atmosphere was tense, until Shan added, "Iscee will punch you for me. She does that well, don't you Iscee?"

I smirked, but nodded. "Yeah, Nik. Unless he really is being a worthless, scum-sucking grawlix. Then I'll punch him instead."

"Iscendra Cole!" my mother exclaimed. "Is this the way I raised you?"

No cursing, no punching people, no facial tattoos. Still one out of three.

"No," Nik cut in. He was watching me with a speculative expression. "But Iscee's always mean to boys she likes."

I felt my cheeks turn burning hot again. "I am not! Or that

would mean that I like *you*, Nikolai Cole, and right now I do not!"

"You *love* me," Nik taunted, stepping away out of reach. "Now I'm going to get a drink, because it's a party. Stay in the doorway for all I care." He vanished, and after a few moments my parents gave Shan respectful nods then followed after.

Then it was just Shan and I once again, still standing in the doorway at the front of my childhood home. His mouth was curved in a slight smirk, and his head tilted back, and if I hadn't known him so well I might have taken that expression for arrogance. But I did know him, and I knew he was covering up nerves. "A party, Older? Is that what all this fuss was about?"

"I told you we have visitors," I said snarkily. "It's not my fault you don't listen."

"You said it was your cousin!"

"And my aunt and uncle. And my friend Lanny and his father. And our neighbours Brant and Trudi, although not their grandson Felix. Oh…and about fifty people from around Unity." I shrugged again, smiling a little. "People are glad we're back. Do you feel *bad* that you sent us fleeing, Your Grace?"

"You are so mean to me," Shan said. "I don't know why I put up with you." But he was smiling while he said it, his dark eyes flickering over my face. We'd held eye contact this whole time, but unlike with most people, that didn't bother me.

I opened my mouth to make a suitably sarcastic reply, then realisation struck me with the force of a lightning bolt. I doubled over, raising my hands to cover my face as I let out a long groan. "Oh, *nooo!*"

"What is it?" Shan sounded panicked. "Iscee, are you alright?"

"I am." I forced myself to lower my hands, but I could feel my face had heated up again, this time right to the hairline. "I've just realised something terrible. Something truly, truly terrible. I've been told before, but I didn't believe it."

"What is it? Are you sick? Can I call someone?"

"No. No…Shan, I've just realised that Nik was right." I paused. "I *am* mean to boys I like…and I'm mean to you. Really, really mean."

Oh suds. I liked Shan. Not just as an attractive friend that I talked to a lot, but could never see myself with. No, I really, really liked him. Maybe more than that.

There was a silence, and I saw he was smiling. "I guess that means you really, really like me."

I scowled. "Why don't you sound surprised?"

Shan laughed. "Because I've known for a long time what you're like, Older. Why do you think I keep holo-calling you? It's because I know I've got a chance now."

He was so arrogant in that moment, but somehow that didn't bother me either. "Suds," I murmured. "This is serious, Shan. How did this happen? It used to be that I'd always rather punch you than kiss you, because you were such a baby-faced little grawlix. And now…"

"You don't want to punch me? People can change, Older, and I'm not baby-faced anymore." But then his expression became uncertain once more. "Iscee, do you remember that day Derry was captured, how I told you I loved you? I didn't mention it again, but I meant it, and I still do. Is it possible that you…might feel the same way?"

I considered the question. It was strange how in this moment I didn't feel embarrassed anymore, or even feel the urge to be sarcastic. Instead I really examined my feelings. I knew I enjoyed Shan's company, and that he was good-looking. I even trusted him now, even though I'd thought I could never truly get past what he'd done by conscripting me. But perhaps I'd changed. He certainly had.

"I didn't at the time," I replied finally, my tone quiet and pensive. "I think I'd have run screaming rather than consider it. But that was then, and this is now… And I think there's a good possibility that I do love you, at least a little bit. Although that could be just the high of coming back home, so you'll have to wait and see."

His eyes narrowed. "How long do I have to wait?"

I shrugged, but inside my heart was pounding double-time with excitement. He still loved me...and I loved him. Probably. "Let's go have lunch, then if you're not scared away by my family, we'll see."

So we had lunch, and my family and friends alternately insulted and complimented him and asked too-personal questions (that was Aria), and afterwards I managed to drag him away to our tiny back garden and slammed the door on all those curious faces.

The funny thing was, even after all of that he *still* seemed to think that he loved me. Even funnier, I still felt like I loved him too, and maybe not just a little bit.

And then when he asked if he could kiss me, I didn't even have the urge to run away screaming, not at all, and not even an urge to punch him in the gut.

No, I actually kissed him back.

It looked like people could change after all.

The End

◎   ◎   ◎

Dear Reader,

Right now you might be thinking: What the heck did I just read? Was it a romance or a sci-fi? And what the heck is a grawlix? (Also, who says 'heck' anyway?)

So, Dear Reader, let's talk about creative cursing. My goal is to make my books accessible to anyone, even non-sci-fi readers, by using casual language. I've also been reminded that a lot of my readers prefer not to swear at all, so used the good old internet to find some alternatives.

A *grawlix* is one of these things: #@$%!.

Suds actually came from 'sard', which was an extremely rude word in the middle ages.

Shrieking cyborg – well, why not? But that's just the fine print.

SPOILERS AHEAD:

Unshakeable came from this amazing, really detailed dream which set the scene in the future, right down to the landscape. It felt like watching a movie of this Old World and New World, an angry girl whose name meant 'Melody', a 'prince' (that became a High Duke) pretending to be someone's neighbour, a family living on a plantation, failure to sell artwork, farlacs, swamp mares, stealing jewels, then almost committing suicide.

That was where the dream ended, and I remembering lying there awake thinking 'is that it? Where's the rest of it!?' But of course I had to make it up…and so I did. Unlike the storyline, the title changed from 'The Spider Prince' (the dream name for Earth) to 'Twin Worlds' to 'Old World, New World', to 'Breaker', then to 'Unshakeable Melody' and then finally to what you see now. I thought it was a good change.

A final note on changes: Yes, people can change. They often do, especially over time or in response to joy or traumatic events. But I really, truly, absolutely believe you shouldn't stay in a bad relationship because 'he'll change for me if I just wait for him patiently'. (Yes girls, I'm talking to you. Do guys do this to? I don't know.)

If he hurts you, if he consistently shows bad character, then get out of there. It's not your place to change him, and you CAN'T. Either life or the grace of God may change him, and if so, great. But don't stick with your worthless boyfriend because you *looove* him, and definitely, definitely don't take this book as any suggestion that you should.

On that light note, if you liked Unshakeable, please do leave a positive review anywhere that will allow it.

(Also, just because it's fun, have a picture of a classy cat marrying a fish in a wedding dress. I call it 'catfished'. See below.)

M. Marinan